Mabel
the notorious
Dwarf

Also by Sherry Peters

Fiction
Mabel the Lovelorn Dwarf
Mabel the Mafioso Dwarf

Non-Fiction
Silencing Your Inner Saboteur
Blueprint for Writing Success

Mabel
the notorious
Dwarf

Sherry Peters

DwarvenAmazon Press
http://www.dwarvenamazon.com

Printed in the U.S.A.

Peters, Sherry, 1973 –
Mabel the Notorious Dwarf

Print ISBN: 978-0-9920535-7-4
Ebook ISBN: 978-0-9920535-9-1

10 9 8 7 6 5 4 3 2 1

Author Photo by: Siri Kousonsavath
Cover Art by: Jordy Lakiere
Cover Design by: Samantha Mary Beiko
Edited by: Samantha Mary Beiko

For my nieces and nephew
Katarina, Angelica, and Thomas

ACKNOWLEDGEMENTS

This book would not exist without the encouragement, brainstorming, critique, love, and support of so many people.

Evan Braun and Jennifer Ranseth who helped me brainstorm the initial plot on a road-trip home from Calgary.

Gerald Brandt, Bev Geddes, Adria Laycraft, Karen Dudley, Lindsay Kitson, Chadwick Ginther, David Fortier, Barb Galler-Smith, Eileen Bell, S. G. Wong, Ann Cooney, and Ryan McFadden. You are my writing peeps, my writing family. You provide me the place, space, and time to write. You inspire me to do better. You get my madness (and my genius?).

My mentors Jeanne Cavelos, Anne Harris, and Leslie Davis Guccione. Who would have ever thought Mabel would grow into this?

Samantha Beiko, editor extraordinaire. Thank you, thank you, thank you!

My cover artist, Jordy Lakiere, who so beautifully gives Mabel life in images. It is a weird and wonderful thing for someone like me to see her imagined words in pictures. You have a gift.

My parents Jake and Barb, my brother Darrell, my sister-in-law Cheryl, your support means the world to me.

My nieces Katarina and Angelica, and my nephew Thomas, you are the lights of my life. This one is for you.

And a special thank you to you, the reader. You are why I do this.

It is a truth yet to be universally acknowledged that all female dwarves have the right to live a life of their choosing.

—Mabel Goldenaxe

CHAPTER 1

I SCOLDED myself for leaving the Hammer and Chisel so late. I wished Otto had left his cart for me as I half-ran, half-walked the two miles to the River's Edge Gallery. Three years of making this trek regularly and it never got shorter.

Tonight's exhibition opening for Celia, a promising new artist, had drawn a good-sized crowd. Breathless, I made a beeline for Brent, dodging the handful of guests milling around the River's Edge Gallery.

"How's it—"

"Where have you been?" Brent growled, cutting me off.

Intense, blunt pressure pooled at my right temple. The fingers of pain soon overflowed, stretching

into my neck and blooming into the right side of my
head. "I told you, I had to supervise at the Hammer
and Chisel so Sophie and Otto could set up here."

He grabbed hold of my elbow. "The show started
an hour ago. I needed you here." His thumb pressed
against a nerve sending sharp pain down my arm to
my fingertips.

I flinched.

Brent let go of me. His face relaxed. "I'm sorry,
Mabel. I've just been so anxious. You're here now."

I massaged my elbow. "This is a great turnout."
Sophie and Otto served food and drinks from the
opposite corner of the gallery, dozens of guests
mingled, and Celia, a young female dwarf, held court
with a number of Brent's regular clients, showing off
one of her drawings on display. "This is going to turn
things around for you."

"You think so?" Brent shoved his hands in his
pockets.

"I know so. Look at who's here. It's been ages
since Sidney has come in, on his own or for a show,
and he's really interested in Celia's art. You know
word is going to spread."

Brent puffed out his cheeks then slowly released
his breath. "You're right. Of course you're right.
You're always right." He kissed me on the cheek.
"You're the best."

"Go mingle." I gave Brent a gentle push. "I'll be
over by Sophie and Otto if you need me."

I greeted a few of the guests as I made my way to

the food table. Sophie and Otto had been so generous to cater tonight's show. Since I'd lived at the inn and spent most evenings there with my friends, it had become the place to be. Business in both the tavern and the inn was booming. So much so they'd had to hire extra staff. But even so, Sophie didn't trust the catering to anyone but Otto, and he really was the best to grill, so I'd offered them a more than fair price, hand-selected the best staff to work the tavern while they were away, and supervised the staff until everything ran to Sophie's standards.

"Is everything all right at the Hammer?" Sophie asked, handing me a plate.

"You would be proud," I said.

"And ideas for a new movie?" Otto asked.

I shrugged. After several productive years of movie-making, I'd hit a dry spell that was extending into its fifth month. I spent my days working for Sophie and Otto and writing down ideas for movies then throwing them out before long. This afternoon, as Sophie and Otto were leaving to come to Brent's gallery, I thought I finally had an idea to work with. I was wrong. "I don't have any ideas."

"What do you mean?" Otto's incredulity was reasonable. I'd been so confident earlier.

"I thought I had something. I even made multiple pages of notes, but it wasn't anything after all."

"I'm so sorry, love," Otto said.

I loved Otto for his enthusiasm for what I did. "Well, it was more of an idea than I've had in a long time. That has to count for something, right?"

He sighed, unconvinced. "You will find the right thing, I'm sure of it. What can we get for you?"

I practically drooled over the bacon-wrapped pork ribs, skewers of mutton and venison, roasted herbed potatoes, and stuffed mushrooms. "All of it. I'm starving."

"Mabel." I turned—Brent's brow was furrowed, eyes narrowed. "Come here."

The right side of my head throbbed. I hated it when he called me like that, like I shouldn't have ever left his side. My stomach growled. The majority of guests in the gallery had heard Brent and were watching me now. This was not the time to say something. I handed the plate back to Sophie. "Save some for me? I'll have it later, when we get home."

Sophie scowled. I half-smiled, apologetic on Brent's behalf. It was fine. I was fine. Brent was nervous and under a lot of pressure to make this event a success.

"Will do, love," Otto said.

Brent grasped my hand and pulled me over to Celia's statue of a dragon breathing sapphire encrusted fire. Sidney walked with us.

"The underside is equally detailed," Brent told Sidney. "Mabel, can you help me pick it up?"

Pick it up? It weighed more than a hundred pounds. I was not strong enough to lift anything so heavy. If I were still mining, sure. But I wasn't. I didn't have that kind of strength anymore. Brent did.

He lifted these kinds of things all the time. He could easily pick up the statue and talk about it at the same time. It wouldn't be right for him to do that kind of work at a show in front of such an important client.

Brent needed my help and Sidney was waiting.

"Of course." I smiled. I reached around the statue, around the dragon's chest, and heaved.

"Watch the wings," Brent scolded.

I did my best to shift the statue in my straining arms. I focused on my breathing as I bore the entire weight of the statue, while Brent and Sidney spoke at length about the detailed stone work. I kept quiet when Brent asked me to tilt the statue a little to the left and warned me to be more careful, when I could barely hold onto it as it was. I reminded myself that this event, and this conversation in particular, could turn things around for Brent's business. He couldn't effectively talk about the art and finesse the sale if he was holding the statue.

Despite our best efforts, Sidney wasn't convinced it was worth his interest or money.

"Have you seen this piece over here?" Brent put his arm around Sidney's shoulder and led him to a wood etching two feet away.

I grunted as I tipped forward, catching myself before I dropped the statue or fell over completely. Brent glared at me. My heart raced and sweat coated my face.

I set the statue down and shook out my numb arms. The piece was valuable, perhaps not as valuable as Brent wanted it to be, but it still warranted a hefty price tag. Had I broken it, I would have willingly paid for it. It was the anger and blame in his eyes that terrified me. In that one look, it was as if he was telling me I was destroying his night, that my weakness was ruining his gallery, his reputation, his business. I dare not mess this up for him.

Shame, pure and absolute, washed over me.

I deserved better.

It was my fault.

Brent's gallery had never been the same in the three years following that business with Radier, Aubrey, and Sevrin. He needed to make a couple of sales tonight or the gallery was going to go out of business.

I glanced over at Sophie and Otto who smiled at me. My stomach growled but I felt ill. I couldn't eat. I should remain by Brent's side, anyway, in case he needed me again.

If this night went well, he would go back to being his kind, caring self, the way he usually was. Or used to be.

I wandered over to him, hovering a step or two back, close enough for him to know I was there for him. He smiled at me and gently held my hand as Sidney showed keen interest in a wood etching.

Brent loved me.

He was happier.

I wanted him to be happy.

I loved him.

I deserved better.

I TOOK a deep swig from the pitcher of ale in my left hand and readied my axe with my right.

The bullseye blurred. I closed one eye and breathed deep, which only made things worse. I heard the words my brother Mikey had said so often as my coach. "Relax. Visualize what you must do. Pay attention to your technique. You can do this."

I shook my head and took another long, deep pull on my ale. I would visualize, all right. I imagined the throwing post as Mikey standing with his back to me. The image morphed into Emma's smirk, and changed again into Brent as he scolded me then praised me for being such a wonderful support tonight.

I knew better than to throw while angry. Last time I'd done it, I blew out my shoulder. I reached back and hurled the axe. It slipped smoothly from my grip, turning head over handle. Mikey would have been proud. The blade pierced the center of the target. Perfect. I scoffed and drained my pitcher.

The last letter I received from Max had said, "Da knows. Don't write." That was it. Three years ago. If Da had his way, my family will have forgotten about me by now. Mikey would never be proud of me again. He had been, once, when he'd coached me, when I'd done everything expected of me.

Why was it that the one thing I was truly ever

good at gave me the most painful memories?

I ran the pad of my thumb over the smooth sapphires embedded in the handle and really thought about it. Was it, though? Was it really the one thing I was good at?

I couldn't sell my art. No agent had signed me. Brent had finally agreed to sell my carvings as a favor, with at least one of them still sitting in the display window. But no one wanted them. My art had been called 'primitive.'

I tossed another axe. It wasn't such a perfect throw, but the post was swaying, or I was, so I was content to have hit it at all.

My movie career was adequate. I earned a fair living at it. By Gilliam standards I was down right wealthy. I enjoyed the movies I made and still loved the creativity involved, but my creativity had dried up. I had no idea what I was going to do next. No matter how many hours I spent thinking and plotting and planning, I came up empty.

I hurled a third axe at the blurry post, which seemed to grow ever wider, and yet I missed it entirely.

Typical. I started off brilliantly with something, then in no time it became a disaster.

I tipped my pitcher, forcing the last few drops down my throat. Then I retrieved my axes and went back to haphazardly throwing.

I could make a movie about axe throwing…

Brent would loathe that idea. I laughed, bitterly.

He hated anything that took me away from his side. If I wanted a golden ring from him, I could never make such a movie, maybe not any movie. He may have been more demanding of my time over the last few months, but he had also been slower to anger.

After tonight, I wasn't so sure I wanted a golden ring. I didn't think I wanted anything from him.

What did it matter? It was a stupid idea. A movie about axe throwing would be the most boring movie ever.

I threw my final axe and hit the post beneath the target.

It might not be that boring, though. Not if I could think of a good story to go with it.

What kind of story could possibly make axe throwing exciting? It would have to be about some kind of competition. But who would want to watch that in a movie theater when they could watch it in person? We received flyers every week for tavern competitions around Leitham. Mind you, watching a bunch of drunk dwarves throw axes was hardly worth paying to see, unless you were as drunk as the competitors.

Oooo. I needed more ale.

I grabbed my pitcher and staggered inside.

Hadn't we received one of those flyers today? I dug through the garbage can behind the bar. I pulled out the crumpled, slightly soggy parchment and flattened it out in front of me.

The event was labeled as a Dwarf Games-track

competition. Those who won enough of these qualified for the city championships, and from there kept
moving up to qualify for the Dwarf Games.

Whatever happened to plain old tavern competitions for bragging rights? Like when I'd beaten
Ricky in Gilliam, and imagined throwing axes to
save Aramis?

Aramis, whom I hadn't seen since our movie
premiere. He'd said I'd saved his life when we ended
Aubrey and Radier's reign of terror. He still left to
take Aubrey's place as Lord of the Elves.

Yet another good thing in my life that had gone
so very wrong.

I tucked the flyer into my pocket next to my last
letter from Max, refilled my pitcher, and carried it up
to my room.

CHAPTER 2

I WIPED the sweat off my brow as I mopped the floor of the Hammer and Chisel. The physical effort of setting up for the evening crowd helped me feel useful.

The door slammed open.

"Mabel!" Sam declared, marching over. "Guess who's retiring from the movie business?"

"Not you, I hope." I set the mop aside and pulled the chairs down from the tables.

"Pff, no. Of course not me! Dakkar."

Dakkar, the first and only dragon I'd ever seen, tamed by Sevrin, trained to be in movies, adored by Sam for years. "Didn't she just finish a movie? And didn't you say she was still in great health?"

"She did, I did, and she is," Sam said. "But she

is slowing down and her trainers would rather retire her while she can still enjoy life, rather than wear her out."

That sounded lovely, but it didn't sound right. Not from what I'd seen over the few years I worked in movies. Most actors, and especially creatures, were worked until they couldn't work anymore. Sam's announcement seemed especially suspicious to me considering Dakkar was the only dragon in Leitham, or anywhere as far as anyone knew, so she was in high demand.

"Is she really in as good health as you say?"

"Dakkar has two movies left, then she's retiring. And I've applied to adopt her."

Sam was actually going to do it. She'd said she would after she spent her first day working with Dakkar, but I hadn't thought she'd stick to it after this many years. I should have known better. Sam didn't give up on anything, no matter how long it took to get it done.

"That's fantastic." I pulled down the last chair and moved behind the bar. I sorted through the stack of mail waiting there: a couple of bills, a few reservation requests, a letter or two for Sophie and Otto from friends or past guests, and another flyer for a local axe throwing competition.

My drunken musings of last night came back to me. I used to wish my axe throwing career had been recorded, made into a movie so that Aramis and Mam would see me. Maybe I should start competing again and record it, make a movie of it, and hope that my family and friends in Gilliam would see it and remember me. I smiled and tucked the flyer into my pocket along with the one from last night. I was too old to compete, not to mention completely out of shape. I hadn't thrown competitively in years, not even here at the Hammer and Chisel when some of the patrons drunkenly challenged each other and everyone within earshot.

I flipped through the letters once more, hoping, as I always did, that there would be a letter from Max. I knew there wouldn't be.

Sam cleared her throat. "Sorry," I said, setting aside the mail and prepped the tankards. "Where are you going to keep Dakkar?"

Sam dropped into a chair at a table nearest the bar. "I've had my eye on a property at the outskirts of town. It will take some work to fix it up and make a nice home for Dakkar. I'm pretty sure if I get custody, I can arrange with the studios to keep her where she is until my place is ready, if I have to."

I filled two tankards. "What about when you're working? How are you going to look after her then?" I placed one of the tankards in front of Sam.

"Lil and I are doing all right," Sam said. "We can take care of whatever medical treatments Dakkar might require. And we can hire someone to look after her while we're working."

I'd met Dakkar a few times. She was sweet, something I never imagined I would ever think about a dragon. "You can hire me to look after her," I said. "Then I wouldn't have to think about what movie to make next."

"Still struggling?" Sam asked.

"I've got nothing." I sank into the chair beside Sam. "Absolutely nothing. The more I think about it, the more I do to let my creativity flow, the worse it gets."

"What do you mean?"

"I come up with ideas but each one is more laughable than the one before."

"You're being too hard on yourself," Sam said. "Maybe you should share your next idea with some-one else and hear what they think before you dismiss it. Like me, or Lil, or any one of us. Try some out on us tonight."

"Or maybe I should just quit. Forget about mov-ies altogether."

"You can quit if you want, but I know you have at least one more movie inside of you."

I CHATTED amiably with our customers as I poured the pints. The interactions were cheerful, routine, and shallow—the weather, family well-being, and work.

I took Sam's advice about giving my ideas more of a chance and thought more about the flyers occupying my pocket. I had no need to be discovered by Mam or Aramis, nor did I need to send some kind of message to Da and my brothers. Maybe there was something there, though, to the notion of axe throwing in and of itself. I couldn't recall if any documentaries had been made about axe throwing, following the rise of a thrower from the bottom ranks to the Dwarf Games. Of course, what I thought would have made a good movie back when I was throwing, was that I was pretty much the only female competing in Gilliam. My brothers had often talked about there being other female axe throwers out there, yet I'd never heard them talk about any specific ones, not even any that Mikey may have competed against when he'd won the Dwarf Games.

"Hi hun," Brent said, breaking my focus. He leaned over the bar and kissed me.

"Hey, Brent," I said, kissing him back.

I looked over to Sophie and she nodded while serving a customer, releasing me to join my friends.

I poured a tray full of tankards for my friends and joined Brent. My friends when Brent and I arrived with the drinks. Jeff and Hannah jumped to their feet and took the tray from me.

Brent was in a very good mood. A couple of sales last night, including a big one to Sidney, made all the difference. He was smiling, calm, happy. Things were finally back to the way they used to be.

"I've been contacted by Fion about a new artist," Brent said.

"That's fantastic."

Brent shrugged. "I agreed to look at the work, but

even if it's a good fit for my gallery, I worry."

I nodded, but my back muscles automatically tensed. Brent worried the decline in his business meant that the artists he showed and sold weren't getting the market value they deserved, if they sold at all. He worried that the decline in his business meant that agents weren't sending him the top artists anymore, which devalued his gallery, which added to the decline of his business. One good night wouldn't automatically mean the struggle was over, but it was a sign that business was improving—wasn't it?

"Did you hear about Sam and Dakkar?" Hannah asked.

Brent shook his head. "No, what's happening?"

I smiled. Brent was worried, but he wasn't upset. I could relax. Knowing Sam wouldn't mind, I half-listened as she told Brent about her plans, and how she had enlisted everyone to help her out in their own specific way. I again allowed my mind to wander to the flyer for the axe throwing competition.

It might be worth going, having a look, see if there were any female throwers there who could carry a good story. I didn't want to simply go to such a competition and flat-out ask if I could record the competitors. I needed to scout out the competitors first and find out if there was someone worth recording. It would be much easier to do if I had a connection, some way to gain their trust.

"Hey." Jeff nudged me, interrupting my train of thought. "Where'd you go?"

"Nowhere," I lied. Sam glared at me. Now was as good a time as any to test my idea. "I was thinking about my next movie. It's a terrible idea." Sam cleared her throat and I sighed, giving in. I pulled out the flyer and passed it around, and picked up where my thoughts had left off. "I can't just go in there and ask to record them. It's a serious competition, and outside distractions will not be welcome."

"So what do you have to do?" Sam asked.

I thought for a moment. "The fastest and easiest thing to do would be to talk to the organizer and get permission to record, but there is no guarantee I'd find what I'm looking for. I'd rather find a subject to record before I do that. Even then, it might not be worth the trouble."

"So why don't you go in as a competitor?" Hannah asked.

"That is a great idea," Jeff said.

I shook my head. "I haven't competed in years."

"You don't have to be good, do you?" Lil asked.

They hadn't said it was a ridiculous idea. I absently massaged my right shoulder as I absorbed the idea, spinning it around in my mind.

"I don't think you should do it," Brent said.

My back tightened even more, making it painful to sit. I could feel Brent's displeasure. His demeanor hadn't changed. Nothing had changed. I could just tell he was getting angry. I shrank away from him.

"Why not?" Jeff jumped on him.

I didn't want Jeff provoking Brent.

"Mabel," Brent took my hand, holding it too tight. "I don't want you to get hurt. Physically or emotionally."

"It's only one competition," Hannah said. "She'll be fine."

"In a tiny, out-of-the-way tavern," Jeff added.

"Brent," Lil said, "None of us want Mabel to get hurt. She won't. She has us for support, and this isn't like it was for her in Gilliam. It's one competition. She won't attract any unwanted attention."

There really was nothing to worry about. "Aubrey's out of the picture," I said. "Radier won't bother me, neither will Sevrin."

Brent let go of my hand, leaving it cold and neglected. He cleared his throat and leaned back.

I'd known he wouldn't approve and yet I'd brought up axe throwing anyway. At the same time, I'd been unable to come up with a decent movie idea going on five months. This was the first real possibility of something good for me. The more I thought about it and talked about it to my friends, the more I liked it. Brent didn't have to be my biggest cheerleader, but he could, he should, support my happiness. Still, I didn't want to make him upset. That would ruin the evening for everyone, especially me.

"I'm not saying for sure that I'm going to do this," I said. "I haven't thrown in ages. While it's true I don't have to be good, I have to be somewhat decent to gain the respect of the other competitors, and I'm far from being somewhat decent. A better documentary might be following Sam's adoption of Dakkar. Starting with the history of dragons."

"I like that idea better," Brent said.

I breathed easier.

"It's a nice back-up plan," Lil said. "But I think you should give this axe throwing idea a chance. It's what you're more interested in, anyway."

"What makes you say that?" I asked.

"I've been watching you," Lil said. "You've been thinking about it for the past few hours, strategizing, figuring out how to make it work. You love the challenge, and you love axe throwing. I remember you telling me about the dream you had when you were younger, about your throwing career being made into a movie."

I looked away, blushing.

"See?" Lil pointed at me. "You love it. You didn't get your movie, but this could be the perfect chance to make it happen for someone else."

I sighed. I loved the idea. I didn't know if I could do it, though. Brent exhaled loudly, his irritation simmering.

"All right." Jeff slammed down his empty tankard. "You don't know if you'll be good enough to gain their trust. Let's find out. I challenge you, Mabel Goldenaxe, to an axe throwing contest, here, tonight, right now, at the Hammer and Chisel. Let's see how bad you really are. I think you'll be fine, but prove me wrong. And if it is too emotionally painful out here, then you know you don't have to pursue this idea."

"Jeff, don't," Brent said.

"Come on," Jeff said. "It's a couple of axes, out back, for fun, among friends."

It wasn't the worst idea Jeff had ever had. I could see how bad I was and put this plan to rest once and for all, and have some fun while doing it. "All right, Jeff. I accept your challenge." I drained my tankard and set it down. "Let's go."

My friends cheered, and Brent quietly followed us out to the back. His silent disapproval weighed on me, made me feel guilty. I shouldn't hurt him like this. Knots twisted in my stomach and I considered backing out. We exited to the empty back garden, the throwing post standing in the far corner. There was no one else here to watch. Surely Brent could see that there was nothing to worry about.

I dug out a few of my throwing axes I had tucked away in the back shed when I first moved in here. I gave a random set of three to Jeff, and kept the axes Mikey had given me for myself.

"Okay," Jeff said, holding the axes, swinging his arms in gigantic circles. "How do you do this?"

I burst out laughing. "You've never thrown before and you challenged me?"

"If I remember right, you'd never thrown before you accepted your first challenge," Jeff countered.

"Fair point. Guess I'll be coach and competitor," I muttered with a smile. "First of all, stop swinging your arms like that."

Jeff listened as I told him how to hold the axe, how to move his arm, reaching back then bringing the arm down from the shoulder first, elbow second, and finally the wrist for the release.

We'd gained a small gathering of spectators by the time I permitted Jeff a few practice throws. The knots in my stomach twisted harder. I glanced at Brent who stood to the side, arms crossed, scowling. My shoulders slumped under the weight of his disapproval, draining my enthusiasm. Jeff was having so much fun, though. I couldn't stop now. I'd make it up to Brent later.

When Jeff finally hit the throwing post on his fifth throw, he declared himself ready for competition.

I stood at the throwing line, focusing on the post. Preparing to throw my axe drove Brent from my mind. My breath caught and my stomach clenched. I shouldn't be nervous. I'd done this before. I had nothing to fear. I blinked rapidly a few times, trying to get into the competitive frame of mind. To focus on the target and make my best throw.

The chatter of the spectators was too loud. It had never bothered me before, but now they sounded like the birdsong in the Gilliam forest, back when I hated it, when it was loud and intrusive and a constant reminder that my family wasn't wealthy enough to live under the mountain like proper dwarves.

I automatically looked to where Mikey always stood when I competed at The Bearded Prospector. He wasn't there. Of course he wasn't there. I was at the Hammer and Chisel, in Leitham, I wasn't in Gilliam.

Why was I putting myself through this? For a movie?

I wasn't really competing. Not like I used to. This was for fun, nothing serious. I didn't have to be great. I just had to be good enough.

I held my breath and threw, barely hitting the target. I'd thrown better last night when I was drunk. "I guess I was the one who needed the practice throws," I joked. "Your turn, Jeff."

Jeff stepped to the line and prepared to throw. Brent moved to my side and whispered. "Are you all right?"

I nodded. "You can do this, Jeff," I called out.

Jeff smiled at me and threw. His axe hit the target on the exact opposite side from mine. Jeff threw up his hands and cheered. "Woohoo! I'm as good as the Gilliam champion!"

"I wasn't quite champion," I said taking my place at the throwing line.

Jeff shrugged. "Second? Third? Whatever. Close enough."

My next throws weren't much better than my first, but then neither were Jeff's. I won, just barely, and a part of me suspected Jeff might have let me win to boost my confidence about competing again. My shoulder was fine, maybe a little tired from the exertion of both now and last night's drunken throwing, but that wasn't a bad feeling. It had actually been exhilarating.

At Jeff's insistence, I bought a round of drinks for my friends in celebration.

"Mabel." Brent pulled me aside. "I really think this is a bad idea. I don't want you to injure your shoulder again. I don't want Radier or Sevrin to use you for their organizations."

I shrank from his anger and I hated myself for it. I'd never let anyone dictate my life. Why was I letting Brent do it now? I jerked my elbow out of his painful grip. "I'm only going to be in enough competitions to gain the trust of the other throwers, so I can find a good subject and make the documentary I've always wanted to be made. I'll be fine."

I couldn't really make that promise. There was always a chance Sevrin or Radier could come after me, but I didn't think they would. More than that, I hoped they wouldn't.

CHAPTER 3

I SLAPPED the flyer and my entry fee onto the bar. The bartender swept the two gold coins into his palm and pointed me to the back garden. Hoisting my bag of axes higher on my shoulder, I nodded my thanks and headed to the throwing range.

It was strange to be at a competition without a coach or any friends. There was something I liked about it. I didn't know anyone and no one knew me. I had no reputation to live up to. I was just another dwarf looking for some action.

I signed in along with six other competitors, including another female. I guess Mikey had been right about there being other female throwers.

The competitive space was small. It was like any other tavern competition, except this one had an entry fee, and no one was drinking. There was only the one throwing post and it was at the furthest distance possible given the space, which was equal to that of the first round of a major competition. There was no way it could be moved for round two, and there was definitely no room for the pop-up targets of round three. How was this a Dwarf Games-track competition if there weren't any pop-up targets?

I took my place on the sidelines and set down my axes. I sized up the others as I stretched and warmed up the way Mikey had taught me: rotating my shoulders and moving my head from side to side, loosening my neck muscles. I drew return stares and I welcomed them. It was all a part of the gamesmanship. However minor my actions were, if the others were intimidated by them, then it worked for me.

I smiled to myself. I was attempting to play mind games like a real competitor. I wasn't here to see if any of the others were interested in mating. I was here to prove myself to myself, period. Still, I ran my fingers through my meager beard.

A couple of the contestants had coaches with them, whispering last minute instructions and tips. I glanced down at the axes in my hand. I missed Mikey telling me to relax and pay attention to my technique.

This was no time to be sentimental about my family or maudlin about how they'd turned their backs on me.

One more competitor arrived, an older fellow,

much older, with a fully grey beard. I guess Mikey didn't get everything right. He'd said he was too old to go back to competing. Apparently there was no age limit, at least not to these low-level competitions.

One by one we were given a few minutes to take a handful of practice throws. The shadow pain returned to my right shoulder and my throws were well off the target. I rotated my shoulder some more as I collected my axes. Mikey always said it was better to get the poor throws out of the way during the warmup. Even so, the tightness worried me. I massaged my shoulder as I waited for my turn.

The first few throwers barely landed their axes in the target area. I couldn't do much worse than they had. That took an enormous amount of pressure off me.

The other female was good. Her axe hit the bulls-eye dead center.

I selected my first axe and stepped to the throwing line. The shadow pain was still present. I kneaded my shoulder once more. I reached back, focusing on the target, breathed deep three times, and threw. The axe came out of my hand too early. Fortunately the axe hit the target rather than flying over it, or falling entirely too short and hitting the ground. It wasn't the worst throw ever, but it was far from the best.

As I took my place on the sidelines, I coached myself. I could make up some ground with the two throws I had left—I usually did, as long as I paid attention to my technique.

The old guy was pretty good. He and the female were both ahead of me. I improved with my second throw, but so did everyone else. By my third throw I was too far back to move up from fourth, and the person in fifth was close in points. I could be satisfied with placing fourth, but that didn't mean I had any desire to move down a spot.

I stepped to the throwing line one last time. The shadow pain was stronger. I considered that maybe it was real, not imagined and I should take something for it when I got home. Not some strange old family recipe though, like the poison Emma had given me. On the other hand, it was probably nothing. It would probably be fine in the morning. Aramis's father, Aubrey, had healed me. I was fairly certain pain couldn't come back unless I did something to cause new damage, which I hadn't. The competition was bringing back the bad memories of the poison Emma had given me, and how I'd ruined my axe throwing career. That was all.

One last time I rotated my shoulder, breathed deep, and hurled my axe. The release was my best one of the night. I hit the ring next to the bullseye. I pumped my fist. I'd secured my fourth place.

I was the only one, besides the winner, happy with their result.

"What's your story?" The female thrower approached me as I packed up my axes.

"It's been a few years since I've competed," I said. "I had an injury that kept me out of it for some

time, and then life got in the way. I didn't know if I
could still throw."

"Huh," she grunted. "I expect it won't be long
before you're beating all of us."

I shrugged. "We'll see. You're pretty good yourself."

"Thanks, but this is the remnants of my lack-
luster throwing career. The name's Reede, by the
way." She stuck out her hand.

I shook it. "Mabel. Nice to meet you. Will I see
you at the next competition?"

We hefted our bags and walked to the front street
together.

"I hadn't planned on it, but it's so rare to compete against a female, you just might see me there."
Reede smiled.

An interesting comment. I was even more curious now about the existence of female axe throwers.
How many were there? "You've competed against
other females?"

"Not many but some. Haven't you?"

She just might be the one I wanted to make the
movie about. I wanted to get to know her a little
better before asking. "No. I was told that there were
others, but I've never met any. Not where I'm from."

"Where's that?"

"Gilliam, in the Black Mountain region."

"Oooh, no, there aren't any. Wow. You came out
of there? That's impressive. It's kind of an unwritten
rule that the Black Mountain region doesn't gener-

ally approve of female competitors. You must have had a pretty liberal coach."

Mikey, liberal? That was the last word I would have used to describe him. "I don't think so. He was my brother, and to be honest, probably the only reason he coached me was because I'm not sure he always remembered I was female."

Reede chuckled. "Brothers can be that way. Mine are the same. At any rate, I'm impressed. It was nice meeting you, Mabel. I look forward to throwing with you again."

I watched Reede walk the other way. I didn't just want to record her. I wanted to beat her. I would have to practice extra hard for that to happen. I needed to prove that females from the Black Mountains could throw axes, and win.

Dear gods of iron and stone, the pumping adrenaline of competition was a rush!

THE EVENING press at the Hammer and Chisel was in full swing by the time I returned. Sophie was swamped behind the bar.

I hugged my bag to my chest as I pushed through the crowded tavern to the bar. I stepped around it and put my bag down. "What can I get you?" I asked the nearest patron as if I had been there all along.

"Five pitchers of your stoutest ale," he said, his speech on the edge of slurring.

"Where were you?" Sophie asked, beside me.

I filled the pitchers from the cask. "I had some things to take care of." I wasn't sure why I hesitated telling her I'd been throwing axes. There was no need to keep it a secret.

"Things, huh? There's a glow about you. Have a good time, did you?"

In Gilliam, coming in fourth in a similar competition would have been a humiliation. After all I'd been through, fourth felt incredible. My cheeks burned. "I did, thanks."

"Good. Does this glow have anything to do with those throwing axes of yours?"

"It does." I grinned.

"And movies?"

"Maybe." There were so many ideas bursting to life, I couldn't possibly say more without running the risk of jinxing everything. Sophie knew me well enough not to push for more.

I handed the last of the pitchers to the patron and took his payment. I watched him as he swayed the first few steps away from the bar. I held my breath, hoping I wouldn't be cleaning up all that ale off the floor. He straightened soon enough and I breathed a sigh of relief.

"Hey," Brent said, approaching the bar, a flyer in his hand. He leaned over and kissed me on the cheek. "I've been looking all over for you. No matter, you're here now. Look."

Had he forgotten the axe throwing competition

had been tonight? Or was he just going to pretend it didn't exist? He was in a good mood. I needed to let it go.

He placed the flyer in front of me. It was a poster advertising The Gilliam Dragon Killers, my hometown's battle-axe team, coming to take on the Leitham Brigade two months from now. Of course I knew about it. I'd been watching the battle-axe schedule for years. "I know."

Brent smirked. He slipped two tickets on top of the flyer. "Want to go with me?"

I squealed as I jumped up and planted a kiss on his lips. "As if you needed to ask."

A moment of sadness washed over me. I bit my bottom lip.

"What is it?" Brent asked.

"I used to have the full Dragon Killers uniform, including the shield." I assumed Da had burned it all since none of it had been among my few possessions Max had managed to save for me. I shrugged and shook off the melancholy. "I'll just have to buy it all new. I'd pretty much out grown it, anyway."

Brent gave me a blank stare. He didn't know much about sports. He basically tolerated me talking about them. I was sure the only reason he was taking me to the battle-axe competition was because he knew how much I loved the Dragon Killers.

"Most everyone who goes to this kind of thing wears the uniform of their favorite team," I said. "It's custom. Expected. I'll get you something, too. You'll love it."

"Are you sure you want to be wearing the uniform of the enemy team?" Brent asked.

"Enemy?" I said with intense indignation. I poured a few tankards of ale for another customer. "The Dragon Killers are heroes. They may be the opposition here in Leitham, but I wouldn't be caught dead in the uniform of any other team."

Brent's expression scarcely changed. He didn't share my passion. That was fine. What mattered was that he was taking me to see the Dragon Killers.

A line of patrons five deep had formed around Brent. "Can we talk more later?" I asked as apologetically as I could. "I really should help Sophie a little while longer."

"Oh, yeah, sure."

"Wait, Brent," Sophie said. "May I see one of those tickets?"

"Um, all right," he hesitated but gave her one.

"Wow," she said. "These are really good seats." Sophie showed it to me and pointed out the section and row number to me. "Otto and I used to go all the time. We'd sit near here. You can see everything. You feel like you can reach out and touch the teams."

Never in my life could I ever have dreamed of seats like that to see the Dragon Killers in Gilliam. "We definitely have to get the right gear now."

Sophie handed me the ticket and I tucked it in my pocket.

Brent's eyes widened for a moment. I could tell

he was trying to find a way to get the ticket back. Normally I would have given it to him, but I decided to leave it in my pocket this time. If it really was for me, then he should have no problem letting me hold onto it.

To my surprise, Brent walked away. I had a feeling he was going to get upset with me later, but for now, everything was all right.

I found myself breathing easier as I rushed to serve the impatient customers.

I busied myself tending the bar, spying Brent every now and then out of the corner of my eye, holding court near the fireplace, regaling a crowd with his stories of his encounters with one famous artist or another. I smiled as I watched him, admiring his storytelling ability. He commanded a room better than anyone I'd seen.

We were busy right up to closing time. I ushered out the last of the patrons and locked the door. Brent usually stayed behind but he wasn't anywhere to be seen. I wondered if he was out back.

"I'll clean up," I said to Sophie and Otto. "You've had a long night. Why don't you go on home?"

"You sure?" Sophie asked, coming around the bar.

"Of course. It should be a quiet night. Our few guests have gone up already."

"If you need us, you know where we are," Otto said.

"I'll be fine," I said, shooing them out the door.

I didn't have to clean up right away. I needed to find Brent after neglecting him all evening.

"Brent?" I called, walking out back. He wasn't there, either. He must have gone home. My heart sank, hurt that he hadn't said good night.

I picked up the tankards left by the customers and carried them inside. I'd make an extra effort to see him tomorrow. I put up the last of the chairs and pushed Brent's silent departure out of my mind. The floor wasn't too bad. I needed to mop it but I wanted to get some practice in. I grabbed my bag of axes and took it to the throwing range. The chilly air made it a perfect night for throwing. I needed to put in plenty of hours on the range. I may have entered tonight's competition hoping to perform respectably. I'd done that. Now I wanted to push myself to improve on those results. I wanted to win.

I worked my way through the exercise routine Mikey used to make me do: sprints, push-ups, weight-lifting with the axes, and stretches. I stopped in the midst of a push-up. Mikey's coaching was loud in my head, "Breathe. Push yourself. Give me five more."

I set my axes aside, closed my eyes, and followed his instructions.

"Stretch out again, keep your shoulders loose," I heard him say. I couldn't picture his face. All I could see was the back of his head as he spoke, his back turned to me, blocking the walk to our family home.

My stomach churned. I rested my hands on my

knees. What was I doing to myself?

I straightened up, took a deep breath, and rotated my arms in big circles to loosen up my shoulders. "I'm not doing it for my family or to find a mate," I muttered. "I'm doing this for me."

Tonight's competition had been fun. For the first time in my life, the only pressure was what I put on myself. There was no need to impress anyone in hopes that they would want to be my mate, I didn't have to prove my strength. I didn't have to please Aramis, or any other director or agent. I had been on my own. I only had to impress myself, and do the best I could. I'd enjoyed it enough to try it again.

Mikey had been a great coach. Thinking about him hurt, but I could still benefit from what he taught me. I'd take his instruction as far as I could go.

I had nothing to lose.

Nothing except Brent.

He would come around. When he recognized I wasn't competing in big tournaments or actually going for the Dwarf Games, that is.

CHAPTER 4

MY CARVING of Sevrin stood on the shelf in the display window of the River's Edge Art Gallery. It wasn't the only one that hadn't sold, but it was the only one on display. Knowing what I knew now about Sevrin, it didn't surprise me no one wanted it. Having a statue of Sevrin in my home would be the last thing I'd want. I wondered how many of Brent's clients, and the dwarven community in Leitham as a whole, knew about Sevrin. As I walked in, picnic basket in hand, I wished for the millionth time that Brent would take the statue down.

"Brent?" I called. The gallery was devoid of patrons yet again. This was not good. He was going to be in a bad mood. My head hurt, an intense pressure at my temples. I'd really thought the opening of

Celia's exhibit the other night had made a difference.

"Hey, Mabel," Brent said, coming out of his office. "What brings you by?"

"I was so busy yesterday and I felt bad for not getting more time with you, so I thought I'd make it up to you by bringing you some lunch."

"Aren't you the sweetest." Brent kissed me on the cheek. "And such good timing, too. I'm starving."

We walked back to his office. I yawned as I set out the roast pork sandwiches, deep fried mushrooms, and two jars of mead.

"You look tired. Everything all right?" he asked, caressing my arm, concern in his voice.

I considered telling him I'd practiced my axe throwing for a couple of hours after I closed up the tavern, but I thought better of it. I was here to make up for not spending time with him yesterday. He seemed to be all right and I didn't want to antagonize him.

"Yes, of course. I just had some trouble falling asleep last night, that's all."

"Anything in particular bothering you?"

Only his reaction to my axe throwing. I'd enjoyed my practice so much that mentally and emotionally I could have carried on for a couple more hours if I hadn't been so physically exhausted. I may love axe throwing, but that didn't mean I was willing to risk injury by pushing myself too hard. "No, no. Probably because work was so busy. That's all."

"If you're sure."

"Yes, of course." I waved a hand dismissively. He was in a decent mood. The absence of clients in the gallery was hopefully just a lunchtime lull. My head hurt more. We began to eat. "When are you going to take my carving out of your window?"

"Never," Brent said, matter-of-factly.

"You really should. You know I won't be upset. It isn't selling, and it isn't bringing in any more clients either. In fact, I'd venture that it's driving them away. No one wants to look at, and especially not buy art, where there might be any association with the Dwarven Mafia."

"Most dwarves don't know that Sevrin is the head of the Dwarven Mafia. To them, he is still the adventuring hero. Your carving is not scaring off potential clients." He put his sandwich down and brushed the crumbs off his hands. "I think Sevrin, the real Sevrin, and his connections, are."

Brent's pointed statement made me uncomfortable. Why hadn't he said something if Sevrin had stayed involved in the gallery all along? "He promised he would leave you alone," I said.

"You are so trusting, Mabel. It's one of the things I love so much about you. But, love, he's crooked. If he can break the law, you can be sure he has no problem breaking promises."

His arrogant condescension was as good as a slap in the face. If Sevrin was back bothering Brent, causing problems, then it was my fault and I needed to make it right. "Has he been in here? Has he threatened you?"

"No." Brent shook his head. "He has left me alone. The problem, I suspect, is that he's making everyone else leave me alone, too."

I put my fried mushroom down. "How long has this been going on? Why haven't you told me before?"

Brent sighed. "For a couple of years. You're happy, Mabel. I didn't want to say anything that might make you unhappy. Quite frankly, I'm willing to let it go because I don't want us to ever have to deal with Sevrin or any of that turmoil again."

If that were true, he wouldn't have mentioned it at all. "Is that why you're keeping that carving in the window? You're hoping he'll see it, and see that you're loyal to him? If he believes you're loyal to him then he'll stop hurting your business?" If that were the case, it wasn't working very well.

Brent shrugged. "I'm keeping it there because you made it, and I love you. If that other stuff were to happen, then that would be a bonus. That is all." Brent leaned forward and held my hand. "I'm sorry. I shouldn't have said anything. Everything is fine. Trust me. I am fine. My business is fine."

It was not fine. If it was, he wouldn't have told me and heaped the blame of his troubles on me, which hurt worse than a pick-axe to the heart. The pain didn't matter if he was right. It was my fault and I needed to fix it.

"Brent, I trust you, but you do not have to continue to suffer because of me."

Brent stood, pulling me with him and into an embrace. "I am not suffering because of you. Don't ever say that again."

I pushed him away. "You are being punished by Sevrin because I refused to work for him."

"Mabel—"

I held up my hand. "We have both paid enough of a price to Aubrey, Radier, and Sevrin. I'm done with it. And that, my love, is all."

"What are you going to do? Scratch that. Don't do anything, Mabel. Leave it, please."

"I'm not going to do anything yet. I don't know what, or even if, I can do anything. All I am saying is that Sevrin needs to stop. It's been going on far too long."

"Please, leave it."

Brent's grip on my arms had tightened to the point of hurting me. I felt his terror, even though he tried to hide it behind a smile.

He couldn't lay this on me then tell me to leave it. I broke from his hold. Walking out I said, "No."

I HAD intended to walk back to the Hammer and Chisel to exercise and get in shape for axe throwing. Leaving Brent's gallery, what he had said about Sevrin infuriated me. I was pretty sure there wasn't anything I could do to stop Sevrin, short of promising to work for him, which I would never do. On the other hand, Mam ought to know what Sevrin was up to. If she did, I hoped she would be willing to tell me.

I hired a taxi to take me to Studio City.

The menagerie of creatures and species walking around never ceased to amaze me, much like walking into the entrance of the Gilliam mine and soaking in the beauty of the crystals and stone. I reveled in being a part of such a diverse society, experiencing our differences first-hand rather than through stories. I lived in a world that had been beyond anything I could have imagined in Gilliam.

Some of the sound stages were in use. Others had their doors closed and pieces of unused sets sat outside.

I walked to studio twenty-two where Mam had started making a new movie. The first days on set always put her in a good mood so it was the perfect time to talk with her about anything, especially Sevrin.

The main doors were closed so I walked around to the side and slipped in. I checked out the set but she wasn't there. I found Mam's dressing-room and knocked on the door.

"Be right there," she called.

I opened the door and poked my head in. "Hiya, Mam. Got a few minutes?"

Mam jumped up from her seat, rushed over to me and yanked me inside. "For you? I have all the time in the world! How are you, my darling? How is that lovely fellow of yours?"

I extracted myself from her. "Everything's grand, really. I have an idea for a new movie. It is too early to talk about, but it has some real possibilities."

"I have no doubt."

"It's Brent that I'm here about, actually."

"Oh?"

"It's his gallery. It seems that…" I sighed and started again. "It's about Sevrin."

Mam leaned back and narrowed her eyes. "What's he done now?"

"I'm not sure he's done anything. For the past few years, Brent's gallery has been losing business and it shouldn't be. He has new and innovative artists exhibiting there. He has a great reputation. The only explanation, the one that seems most logical, is that Sevrin isn't the only one leaving Brent alone."

"What are you saying?"

"I'm wondering if maybe Sevrin, when he made it known to his organization that Brent's gallery is off limits, that it was interpreted as stopping anyone from going there. Was that his intention? Or is it a misunderstanding he isn't aware of?"

"Is it possible there isn't a need for what Brent offers anymore? These things can come and go, you know."

I expected her to take Sevrin's side. Arguing with her or showing my disappointment wasn't going to help me find out what was really going on. Showing my frustration and helplessness might. "Sure, sure."

I shrugged and looked over her shoulder at the wall behind her. "You're probably right."

"Sweetheart, we can figure this out, together."

I nodded and turned my gaze to the floor.

"I'll talk to Sevrin," Mam said. "If it is because of him, I'm sure it was a misunderstanding. I'll ask him to look into it."

"That would be great. Thanks, Mam."

"Anything for you, love. Why don't you and Brent come over for dinner one evening next week? My recording schedule ends fairly early each day, and I'd love to have the two of you over."

Time to give myself a guarantee she'll talk to Sevrin. "I'd love to, Mam, but I need to figure out how I'm going to make this movie, and Brent is putting everything he can into keeping his gallery open. It's putting a lot of strain on us right now. I don't know if we'll last to next week, if things keep going the way they are."

I sagged into a chair and hung my head. Maybe I was laying it on a little thick, but as an actress, Mam needed the dramatics to be able to relate and understand.

"Oh, honey, is it really that bad?"

"He hasn't had business in ages. I don't know how he's managed to stay open this long. I think he's almost exhausted his savings. He blames me for all of it. He says he doesn't, but I know, deep down, he does."

"Business will improve soon, I'm sure of it. He

can't hold it against you forever. If he does, he isn't worth your time."

"I know, Mam, but I love him so much, and it is my fault. I want him to be happy."

"Of course you do, but it goes both ways. Does he make you happy?"

A pang of anxiety ripped through me. He used to. He had the other day with tickets to see the Dragon Killers. "He does."

"Honey, it will be all right."

"I hope so." I sniffed and stood up. "Thanks, Mam. I should let you finish getting ready. I'll talk with Brent about coming to your place."

Mam hugged me again.

I clung to her for a moment, fighting back the tears. I hadn't lied about Brent blaming me and I wished I could talk to Mam about it. Really talk to her like daughters should be able to with their mam, like I'd thought I would be able to when I first moved here with her. As long as Sevrin was in her life, I would never allow myself to get that close to her again.

WHILE I was in Studio City, I decided to stop in and see Sam. She wasn't working today, so there was only one place she would be: with Dakkar.

I almost felt bad about using Mam. The way she'd used me when I first moved to Leitham had nearly destroyed me. It was hypocritical of me to use her now. Even so, I hoped if she ever realized what I'd done, she would find a way to forgive me.

Dakkar's imitation-mountain home loomed at the back of Studio City. Dakkar knew my voice and my scent. I didn't have to be super careful in approaching. To my surprise, Sam wasn't outside Dakkar's protective fence.

From twenty feet away, I called out. "Hiya, Dakkar. It's me, Mabel Goldenaxe. Is it all right for me to visit with you?"

I waited a full minute, wondering if Dakkar was here. She did have a couple of movies left to make. It was possible she was still working. I heard a snort, and her snout poked out the entrance of her cave.

I walked a little closer and repeated my greeting.

Dakkar poked her head out, took in a big sniff of my scent, pulling me toward her in the suction of her intake of air, and lumbered out to the fence, her face leaning over, smiling, ready for me to pet her.

"Hiya, sweetheart." I stroked her cheek and her chin. "I hear our friend Sam is hoping to take you home."

Dakkar nudged my head and purred when I mentioned Sam. If I hadn't been standing where I was, knowing it was a happy purr rather than a roar, I would have been terrified. As it was, there was a ringing in my ears for several seconds.

Her happy snorts and grunts grew in frequency. Out of the corner of my eye, I saw Sam approach.

"Hey, Sam."

"You're not trying to take Dakkar from me, are you?" she asked with a smile.

"Hardly. We were just talking about you. Weren't we, Dakkar?"

She purred again.

"Aww. That's sweet. And so good. Because I have officially put an offer on the property I was telling you about. Hopefully I'll get it soon so I can start building you a proper home."

Dakkar's wings flapped, she thumped her tail and licked Sam with her forked tongue. The ground shook and the left side of Sam's face and hair was soaking wet.

"Okay, okay," Sam said, patting Dakkar's snout. "Maybe let's not do that again."

"You two are adorable. Any word on the adoption?"

"Unfortunately, yes. There's another applicant wanting to adopt her."

"Do you know who?"

Sam cleared her throat, kissed Dakkar's snout, and said, "Sevrin."

Dakkar reared back, snorted and stomped her back foot causing the ground to vibrate.

Sevrin, again.

"Dakkar," I said. "You don't like Sevrin, do you?"

She shook her head and stomped both feet so hard I had to grab the fence to keep my balance.

"But Sevrin is the one who introduced me to you. I thought you liked him."

Her body relaxed and yet seemed frozen in fear, subservient, obedient, on the verge of trembling, devoid of energy or will. She nudged me, snorted, then fell back into that horrible state. I saw it now. I hadn't seen it then. This was the same posture she'd had with Sevrin: friendly but subservient.

"He took your mam from you. He took your fire from you."

Dakkar rested her head on my shoulder, the weight of it crushing me. I couldn't help but hug her and share in the affection. She knew, she understood, he'd done the same to me.

"We can't let him have her," I said. "What can I do to help?"

"I don't know," Sam said. "I'm hoping that by being proactive in getting the property and building the beautiful home for Dakkar, the committee determining her adoption will see how committed I am. That has to work in my favor. Surely they'd have to take Dakkar's wishes into account, wouldn't they?"

Dakkar licked Sam again. "Okay. I appreciate the gesture, but please, a nudge or a snort will do."

I couldn't help but laugh. "But Sam, this is a great look for you, really."

"Shut up," she said, drying her face with her sleeve.

"How about if I write up a character reference

for you? I'll be happy to tell them how much you and Dakkar love each other, how you'll care for her, and I might even slip in that Sevrin would be terrible. I don't understand why he wants her."

Dakkar smacked her foot down.

"I don't know," Sam said. "It isn't like he ever comes to visit her. The only thing I can think of is that she's his prize. He captured her and tamed her. My guess is he thinks she belongs to him."

Big tears fell from Dakkar, splattering in puddles by our feet. My heart broke for her. "I can't believe I used to look up to him, like he was some kind of hero."

Dakkar looked at me, her eyes narrowing, suspicious of me.

"I know better now," I said to her.

"We all grew up worshipping him," Sam said. "How could we not, given the stories we heard? Most dwarves still worship him because they don't know what he is or what he's done."

"Or what he continues to do," I added.

"What do you mean?"

Dakkar's head was back on my shoulder, my knees threatened to buckle under the weight.

"It's likely he's the one responsible for Brent's gallery failing."

"Brent hasn't said anything," Sam said. "He's only said artistic tastes must be changing."

"They may be, but they don't change that dramatically, or that instantly." I told Sam about my conversations with Brent and Mam.

"You think she'll actually confront..." Sam stopped herself from saying Sevrin's name and upsetting Dakkar again.

"If she wants to see me again she will. Mind you, she walked out on me once and she may have no problem doing it again. I hope that over the past few years she's gotten to know me enough that the choice is a little harder for her this time."

"And if she doesn't confront him?"

I shook my head. "Then I have no idea what I'm going to do."

Aramis and his gratitude at our movie premiere came to mind. He'd said I'd saved his life, that he'd so anything for me. I hadn't seen him since then.

News of his whereabouts was scarce. He'd returned to his people and taken over from Aubrey as Lord of the Elves in an attempt to repair the damage Aubrey and Radier had done. At first I'd been glad he was gone. I'd needed the time to heal from the hurt he'd caused. After a year or so, I'd thought I would have heard something from him.

I didn't know how I felt about him now. I didn't know him anymore. I wasn't sure I'd ever known him. He could still be fighting to save his people, or he could have fixed everything. For all I knew, he could be ruling them the way Aubrey had. No one talked about him. Not even the elves from his own clan who passed through Leitham.

I wondered if I found him, if I talked to him, if

Aramis would be willing to help me. I couldn't picture him turning on his oldest friend. Then again, he was immortal. He was going to outlive Sevrin, and wasn't it the responsibility of the elves to be stewards of the earth and look after the peoples on it? How many times had Aramis protected the interests of the next generation over those of a friend?

I didn't know how to find him. I didn't need Aramis's help. Mam would talk to Sevrin, get him to stop hurting Brent. If she didn't, well, I didn't really like going to her place, anyway. It brought up too many painful memories. I had no difficulty coming to visit her at Studio City. Brent and I would find a way to make his business succeed again, and find a way to protect it from Sevrin.

CHAPTER 5

I WALKED to the back of the tavern to the throwing range. Nearly all of the participants were the same as the last competition. I spotted Reede and waved. She smiled back, and motioned for me to join her.

"So, is this it for axe throwing competitors in Leitham?" I set down my bag of axes and began stretching.

"Yes and no," she said, doing her own warmup. "We all live in or near this neighborhood so that's where we tend to compete. There are competitions in other dwarven neighborhoods where the locals compete against each other. These tavern things are too small to be worth traveling for, even within the city."

I'd see how tonight went, and if Reede was a

suitable and willing subject for my documentary, then great. If not, I might have to look into these other competitions.

We were called to attention. As I listened to the official go over the rules, I noticed the handful of spectators. There were actual spectators here, friends of some of the competitors. I hadn't realized friends were allowed. I might ask my friends to come to the next one.

I was the first one to throw. I hated being the first one. I stepped to the line, axe in hand. The spectators shuffled and mumbled into their ale. It was weird. I expected them to be drunk and loud like they'd been at the Prospector. I would have loved it if Max or Jimmy showed up, but that was never going to happen.

I smiled. It could happen, sort of.

I readied the axe on my shoulder, breathed deep, and shut out all the noise and activity around me, focusing on the target, imagining I could hear Max and Jimmy cheering, raising their tankards of ale to me. Then I remembered Max's last letter to me and they vanished from my imagination.

I was alone.

I didn't need anyone cheering for me.

I lined up the axe and threw. The release was remarkably good considering how stiff my arm was. The axe rotated nicely head over handle once, then pierced the second inner-most circle. Unlike last time where my throws were either too high or too low, this one was to the right.

"Nice," Reede said when I took my place beside her on the sidelines.

"Thanks," I mumbled, trying to figure out how I got the release so good with such bad technique.

"You've been practicing," Reede said.

"A little. At night, when I can. I'm surprised you can tell."

"Your release is a lot better than last time."

"Yeah, but my technique is off."

"It wasn't too bad. You were a little tight, but who isn't on their first throw?"

I shrugged and watched the others, one after another, hit the center of the target. Some were a little too tight, or too loose, but they were all better than me.

This was going to be a tough competition tonight.

Reede was the last one up for the first round. Her technique was impeccable.

"Wow," I said when she sat down. "I thought you said you were on the decline of a lack-luster career."

She chuckled. "Trust me, I am."

It was my turn again. I closed my eyes and did my best to remember Mikey's coaching. Keep my shoulder relaxed, all the motion should be from my elbow and wrist. My technique and my release were much better but I still hit the second inner-most circle.

"Did you ever make it to the Dwarf Games?" I asked Reede, standing next to her once more.

"I did, a couple of times, many years ago. Second was my best placing."

"Really? That's incredible." I definitely had to make the documentary about her. I wondered how it was that I had not heard of her. My brothers knew every axe thrower to ever place at the Dwarf Games. They used to talk about them non-stop when I was younger. At least they had, until Mikey stopped competing. I couldn't remember them ever talking about a Reede or any female thrower for that matter. She must have competed after Mikey.

"It was all right," she shrugged.

"You placed second. That's huge! You don't like competing?"

"That's not it," she said and she got this look in her eyes, like she was thinking about something that happened long ago, something that hurt. Mikey had that same look when he talked to me about why he stopped competing. "I love throwing. There were some...other things that happened that I'm not so fond of."

I understood. "It's always the external troubles or expectations that ruin a good thing." I thought of my desperation to find a mate, and my need to prove my strength, which had pushed me so hard and ruined everything: my shoulder, my love of throwing, and my mining career.

"Truer words have never been spoken, my friend," Reede said as she stepped to the line, once again making a perfect throw.

"Nice," I complimented her.

"Thanks. You're pulling to the right when you raise up your axe. Keep your arm tight to your ear."

I glanced at her, skeptical, surprised she was giving me advice. "I will, thanks."

I strode to the line and lifted up my arm. There was no pain in my shoulder, not even phantom pain this time, but I had difficulty bringing it in as close to my head as I needed too. I grit my teeth and held my arm there, breathing through the muscle strain, then released.

It was as close to a perfect throw as I'd ever made, hitting dead center of the bullseye. I pumped my fist in celebration.

"Nicely done," Reede said.

"It's all down to you. Thank you. But, why help me? We're supposed to be opponents."

Reede shrugged. "The stakes aren't huge, and it isn't like others aren't being helped. Besides, I like you."

"Well, I appreciate it. I guess I've been compensating for my old shoulder injury even though it's been fixed for a long time."

Reede won and received a little pouch of her winnings. I came in fifth and I was not happy. Though the competition had been tougher than last time, I had practiced and I demanded more of myself.

I cheered for Reede and reminded myself I wasn't here to compete—at least that wasn't my main purpose.

"Listen, Reede," I said, walking with her through the tavern to the street outside. "I make movies and I would like to make a documentary about you, competing, aiming for the Dwarf Games. Whether you make it to the Games or not, doesn't really matter. It would be great, of course, if you did. Even better if you won. But really, I want to document the life of a female axe thrower, and I want that axe thrower to be you."

"Oh, wow." Reede's cheeks turned bright red. "I'm flattered, but I don't think I'm the best subject for your documentary."

"I think you are," I said, readjusting my bag of axes on my shoulder. "Take some time. Sleep on it. You can find me at the Hammer and Chisel. Leave me a message if I'm not there."

"No, Mabel, you don't understand. I am incredibly flattered, believe me, but I'm not aiming for the Dwarf Games. In fact, I may not be competing much longer. I am getting far too old for this. I'm doing these little competitions because I still like the rush of it all, but to go for more than this? I'm not good enough for that. Not anymore."

I nodded, disappointed. "I think you are, but I get it. I won't push. I don't suppose you know of another female axe thrower who might be a good candidate for my documentary?"

Reede hesitated. "I might," she said.

"Great." I was relieved. This hadn't been a waste of time. I'd at least made a good connection. "Where can I find her?"

"You."

I sputtered. "Excuse me?"

"You. You're young enough. I see the hunger in you. And you have the talent."

I shook my head. "I don't compete any more."

"Yes, you do." Reede pointed back at the tavern. "You just did."

"Well yeah, here, but this was to make connections and find a subject for my documentary. This isn't my story."

"It should be."

"What do you mean?"

"You're from Gilliam, where not many females compete, if any. For whatever reason, you're here now, and you still have a chance to compete in the Dwarf Games. Win or lose, that's the story you should be telling. The story of a female dwarf who is beating all the odds. Females in places like Leitham don't understand what you and others like you have had to live with. And maybe those at home, when they see your story, will understand the pain they've caused you and so many other females and maybe things will change. That's the story you want to tell, isn't it?"

It was as if she'd been with my whole life. "How did you—"

"You're Mikey Goldenaxe's baby sister."

She was full of surprises. "You know Mikey?"

"He defeated me at the Dwarf Games."

None of my brothers, especially Mikey, had ever mentioned her. I had to tell her story. How could I convince her? "Wouldn't you like to compete again? Show Mikey you're still great at it?"

"But I'm not great at it. You, on the other hand, are. You're just a little rusty."

"I can't make a documentary on myself."

"Why not?"

"It's too complicated."

"I'm sure you can find others who will help you. You don't make any movie all by yourself. So for this one you need one or two extra helpers." Reede smiled and patted me on the shoulder. "It's your story that needs to be told. Not mine. You'll see I'm right."

My story? Did I have a story? I could get Jeff to help me. I did like the feel of competing again. If the documentary failed, at least I would have tried. "If I do this," I said, "I'll need a coach."

"I expect you will," Reede said.

"Then coach me."

"Excuse me?"

"Coach me, Reede. You did tonight. I could use your help. It wouldn't have to interfere with your own competitions. We would compete separately." I started walking away. I turned back. "Think about it."

"WELL?" JEFF asked, as he and my friends waited

for me outside the Hammer and Chisel. "Have you found a subject for the documentary?"

"Maybe." I walked past them, through the tavern, and out back. I stood at the throwing line, set my bag down and stared at the post.

"So Reede said yes?" Jeff asked.

"She said no."

"Did she recommend someone to you?" he asked.

I nodded. Could I do this?

"Who is it?"

I drew in a shaky breath. "Me."

After a moment or two of dead silence, Jeff said, "That's brilliant."

"No," Brent cut in. "No way. You're not doing it, Mabel."

He sounded like Da telling me I couldn't go to the movies with Emma. Brent wasn't my da, and yet I felt just as cowed as if he were.

"You're being ridiculous," Jeff said. "Mabel, it's a brilliant idea. It won't be easy to record yourself, but I'd be happy to help you, if you'd like. Any one of us will. Or you can hire others to help you."

"None of that matters," Brent said.

"That's all that matters," Jeff said.

"Mabel," Brent stood in front of me, holding me by the shoulders. "Do you really want to compete in axe throwing, going for the Dwarf Games? Do you really want to be back in the public eye like that? With Radier and Sevrin out there?"

I didn't want their attention, but... "I'm already

in the public eye, Brent. If they wanted to come after me, they would have done it already."

"Maybe they have," he whispered.

His business. Sevrin was after his business, shutting him down. I was taking care of it. I'd talked to Mam and I expected to hear back from her soon. If I didn't hear from her, or get an answer I liked, I'd find another way. If Sevrin was indeed going after Brent, I had no problem putting an end to it. Sevrin and I had an agreement and I would remind him of it. Of course I didn't want to have to do any of that.

Unlike Brent, Sevrin's involvement or interest wasn't what worried me about the idea of telling my story.

I worried about how such a movie would affect my family.

I didn't know if I could get back into competition. What if I destroyed my shoulder again? Could I survive the painful memories competing brought back to me? I did love the rush and the camaraderie of competing. The Dwarf Games were a long ways away. I had time to work my way up. I wouldn't have the intense pressure of competing at such a high level so quickly.

More than anything, Reede was right. It was my story that I wanted to tell, for myself, and for my family and others like them, to understand me and what I'd gone through.

I broke loose from Brent's grip.

"I've asked Reede to coach me. If she says yes, or

finds me another coach, then I'm going to do it. And Jeff, Hannah, I'd love it if you would help me with the documentary, from recording and interviews, to creating the story, the narrative."

"You got it," Jeff and Hannah said together.

"I'd like your support," I said to Brent.

He sighed. "I don't know that I can give it. I'm sorry."

My stomach sank at the disappointment in his face, his voice. Something had broken between us. We were pulling apart. We had been for a while, but now it felt like we were too far apart and I was flailing, desperately trying to keep us together. "Brent, please, try to understand."

"I understand just fine," he said.

"I don't even know if Reede will coach me."

"I'd be happy to coach you," Reede said, walking toward our circle.

I turned. "You will?"

"I'd be honored to help you get to the Dwarf Games, if that's what you really want to do."

"I can't support this." Brent turned on his heel and walked away.

Lil stood firm beside me. "Don't worry, Mabel. He'll come around. This documentary is brilliant and he knows it."

I should have gone after him, persuaded him, given in . . .

No. Not this time. I set my jaw. "Reede, let's get to work."

"Are you sure?"

"Absolutely."

"All right. If you're going to go for the Dwarf Games, then you need to train at a proper throwing range." Reede handed me a piece of parchment. "Here's my address. I have a competitive-sized throwing range in my back garden. We'll train there starting tomorrow afternoon. Bring whatever you need for training, and your movie."

"That's too soon," Hannah said. "We need at least a couple of weeks to work out the story, hire the right people, get the right equipment, plan the interviews."

"The longer it takes to start the training, the harder Mabel will have to work if she hopes to have a chance at qualifying," Reede said.

"I'm not putting that kind of pressure on myself, not again," I said. "I'll be there for training. I have a couple of wizard's crystals and a staff. Jeff, you can come with me and we'll start the recording. It will be rough at first, but we can edit as needed later. Hannah, while I'm training tomorrow, sketch out ideas for the story. We can talk about it when I get back. At that time, we can also talk about the details of who we need to hire."

Reede smiled. "Good. I'll see you tomorrow."

"You absolutely will."

CHAPTER 6

OTTO CARRIED the last of the morning's dishes to the kitchen for washing. Sophie was already there preparing food for our lunch customers. I put the broom away and took my bag of axes outside. Brent's refusal to support me weighed heavy. I questioned my motives. Was I really interested in making a movie about axe throwing? Or was I railing against Brent's stubbornness? I didn't know what I would do if Brent was right, if Sevrin or Radier came after me.

One after another I tossed my axes at the target, collecting them and tossing again. What did it matter? It wasn't like making movies kept me safe from the attention of the Dwarven Mafia. Brent had no problem with me making movies. If he loved me as much as he said he did, he ought to support me. I deserved that much from him.

I was due at Reede's in a few hours. If I wanted her to think I was better than a beginner, I needed to focus on my technique, not Brent.

The axe head thudded into the target and I grabbed the next one, readying to throw.

"Mabel," Mam said, behind me. "Sophie said I would find you back here."

"Mam," I said, putting down the axe and facing her. Had she talked to Sevrin already?

"You're throwing axes again?" she asked.

I shrugged. "For fun, mostly," I lied. "Getting some exercise." I walked over and gave her a quick hug. "It's nice to see you here, but I am a bit surprised, to be honest."

"Yes, well, I wanted to see how you're doing, really."

"I'm fine. Come in. I'll get you a drink, some food, maybe?"

"That would be lovely," Mam said, patting her belly. "Could always use a bit more girth around the middle."

I had Mam sit at a table while I fetched some leftover bread and cold meat.

"It isn't much," I said, bringing the food out and setting it in front of Mam. "Sophie's busy preparing lunch but it won't be ready for an hour or so."

"It's all right, love," Mam said, helping herself. "And how about Brent?"

The mention of his name was a stab in the heart

after last night. "He's . . . I don't know."

"I'm so sorry, Mabel. He hasn't hurt you, has he?"

I looked away. Not physically, he hadn't. "No, of course not. Have you talked to Sevrin?"

Mam pushed the plate toward me. "Help yourself."

I picked at the roast beef. "You have, haven't you?"

"It isn't him, Mabel. In fact, he offered to look into it and help find out what is happening to Brent's business."

"No," I snapped. I took a slow, calming breath. If Sevrin really wasn't the one responsible for the downturn in Brent's business—which I highly doubted—I still was not going to provide an opening for Sevrin to get involved and control it again. "No, that's all right. If it isn't Sevrin, then it really does mean the public's taste in art is changing, that's all."

"Love, I'm sorry he blames you for what happened, with Radier and Aubrey and Sevrin. He should not hold that against you. That's not the love and respect you deserve."

It really wasn't. I wiped my hands on my trousers. "I'm sure we'll be fine. He's going through a rough time and trying to find an answer. Sevrin seemed like an obvious choice and I thought I'd ask about it."

"Hey Mabel," Jeff said, bursting into the tavern, Hannah hot on his heels. He paused when he spotted Mam. He blushed, ran his hand over his clean-shaven chin, and adjusted his cap. "Frerin, it's nice to see you again."

"Nice to see you, too. What are you all up to?"

"We're helping Mabel on her new movie project," Hannah offered. "Thought we'd plan a few things before we go do some recording."

"Oh yes. Your movie," Mam said. "Can you talk about it yet?"

"It's a documentary on dragons," I said before Jeff or Hannah could tell her what we were really doing. I didn't trust her or Sevrin. I wasn't ready for her to know. "The history of dragons in general, and Dakkar specifically."

Mam grinned. "Come over for dinner tonight, after you've finished your work for the day. Sevrin would love the chance to talk about dragons."

I could go and ask him directly, if he was affecting Brent's gallery. I really didn't want to see Sevrin and I had no expectations that he would be honest with me. I could try and read him, though. I could tell if he was lying. If I saw the signs, it didn't matter what he actually told me, I'd know he was involved. Maybe if I could give Brent some kind of indication of Sevrin's activities, he would change his mind and support me.

I couldn't promise anything. I had no idea how tired I would be after training with Reede. I had no idea if I would be up to seeing anyone. "I'll, um, do my best."

JEFF HELPED Hannah and myself into his cart. "I came up with some story ideas last night that I wanted to run past you, see what you think," Hannah said.

"Let's hear what you've got," I said.

"I was thinking we should open with your first training session, today, obviously. We'll show your first throws and have you doing voice-over about why you decided to aim for the Dwarf Games, why it is important to you and all that. I want to highlight the missed opportunity before with your injury. We'll flash back to the training you had with Mikey, your life in Gilliam. We may have to do some re-creations, or show some news articles if there are any."

"I can search the archives in case there was any news coverage," Jeff said.

"There wasn't any," I said.

"We can figure that out later," Hannah said. "We'll have to talk about your family, of course, and you being the only female in it, your expected role in your conservative town, and how you broke the mold by being the only female axe thrower from Gilliam. The main features will be your competitions as you move up the ranks, including whatever other media coverage you get. I'll want to interview your family and friends in Gilliam to add some color. You know, have them talk about—"

"No." I cut her off. "No interviews with my family. Mam, maybe. But no one from Gilliam."

"You can edit the interviews in whatever way you want, but we need to have them tell the audience about you, what you were like growing up, when you started throwing axes, and all of that. It's especially important if there are no articles or anything else about you from the first time you competed. That's the story we're trying to tell."

"I get that, but my family won't talk to you."

"It isn't like Jeff and I would show up on their doorstep, wizard crystal in their faces, peppering them with questions. I'll write first."

"They won't get your letters, and if they do, they won't open them or respond." I fingered the note from Max. Da knows. Don't write.

"They kicked you out years ago. Surely they've moved on, forgiven you."

"They've moved on, all right. By now it will be like I never existed in Gilliam."

"How is that possible?"

I shrugged. "Da has his ways."

Hannah studied her notes, flipping pages of parchment. "What if we were to highlight that your family had exiled you for throwing axes?"

"They didn't have a problem with me throwing axes. Well, Da kind of did because he thought it was taking me away from mate-finding activities, but that's not why he disowned me."

"What if we were to say it was the reason for your exile? It will heighten the tension; we can say you're going against your family even now, and everyone will love you. Likely no one in Gilliam will watch the documentary when it's done, so they'll never know."

"I'll know," I said. "I'm sorry, Hannah. I'm not trying to be difficult."

"Your family, your life in Gilliam and what happened there, that's the story, Mabel. How can we tell it without any interviews from them?"

"It isn't the story."

"It is," she persisted. "The pressure they put on you to find a life-mate and to win, resulted in your injury which changed everything for you. But it also instilled in you a love for the sport and competing and you're getting your second chance. The female dwarf who competes to please her family and society's expectations in a sport dominated by males."

"Hannah—"

"I know you think the story is that there aren't many female competitors. In itself, that's boring. No one cares. What makes it interesting is your history with your family. The reasons they pushed you to compete are the reasons so few females compete. If I can't interview your family, we'll find another way to tell that history, but we have to tell it."

I sighed. "Come up with a way to do it without needing my family and friends. I'll have a look at it and decide then."

"I'll do what I can."

"Jeff?" I asked. "Do you think you can get some

decent recordings out of today with the equipment you have?"

"I expect so. I was doing a little research this morning and I think Reede might be the first female throwing coach. I'm going to look into it some more to make sure it's true, if you think we can use it."

Hannah's face lit up. "I can."

"I like it," I said. "See what you can dig up."

We arrived at a large property on the outskirts of town. "Start recording," I told Jeff.

The house was a lovely stone bungalow with a thatched roof, perfect for a small family. A small hedge full of honeysuckle blossoms lined the drive to the house. We walked around back to find a small shed and a large, flat open area containing a full-sized throwing arena, where Reede tossed a couple of axes. "Keep recording," I whispered to Jeff.

She was spectacular. Random targets popped up and she gracefully spun and threw, hitting them dead center.

I found it difficult to believe she was really on the downward swing of her career.

When she finished I called out, "Looks like you have a few more years left in you, Reede."

She smiled and bowed to me. "Hardly. I've been doing this for so long I know which ones will pop up when," she said with a grin. "Let's get started."

"You got this," Jeff whispered.

I walked into the throwing arena. "This is impressive. Mikey would be, I mean, would have been, jealous."

Reede cocked her head to the side. "Why is that?"

"We had a throwing post in our back garden, but the pop-up targets were improvised, make-shift, not nearly as professional as these."

"Well, years of competing for prize money allowed me to build this. Even the low-level competition prizes add up after a while. Show me what kind of warmups Mikey put you through."

I glanced over at Jeff. I wasn't sure I really wanted this embarrassment to be recorded. I cleared my throat and began stretching, working my way into push-ups, and finished with some practice throws, panting after putting myself through the paces a little harder than I had been doing on my own. I wanted to show Reede I was keen to put in the effort, and maybe also come across as impressive on the recording.

"I was right to agree to help you. Mikey did a good job. You're out of shape, though. We'll have to work on that, but you are in a better place than I expected. Give me thirty throws to the post at twenty feet."

I paused. Last time I was given that instruction, I'd hurt my shoulder. No, that wasn't quite true. Mikey had told me to give him thirty more throws, after an already long and grueling session, because I was trying to improve at an exponential rate. That had only been the start of the pain. The injury had been a result of undisciplined throwing.

"Is there a problem?" Reede asked.

"No problem." I set my shoulders and threw.

After the first five throws, Reede said, "Keep your elbow in tight. Throw again."

I threw twice then she stepped up to me as I prepared to throw, and held my arm in position, elbow in tight to my head. "Now make the beginning of the throwing motion."

It was tough to do with Reede holding my elbow in place. The strain in my muscles concerned me, but it also felt great.

"Do you feel it?" Reede asked.

"I do."

"Good. Now throw again."

I kept my elbow in place, but my throws were way off. I shook my head. "That's terrible. Why is it so terrible?"

"Because we haven't worked on the rest of your technique yet. This is a good start. Keep your focus only on your elbow. Don't worry about where your axe lands."

I chuckled and sighed, remembering my first practices with Mikey. "My brother said the same thing. You said he beat you at the Dwarf Games," I said, still practicing my throws. "He never spoke of you. Mind you, he never talked about throwing axes after he quit competing."

"I'm not surprised you don't remember. You were a wee dwarfling back then," Reede said.

"Quite. I know I'd traveled with the family to the Dwarf Games, but I don't remember much about it."

Reede grinned. "I remember you sitting on your brother Frankie's shoulders."

Frankie? "You met my family?"

"Mikey and I courted for a few years."

I shook my head. "That's not possible. Mikey never courted anyone."

"Sure he did."

Why would he lie? "But I asked him about it. He said he was never interested until it was too late. He quit axe throwing to focus on mining to impress the fellow he was interested in, but by then that fellow had found someone else."

"There may well have been a fellow in Gilliam. Probably more than one, and a few females, I suspect. But we definitely courted, soon after your da exiled your mam."

Mikey had lied to me. Reede knew my family and she seemed willing to talk. Would she tell me the truth? "Do you know what really happened? Why he quit? He never threw an axe again. It was a huge shock to everyone when he offered to coach me."

Reede instructed me to cool down. "I don't know why he quit. Not exactly. Those external factors we were talking about the other day, the ones that I'm not so fond of, were a big part of it."

"Jeff, that's enough for today," I said. "Pack up and meet me out front."

"You got it."

Reede waited until Jeff left. "Mikey never told me what happened. I know he met with some fellows and soon after the finals, when we were celebrating, they met with him again. He came back, broke up with me, and quit throwing."

I bit my bottom lip. I wondered if those fellows had been working for Sevrin. I'd almost be willing to bet they had.

I thought of Mikey, his back still turned to me, but I saw a sag in his shoulders I'd never noticed before, like he carried some bigger, darker burden that no one could lift off him. "Did my da or any of my brothers know about these meetings?"

"Not as far as I know. Mikey never told me who they were or what they wanted, and you know how tight-lipped he could be. If he didn't tell me, I doubt he told anyone else."

"That sounds like Mikey, all right. There must be more to it. You said there were things you did you weren't proud of. What was your part in it?"

Reede looked to where Jeff had stood, making sure he was gone. "After Mikey came back from one of the meetings, he asked me to throw the competition, to let him win. I did, because I saw a desperation in his eyes. I loved him and would do anything for him. He won, we celebrated, he had another meeting, and then he broke up with me. He never threw again."

"And you lost interest in going for the Dwarf Games, yet you still compete."

"At low-level competitions."

"Competitions you know you can win. You could

have, should have won the Dwarf Games. He'd stopped competing. You could have won it the next time."

"He broke me."

Sadness hung over me. Mikey had a strong record of hurting others. Mam, me, Reede. "If I get to the Dwarf Games, with you as my coach, and if I win, it will be your redemption, and your revenge, won't it?"

Reede lowered her gaze. "Yes. I suppose so. You can change your mind. I don't want you to think I'm using you the way Mikey used me."

I smiled. "Hardly. I think it's a great plan."

"I don't want this in the movie."

I thought it over. This would add an extra dimension that could really add to the story. If I failed, it would make both of us look petty. "You got it. This little element of revenge, and redemption, will be between us."

I LEFT Reede's, lost in thought.

I desperately wished I could run straight home and write to Max, tell him everything Reede told me. I wanted to ask if he remembered anything from Mikey's competitive days because I couldn't. I didn't dare write Max in case Da found it and Max got in trouble. That is, if Max even went to the trading post anymore for mail. I doubted he did. He wouldn't take that risk.

"Everything all right?" Hannah asked, as she and Jeff pulled alongside me in the cart.

I stopped and looked up at them. I'd completely forgotten about Jeff and Hannah and that we'd come in Jeff's cart. "Oh, yeah. I was just thinking over the instructions for my practices this week."

"You are far too distracted for practice instructions," Jeff said as I climbed in.

What about Jimmy? Could I write to Jimmy and get him to pass the letter to Max? The last time I saw Jimmy, I was leaving Gilliam with Mam, and he was undoing the braid from his beard.

I wasn't going to write to Jimmy, either.

"Hey," Jeff nudged me.

If Sevrin had been at the Dwarf Games and for some reason threatened Mikey, then maybe Aramis or Radier had been with him and recorded the axe throwing competition, as leverage. "She gave me an idea for the documentary," I said. "I want to go to the archives and see if I can find a recording of the Dwarf Games M—Reede competed in."

"If there is anything," Jeff said, "I know where it would be."

We dropped Hannah off at Studio City and drove on to the Archives.

I missed Percy's friendly greeting. This place had never been the same since he retired.

Jeff and I walked down to the archives and he ushered me into a viewing room. "You stay there, I'll get what you're looking for."

"Thanks."

I waited for him to come back, drumming my fingers on the table, wondering what I might find on a recording of the Dwarf Games, worried at how I would feel at seeing my family again even if it was only on a screen. Wondering if Sevrin was somehow behind Mikey quitting axe throwing and what Mam knew about it. I really was going to have to go visit her, have dinner with her and Sevrin, after this.

"Here we are," Jeff said, bursting in, carrying a box with a handful of crystals.

He took the first crystal and set it in the projecting fork. Jeff tapped the tines. They vibrated against the crystal perfectly. The screen lit up.

We were watching the axe throwing portion of the Dwarf Games, and there was Mikey.

I gasped, and quickly covered my mouth with my hand. It hurt both more and less than I had thought it would.

Jeff put a hand on my shoulder. "Are you all right?"

I nodded and leaned forward. "He's—Mikey's —so young." I moved closer to the screen. "And so happy," I whispered.

"Happy?" Jeff asked. "How can you tell? This isn't a close-up of him."

"No, but he's standing taller. I see a spark in him. And look." I pointed to Mikey walking up to the throwing line. He was also a lot thinner than I remembered. He must have gained his stoutness after he finished competing. "That is a smile."

I missed my family so much as I watched him compete. It was so good to see them after all this time. Tears threatened until I remembered the pressure he and Da and the others put on me—that I didn't miss.

Mikey prepared to throw. His form was perfect, and so was his release. "Wow. Mikey was really good," I said.

"Is that—?" Jeff asked.

"Reede? Yes," I said, mesmerized by what I was watching. If Mikey was good, Reede was perfection. I bit my bottom lip. She was clearly the better of the two.

The video moved in close on Mikey and Reede as they sat, awaiting their next turns. They said nothing to each other, but I could tell, maybe I imagined it because of what Reede had told me, but I was almost certain I could see the connection between them. What I didn't see was any reason Sevrin would have approached my brother. Mikey was holding his own, so why would he have asked Reede to throw the games?

The movie finished and Jeff removed the crystal. "I hope you don't mind me saying, but you look a lot like your brother."

I smiled. "Goldenaxes tend to have a strong family resemblance."

"You ready for the next one?"

"I am."

I prepared myself for round two, hoping this time to see what drew Sevrin's interest in Mikey.

Jeff tapped the tines and round two lit up the screen.

Sevrin, I assumed it was Sevrin, was probably interested in Mikey for the same reason Aubrey had been interested in me. Using me to earn him winnings and followers, to fix matches. Had Mikey asked Reede to lose because he owed Sevrin? Had Mikey needed to win to pay off Sevrin?

Reede was clearly the best, and Mikey was definitely second best. They were far above the rest of the competition. If I hadn't known that Mikey had asked Reede to throw the competition, I would have been proud of him.

Knowing what I knew, made watching the final crystal the hardest. Reede had been so good through the first two rounds. Now there was an unhappiness in her demeanor. She kept looking over at Mikey. He wouldn't look at her.

Mikey's game was the same as the first two rounds. It was great, but not perfect. I'd expected to see him raise his level for the finals. The drop in Reede's performance was noticeable. A moment of hesitation on one throw when she'd been poised for a perfect throw. A waiver in technique on another. It was all Mikey needed to win. Anguish flashed across Reede's face which she covered with a wide grin when Mikey was declared the winner and she was named the runner up. Under any other circumstance, second would have been admirable.

Why was it so important that Mikey win? What had he been so afraid of that he was willing to hurt, to break, someone he loved, to prevent it from happening?

"What happened to Reede?" Jeff asked. "She'd been doing so well."

"She said something about the pressure of the moment, being the first female Dwarf Games champion, was too much for her. She didn't want the same thing to happen to me."

"That's good, but I don't think we can use that in the documentary," Jeff said.

"No," I agreed. "It would not be good for optics, to show her losing like this, probably," I said.

"What do you mean, 'probably'?"

"It depends. If I win, become the first female champion, then I restore honor to her, in which case, I'll ask Reede if we can use this. If I don't win, we forgot it ever existed."

The trophies were presented. Mikey raised his arms in victory. Jeff moved to stop the crystal. "Wait," I said. "I want to keep watching."

"Why?"

"My family. I want to see my family."

"You think you will?"

I shrugged. "I hope so," I said as young Patrick, and Danny, jumped onto the arena floor and rushed Mikey. Da and my other brothers weren't far behind, with me perched on Frankie's shoulders. I laughed at the sight of me, and forgot all about what Mikey had done to Reede as dwarfling me and my family celebrated, engulfing Mikey in our embrace.

"Is that you?" Jeff asked.

"It is."

"Look how tiny you were." Jeff poked me playfully. "Actually, you kind of look the same there as when you had no beard."

I smacked him back. "I know. But shut up."

The video paused on my gleeful dwarfling face, and stopped.

"Aww," Jeff purred, "Everyone loves the image of a proud little sister."

Unless it had been Sevrin who had asked whomever was recording the event, to make sure my face was the last image—for Mam.

"Can I get copies of these?" I asked.

"Consider it done." He set up the crystals and began to copy them. "Reede was good. Nothing against your brother, but she should have won."

"Yes, she should have." I stared at the screen.

Was I really going to get pulled back into this business with Sevrin? Maybe I was just being paranoid. There was one way to find out, and that was to see Mam and Sevrin.

I WIPED my sweaty palms on my trousers and

knocked on Mam's door. She hadn't given me an exact time for dinner and I hoped no one was home so I could say I tried. I didn't want to see Sevrin. I had put that drama behind me as best I could. I didn't want to stir it up again. Not tonight.

"Mabel?" Sevrin asked, opening the door wide.

My stomach lurched into my throat. Of course he would be the one to answer. I forced a smile. "Hiya, Sevrin. Ah, Mam asked me to dinner tonight. I hope that's all right. If it's a bad time, I can come back another night."

"Of course it's a good time!" Sevrin stepped aside to let me pass. "Come in, please. Frerin should be home shortly."

"Oh." I stopped inside the door. "I can come back later. Really."

Sevrin held up his hands in supplication, leaving the door open. "Please stay, Mabel. I know I hurt you. I promise you, I don't do those things anymore."

I snorted. "You and I both know that isn't true."

Sevrin looked like I'd wounded him deeply. "If you're referring to what is happening to Brent's business, I assure you I have nothing to do with it. I've kept my promise to stay away."

"I wasn't referring to Brent's gallery, as a matter of fact." I couldn't believe I was willfully spewing such venom at the Lord of the Dwarven Mafia. "You forget that I've got connections in this town and I am well aware of the control you still wield. I don't know what you've told Mam, if she knows the truth, or if she's in this with you, and I don't care. I will stay, and I will have a pleasant conversation with the two of you, but you have to be honest with me."

"I am being honest. I have nothing to do with what is happening to Brent's gallery. I promised I would stay away, and I am. I haven't told anyone else to stay away from it, either. As soon as we'd made our agreement, I told my people to allow Brent to carry on business as usual. No one was to interfere. I nearly destroyed Frerin's relationship with you. I would never do anything to jeopardize that again."

"Then stay out of her life."

"She came to me."

I set my jaw and glared at him. "You didn't have to take her back."

"What Frerin and I have runs deeper, and longer, than any involvement with the Dwarven Mafia."

I shook my head in disbelief. Maybe he really believed it, but I knew that wasn't the case. Deeper, perhaps, but not longer. They hadn't met until Mam needed his help to get revenge on Radier. He'd seen her as an opportunity. They'd told me as much, word for word.

"Oh!" Mam exclaimed, breathless, rushing through the doorway. "Mabel. I am so glad you made it."

I couldn't do this. I couldn't sit down to a meal with them, and pretend all was fine. He was lying, I could tell that much, but what he was lying about, that I couldn't tell. I was an idiot to think I could figure out what Sevrin was up to. "Yeah, Mam, listen, I can't stay."

"Oh, please, love."

"Really. I stopped by on my way home to tell you how much I appreciated you coming by my place this morning. I would like it if you did it more often."

"Please, stay a little while. A cup of tea, perhaps? One drink and a bit of a snack?"

"I can't, really. It's been a long day and I'm exhausted. I just want to go home."

"What you need is a bit of your mam's home-made stew, and a nice tankard of stout ale to boost your energy. Come," Mam pulled me by the arm to the chairs in front of the fire. "Sit with me. Tell me about the research for the movie you're making, while Sevrin gets us the food and drink."

"Mam, I'd love to, but—"

"I won't hear of it. There is no way I'm sending my daughter home on an empty stomach. Now sit."

I sighed and gave in.

"Tell me. What did you find out about dragons?" Mam asked.

Sevrin paused in the doorway to the kitchen then kept walking.

I had come here for a reason. Besides, there was no way I could keep up the pretense of what I was really doing. I sighed again. "I'm not researching dragons."

"Oh," Mam said, softly. "Well," she said a little more brightly. "If you don't want to tell me, that's fine."

"No, no. It's nothing like that." I wondered if Sevrin was listening from the kitchen, how he was reacting. "I've decided to try and qualify for the Dwarf Games, in axe throwing. Today was my first training session with a coach, and I wasn't sure if it would be a good fit, or if this was something I really wanted to do. I needed to be sure first."

Mam smiled. "That's wonderful, love, but, what about your shoulder? What if you injure it again?"

"That is a concern. My hope is that we have plenty of time to train and qualify, so I won't be under quite as much pressure as I was the first time. Because of the time I have to train, my shoulder should be all right."

"Well, honey, if that's what you want to do, then I am behind you one-hundred percent. I guess you won't be making any movies for a while, then."

"Actually," I cleared my throat. "Jeff, Hannah, and I are recording my training, and my competitions, and we're going to make it into a documentary. I'm sure I'll have one or two other small projects that will come up in the meantime as well."

"That's my girl," Mam said.

"Who do you have for a coach?" Sevrin asked, bringing in a tray laden with bowls of stew, plates of bread and butter, and tankards of ale.

I didn't really want to tell him, but my desire to see his reaction was far too tempting. "Her name is Reede. Apparently she competed with Mikey in the

Dwarf Games."

Nothing. Not a flinch, nor a flicker of recognition at her name. Interesting.

"She knew Mikey?" Mam asked.

"She did. Not well," I lied. "Only as a fellow competitor."

"That should make for a very interesting documentary," Sevrin said. "I look forward to seeing it."

"Its early days. The first day, really. So we'll see how it goes. Sevrin, I hear you're applying to adopt Dakkar."

"You're what?" Mam asked.

Sevrin's jaw dropped. "Frerin, love—"

"We are not adopting Dakkar. We have no place for her. I'm not going to look after her and I know you're not going to. What are you thinking?"

Sevrin looked at me. I smiled as I bit into a thick, buttery slice of bread. The look of panic in his eyes was worth it.

"I was simply making inquiries. No decisions have been made. Dakkar is retiring and I am worried that no one else will want her."

"Aww, that's sweet of you," I said. "But no need to worry. Sam has put in the paperwork, too. She and Lil are buying a place and setting it up for Dakkar and everything. You should see them together," I gushed. "It's incredible."

"That's settled, then." Mam gave Sevrin a pointed look.

Sevrin grunted as he sat. Maybe he had more

respect for Mam than I thought.

I dipped my bread in my stew and savored the rich gravy, satisfied with Sevrin's discontent.

CHAPTER 7

"MABEL," REEDE said. "You're doing fine."

"I'm not paying you to tell me I'm doing fine," I snapped. My practices had been terrible all week. My technique was off and I couldn't focus.

I stood at the line in Reede's back garden hurling my axes. I'd been doing so for forty-five minutes now. I'd stopped improving and I knew I was getting dangerously exhausted and close to risking injury. I couldn't help it. I had an obsessive need to keep throwing until I got it right.

"Mabel," Reede shouted. "Stop throwing right now."

I grudgingly lowered my axe and faced her.

"Listen to me." Her voice was stern. "I am well aware of what you need to work on and we will. You are not going to master anything in one day. If that is how Mikey taught you, made you practice, then shame on him. We have plenty of time to work on your technique and strength. So relax. Drop your axe." She waited until I let it fall out of my hands. "We will work on your strength tomorrow."

I looked from my axe which now lay at my feet over to the throwing post. "Just ten more," I said. "I can't—"

"Go home. And I'm going to ask Jeff to keep an eye on you so you don't try to throw at the Hammer and Chisel."

"Fine." I sighed.

"This is for the best, Mabel," Reede said. "I don't want you risking injury, and I know you don't want to take that chance, either."

"Can't argue with that." I reluctantly packed up my axes and tucked them away just inside the back door of her house.

Leaving Reede's with Jeff beside me prattling on about the material he'd recorded. Part of my obsessive determination to perfect my distance throwing was due to my reluctance to go home.

Brent was more than likely to be there and I hadn't seen him in a few days. I hated the shame I felt when I was with him. Shame for letting him control me. Shame for standing up for myself and doing what I loved. I needed the support of my friends, and if he couldn't give that to me, then I was at a complete loss as to what to do or how to handle the situation. I didn't want to see him until I had some idea of what I could say to him.

Avoiding him was not an option. As I expected, Brent was already at the Hammer and Chisel when Jeff and I arrived. Brent smiled and kissed me on the cheek.

He acted like everything was fine between us. His ever-changing moods set me on edge. My inability to know what to expect from him crushed me.

"Have a good day?" I asked, trying my best to remain pleasant and predictable.

"I did," he said. "Sold a couple of pieces today. They were small, and not a great boost of income, but I guess it's all right. Sales are sales. They were to one of my oldest customers. He's a great client, but there isn't much hope of him sending any new business my way. He hasn't done so in years."

"Still, a sale is better than no sale," I mollified half-heartedly. I should have been more supportive but I just couldn't bring myself to do it. I wanted his business to succeed. I was curious to know if the sales had happened because I'd spoken to Sevrin, although I supposed the specific reason for the sales wasn't really that important. If Brent was earning, that meant Sevrin was either no longer, or never had been, to blame. Brent had no more excuses to not support me. He made no suggestion in that direction.

I drained my pint and stood up. "I'm exhausted. I'll see you all tomorrow."

"What?" Hannah asked. "No, don't go."

"I'm no fun tonight," I said with a shrug. I glanced down at Brent whom I thought might say something. Instead he quietly smirked.

Walking away, I could hear Mam in my head. "He's not treating you with the love and respect you deserve." She was right. I didn't have the energy, or the courage, to do anything about it.

"Hey," Lil said, walking beside me. "Everything all right?"

"Yep."

Lil glared at me.

"No," I capitulated. "It's Brent. He's down there with that smirk that says, 'I'm right, you shouldn't be throwing axes.' He doesn't care about anything but his stupid gallery. I've had a horrible week of practices. I need so much more work and today Reede cut my practice time short. Good gods of elves and dragons. I'm as bad as him, whining about my problems that aren't problems. I'm sorry."

Lil hooked her arm in mine. "Don't be silly. You just need a bit of alone time. We all do every now and then."

She followed me into my room and closed the door.

"What's up?" I sat on my bed and removed my boots. I'd been wearing these thinner, fashionable boots for years now and I still wished I could wear the thicker, more comfortable miner boots, especially if I was going to be on my feet all day. "Is everything all right with you and Sam?"

"Sam and I are fine." Lil smiled but kept her gaze down. "Better than fine. It's pretty great."

"Yeah?"

"Yeah. She's suggested we have a golden ring ceremony, make it permanent."

My bad mood dissolved. I jumped off my bed and threw my arms around her. "I'm so happy for you! When did this happen? Why are you just telling me about this now? When is the big day?"

Lil laughed. "She asked me yesterday. We haven't told anyone yet. I wanted you to be the first to know."

There was a knocking on the door and Sam poked her head in. "I take it you've told her?" she asked, beaming.

I reached for Sam and pulled her into my hug with Lil. "I'm so happy for you both."

"Sam, I need a few more minutes with Mabel," Lil said after a few moments. "I'll be down in a bit."

"Of course. Take as long as you want. I'll tell the others everything is fine."

The joy left Lil's face.

"Hey," I said. "What's going on?"

Lil sighed. "I have a favor to ask. I really don't want to. And I fully understand if you say no, but…" she sighed again and rubbed her face. "Sam and I want to wait until the adoption of Dakkar is complete, which is fine, except that Sevrin is going out of his way to make it impossible for us to adopt Dakkar."

This news surprised me. I'd expected after my dinner with him and Mam, and Mam's disapproval of him looking into adopting Dakkar, he would have backed off, stopped all together. "You know for sure it is him?"

Lil wrung her hands. "Aramis told me."

"He told you?" My mouth dried and I could not focus my gaze on Lil or anything else. She'd seen Aramis? Did that mean he was back? I hoped so. I missed his movies. A part of me missed him.

"He came by the set of my movie."

"What did he tell you?"

"That Sevrin is trying to out-bid us on the property we want for a home for Dakkar, and that he's had a meeting with the committee from the Performing Creature Welfare Societies administering her adoption. We can't even get a response or an appointment with them."

It was admirable of Aramis to tell her all of this, but the amount of detail he had was suspicious. "How does he know all this?"

"He was at the same tavern where the meeting was held."

"So he was with Sevrin?"

Lil shook her head. "He was at a different table. He doesn't want Sevrin to get Dakkar. It's why he sought me out. He's offered to help us buy the property. He wants to help us."

"Lil, it is never that straight-forward with him, or Sevrin."

"I know. And that's the favor I have to ask you. Is there a way you can find out if they are working together? I want to believe Aramis really wants to help us, but after what they did to you, a part of me thinks that somehow they're working together to make me or Sam pay some kind of extra high price for Dakkar. A price we can't afford, one that will ruin us."

"She can't let Dakkar go, if it comes to it?"

"Sam told me how Dakkar reacted when she heard Sevrin's name. She is terrified of him. If we let him have her, we would be forcing her to live out her days in fear, maybe even torture. We can't do that to her. I know what I'm asking of you. I wouldn't ask it if I didn't think there was any other option. I know you're busy with competing and you don't want Sevrin anywhere near you in case he tries to get you involved in the Dwarven Mafia again—"

I held up my hand to stop Lil. "I understand. We can't go after Sevrin directly. He'll just deny it. Mam won't be any help. She believes him, or she's in on whatever he's up to. What we have to do is figure out why he wants Dakkar so badly."

"You're sure you want to do this? I mean, Sam and I would be incredibly grateful if you are."

"Sevrin's likely responsible for the downturn in Brent's gallery; he's going after you two; and I have a strong suspicion he's been after my family for a long time, going back to when Mikey was competing in the Dwarf Games. He's done enough damage to my family and those around us. It is time he moved on. I thought he'd already learned that lesson, but it seems he's merely been quiet, biding his time, hoping I would forget."

"All we want is a fair chance at being able to adopt Dakkar. I'm sorry to have dumped this on you after you already had a not so great day."

"I'm glad you did. I'm not feeling quite so sorry for myself anymore. And you've given me something to channel my competitive energy into when I'm not actually practicing. I can't make any promises but I'll see what I can do."

Lil wiped her eyes. "Thank you. Really."

"Tell you what. Hannah and I are at Studio City most mornings going over what's been recorded, deciding what, if anything, can be used. Next time you see Aramis, ask him to come find me."

HANNAH AND I sat shoulder to shoulder in my editing room in Studio City, making notes of the practice sessions. Though we were marking down which sequences we were most likely to use in the documentary, this was also a great chance for me to study my technique, both what I was doing right and what I was doing wrong. At the moment, everything I saw about my technique was wrong.

"Mabel." Hannah gave me a pointed look.

"What?" Why had she stopped the crystal and interrupted my note-taking?

"You need to be objective right now," Hannah

said. "I get that it's going to be difficult, but you have
to treat whatever we see on screen as if it is any other
subject of one of your documentaries."

I glanced down at what I'd written—a parchment
and a half of thoughts on how to throw better, to do
what Reede has been teaching me from the placement
of my feet to my posture, and even the movement of
my free arm. I finally understood what Reede was
telling me to do.

"You're right. Sorry, Hannah. Let's start again."
I tossed my parchment aside and reached for a fresh
one.

"Hey," Hannah retrieved my discarded notes.
"We can use these. You, obviously, for your practice,
but this might be useful for the narrative. Just don't
make this a habit."

"Got it."

We started again, but it didn't take long before
I was making noises of disgust. Hannah paused the
crystal again.

"Sorry, sorry," I said. "It's just that…look at
me." I pointed at the screen. "My feet are all wrong.
The elbow of my throwing arm is sticking out. It's
like everything Reede teaches me vanishes from my
brain the moment she leaves me to work on it on my
own and I'm back to throwing like a beginner. It's
a miracle I hit the post at all. And the worst part is
that I'm proud of myself. I think I'm doing amazing
out there. How has Reede not dropped me for not
listening to her?"

Hannah set down her quill, leaned back, lips pressed.

"Sorry." I covered my face with my hands. "This was a terrible idea, trying to make a documentary of myself."

"It's a brilliant idea." It wasn't Hannah who said it. I looked up and turned around. Aramis stood in the doorway. I froze, trembling. I hadn't realized how much I had missed him. He was so beautiful, so calm. There was an air of peaceful strength about him he hadn't had before. At the same time, it was as though just yesterday we had been chatting on set in Gilliam. Our connection was instant and strong. The residual emotional pain held me back from running to him and embracing him.

"You have a great story to tell," he said. "Perhaps you need someone else to edit it."

My warmth toward him faded as my suspicion rose. "And I suppose you think it should be you?" This was not why I'd asked Lil to send him my way. How dare he presume.

"I would be happy to suggest someone else, if you would prefer. But you have seen my work. You know me and I know you. I think I would do a good job of it, and you would have final say on every-thing." Aramis paused. "I apologize. Lil suggested I come speak with you. She said I could find you here. I merely overheard your frustration and thought I could offer my services. My apologies. It was wrong of me to do so."

"Not necessarily," Hannah said. "Can you give us a few minutes to talk this over?"

Her voice was more tentative than I'd ever heard it, but also thoughtful.

"Of course." He ducked out of the room and closed the door.

"He is the best in the business," she said.

"Do you want to work with him?"

"I wouldn't say I am excited about the idea given his connections and your history with him. If we were to set some kind of parameters, make the professional boundaries clear, he could make this better than any of us could have imagined. Your story is brilliant. It needs to be told."

Aramis really was the best. We had worked well together. I looked at the image of myself on the screen, frozen in such a beginner throwing stance. Except that I'd come a long way since I had been a beginner, fantasizing about saving Aramis, dreaming he would make a movie of me. I had saved him, though. Or, he said I had saved him from his father and a life in the Elven Mafia. And now he was offering to make a movie of me. I'd come so far only to be back where I started.

I couldn't ignore Aramis's peaceful air. It was different. He was different. I'd missed working with him. I'd missed his friendship. "Brent is not going to like this," I muttered. "Not that he liked the idea of me competing, anyway. Are you sure you'd be all right working with him?"

Hannah nodded. "With strict boundaries, and permission to change my mind at any time if I suspect he's crossed the line."

"I would insist on it." I hesitated. I had doubts. "Give me a bit of time to talk to him before I decide." This was not what I'd expected from him. I opened the door. Aramis stood, waiting patiently.

"I'll be next door." Hannah pointedly looked at Aramis as she passed him.

I ushered him in but remained by the door, my arms crossed. "Lil told me you wanted to help her and Sam adopt Dakkar."

"That is true."

"Are you expecting me to believe you're turning on your life-long best mate, Sevrin?"

"He is not my best mate. He has not been for a few years. Not since…" Aramis broke off and I waited for him to go on.

To my surprise, I felt no anger toward him. Suspicion of motive yes, but not anger.

Aramis pulled out a stool and sat. "Do you remember when we had lunch, it was your first day visiting Studio City, and I told you about my sister?"

How could I forget? "You said I reminded you of her. That the situation between Da and myself had been similar to what happened between your sister and your father. You wanted to help me. Protect me like you hadn't been able to protect her." I scoffed and shook my head at the irony of those words.

"I meant it. I know that, given what happened, it

is hard to believe. I have no excuse, no reason that could possibly justify what Sevrin and I did to you. We said we were going to free ourselves and our people from an ancient tyrant. I hated putting you through it. I hated myself for using you. Sevrin felt nothing. He did not care as long as you succeeded. That was the first time I really saw what he was like."

I crossed my arms and leaned back against the editing table. "The first time?"

"Thinking back, there had been countless times he manipulated those around us, but because they were always for the results we wanted, I never noticed, or maybe I did and I did not care."

"So why care now?"

"You."

I raised an eyebrow. "Me?"

Aramis held my gaze. I fought hard to keep myself from sinking into their blue splendor.

"After Radier had kidnapped and interrogated you, you still came after me, telling me not to give up on the life I loved. You really did save me. By taking down Radier and my father so publicly, I had hoped to show my gratitude, that I understood how terribly I had hurt you, and that I wanted to change."

That was all well and good for him to say, but I needed proof of that change. "You said that was the first time you saw what Sevrin was like. Does that mean he has done worse things since then?"

"Yes, he has."

My heart leapt to my throat. "Is he having his

henchmen go after the River's Edge Art Gallery?"

"No."

My blood pounded in my ears. "You know this with absolute certainty?"

"I do."

I decided to push him. "Did he or his henchmen to go after my brother Mikey when he was competing in the Dwarf Games?"

Aramis was quiet for a moment. "Yes," he said softly. "Though I do not know the details."

I didn't need or want to know more. The confirmation of my suspicions hurt enough. I couldn't look at Aramis. "And Dakkar?"

"She is a project, something to do now that he is supposedly retired."

"Sevrin doesn't need a project or to fill time. Why does he want her?"

"He killed her family and he took away her fire. As with everything he does, it made sense at the time, but it was torture to Dakkar. She survived, but she should not have to live with the one who did that to her." Aramis paused. "Nor should you have to work with me after how I used you. I never should have suggested it. I assure you that had not been my intention when I came here. Thank you for hearing me out. I shall leave you to it."

"Hold on. I'm not sure I believe you. I don't particularly trust you. But I appreciate what you said about Sevrin, and admitting your complicity. Please do help Lil and Sam buy that house for Dakkar. As for working with me, there are stipulations. You will work with Hannah on the story, direction, and editing, coming to me for final approval. You are not to use me, my friends, my competing, any of the other competitors, or this documentary, for any gain, other than what I pay you, for your services, as editor and consultant. If that is reasonable to you, then I would like to offer you the job. You are the best in the business. You know me. And," I shrugged and lowered my eyes, "I would like it if you would make this with me."

"I would like it, too."

I heard the smile in his voice. I could well imagine his dimples. I kept my eyes down to protect myself from forgiving him completely.

I LEFT Aramis and Hannah to work on the documentary. Before I headed to Reede's to practice, and apologize profusely for not following her instructions, I decided to stop in and see Brent. It wasn't going to be easy to tell him I hired Aramis to work on my documentary. He'd hate it and I didn't care to face his disapproval. I needed to tell him before he heard about it from someone else. I also wanted to tell him that Sevrin had nothing to do with his gallery.

This time my carving of Sevrin in the gallery display window tugged at my heart rather than disgust me. Brent cared about me. He didn't want to see me get hurt or used again. I couldn't fault him for that, and I couldn't wait to tell him he had no reason to worry any more.

I was pleased to see a couple of dwarves browsing the gallery. Brent hovered in the back corner, ready to move in should either of them appear to be ready to make an inquiry or purchase.

Brent smiled and waved at me. I returned the gesture and sauntered over to where one of the customers stood, eyeing Celia's dragon. I pretended to study the carving for a few minutes when in reality, I watched the client and what he was focusing on.

"Fine detailing, isn't it?" I spoke softly, pointing to the fine etch marks Celia had made in the stone, the intricate patterning of the scales flowing through to the underbelly.

"It really is remarkable," he agreed. "I am in love with this piece."

"I can see why." I glanced at the price. "It's a steal too."

"Is it?"

"Oh, yes. Celia's brilliant. She is going to be huge. I've heard a carving she did, similar to this one, sold for almost twice as much just last week."

"Really? I am so tempted, but I don't think I should."

"Where would you put it?" I asked. "If you were to buy it?"

"I have the perfect spot for it inside my front

door, to greet guests when they come to visit. There is a little corner that is bare and this would add the perfect ambience."

"Hmm," I looked at it wistfully and said, "I'm sure it would," as if I knew him and his home. "I don't know. It's so stunning. You really can't go wrong, especially if you have a place for it. What would you do if you came in tomorrow and it was already claimed? What if her exhibition closed early?"

"I would never forgive myself for letting it go."

I sighed. "I feel that way now." I reached out as if I was going to touch the dragon's wings, then pulled back. "You'll be the envy of the city."

He bit his bottom lip. "Okay. I'm going to do it. I'm going to get it. Where's the manager?" He looked around.

"I'll go get him. You guard this piece so no one else buys it." I leaned in and whispered, "I saw that other fellow eyeing it when I came in." I pointed at the other customer in the gallery.

"Thank you."

I made my way back to Brent and told him to go close the sale. I browsed the art while I waited for him to finish. Reede was going to be upset with me for being late but I had to talk with Brent.

Finally he was done, the dragon purchased and marked for pick-up at the end of the exhibition. Unfortunately, the other customer was still in the gallery, making it difficult for me to talk with Brent privately.

"Thank you for that," Brent said, sneaking a kiss on the cheek.

"You're welcome. Listen, I can't stay. I have to go practice."

Brent's face fell.

"I came to tell you," I took a steadying breath, "I hired Aramis today to work with Hannah on editing."

Brent stepped back and stuffed his hands in his pockets. "I see." His voice was low, cold, hurt.

"He and Sevrin are no longer friends."

Brent snorted. He didn't believe me. There was no way he would believe that Sevrin wasn't involved in controlling his gallery since Aramis was my source.

"He is the best there is. I need his skill and objectivity."

"If that's your decision...I wish you'd talked to me first."

"It is my decision. I'm only telling you so you don't hear it from someone else and think I'm keeping secrets from you."

"Very thoughtful," he muttered, walking away.

It was very thoughtful of me, even though it hurt him. Hurting him was what I seemed to be best at.

CHAPTER 8

I FOLLOWED Reede to a small community arena. We were in a part of Leitham I'd never been to. In the years I'd lived here, I thought I'd explored most of it, every dwarven neighborhood at least. Apparently I hadn't.

My stomach was in knots as we entered the low stone building. Jeff and Hannah were to have arrived earlier to arrange for and set up the recording. My entire body ached, especially my right shoulder. After a couple of weeks of triple the warmup time I was used to and equally extended practice sessions at Reede's back-garden arena, I fairly expected to blow out my shoulder.

This was what Reede called my first real competition. While I could continue to compete at the local taverns, I would need to have a minimum of ten wins under my belt to be eligible for this competition. The organizers reserved a handful of wild-card spots for competitors like me, Reede had said: an experienced competitor new to Leitham. Though I didn't consider myself new to Leitham, Reede had plead my case as a past Black Mountain Regional finalist who had to recover from a major injury. The organizers generously granted me one of those wild-card spots.

I'd enjoyed competing at the taverns. I'd loved practicing at Reede's. I'd worked hard and I was positive that under her tutelage, my throwing skills had improved exponentially over what they had been when I'd competed in Mitchum.

Though this arena was much smaller and not under a mountain like the Mitchum arena was, I felt the walls pressing in on me, under the same kind of weight as I'd felt in Mitchum, when I ran out of the arena in a panic.

I leaned against the wall and stopped.

"What's going on?" Reede asked.

I shook my head, unable to give voice to my fear. I breathed deep. I didn't have the same expectations placed on me that I had then. My career would survive regardless of my performance or the final outcome. Still, I didn't want to embarrass myself. That was it. I smiled. It was my competitive nerves trying to get the best of me. "I'm fine," I said, stepping away from the wall.

"You sure?" Reede asked.

"Absolutely." I wanted to win. For myself and simply for the sake of winning. "Let's do this."

My knees shook as I pushed off the wall. Once I was in the arena and put in a couple of practice throws, I would be fine. I had no control over how any of the others performed. All I could do was focus on myself and not let my opponents distract me. I had the drive to win, the skills, and the training.

Hannah and Jeff stood near the registration table. As we approached, he whispered the incantation needed for the crystal to start recording. This was different than during practice. With the crystal so close to me now, I was extra aware of my trembling knees and the clammy sheen of sweat coating my face. I did my best to ignore Jeff, to be natural and relaxed. I hadn't realized how difficult a task that was without specific lines to speak and a persona to inhabit. It was probably all the more difficult because I was already nervous.

Then I saw Reede stumbling over her own name as she checked us in. Jeff was smirking. Hannah, behind him, made notes, likely to edit out this part or re-record it later. I appreciated that they were being so detailed in the material they were collecting, but I didn't think I'd need to use images of me registering for any competition except maybe the Dwarf Games themselves. On the other hand, depending on the final narrative, it could provide a nice bookend: see the nerves as I register for my first competition compared to my confidence registering for the Dwarf Games.

First things first. I had to perform well today. Placing was the preferred result. Winning would be ideal but unlikely given I had not been training long.

Reede and I walked past Jeff who then came around to face us, recording us as we entered the arena floor and found our spot along the back wall. Behind the wall and elevated along the sides were two rows of spectator bleachers. A handful of dwarves already sat there. I searched for my friends. I didn't see them. I hoped they would come.

Reede snapped her fingers in front of my face. "Focus, Mabel. Grab two axes and warm up with the throwing motion."

I reached into my bag of axes and glanced up at the bleachers. A few more spectators had arrived, including Sam and Lil, who waved at me. I nodded at them and continued my warmup. Brent wasn't with them. He wasn't working late today. He had no excuse, he just didn't want to support me. Not even for a low-level competition, not for my documentary.

Reede tapped my shoulder and we took our place at our bench, ready for introductions and competition.

I thought about Reede beside me. She was a fighter, which I loved about her. After Mikey had asked her to lose at the Dwarf Games, then broke up with her, she'd continued to compete. That was huge. Brent not being here was minuscule in comparison.

What was I going to do? Allow his lack of support to distract me? Hurt me? Get in the way of competing at my absolute best?

Hardly.

I was going to use it. Let that hurt and disappointment fester into anger and use that anger the same way I'd used my immature fantasies of Aramis when I'd begun throwing. Like Reede, I was going to use this anger as motivation to win.

When my name was called, I took a step forward and waved to the stands, grinning as my friends cheered.

I was up. The first round was always the easiest with the throwing line closest to the post. For that very reason, the first round could also be the trickiest. It was far too easy to become over-confident and complacent, thereby ending up with a terrible result. I'd heard stories of some top throwers completely missing the post in the first round.

My heart thumped in my chest. I took a couple of calming breaths and rolled my shoulders to loosen them up.

I could do this. I had a brilliant coach. I was better at throwing than I'd ever been.

My focus narrowed on the target. I pointed the blade of my axe at it. Reached back then pointed it again, visualizing the path of the axe. I reached back, keeping my elbow in tight, held my breath as I focused on the motion, releasing my breath as I released the axe, and finished with a good follow through.

The axe hit dead center.

I nodded my head ever so slightly. That was how it was done.

I breezed through the first round, but so did almost everyone else. There were fifteen of us tied for first place.

The second round moved the throwing line back a fair number of feet. While the first round was about technique, the second round added the challenge of strength and was sure to put some space between competitors.

My second round was not as perfect as the first, but I sat in third going into my final throw of the round.

I took my time, rotating my shoulders. I reached back and thought I'd felt a twinge in my muscles.

No. No. I couldn't have. I was imagining the pain. I didn't feel anything now.

I pulled my focus back to the task at hand. Reede was teaching me the right technique to use to prevent injury.

I breathed deep, reached back, and breathed out as I hurled the axe.

It landed perfectly, keeping me in third, moving me on to the final round.

"You hesitated," Reede said when I returned to the bench.

"I thought I felt something in my shoulder, but it's gone now."

"Stretch it out while we're waiting for them to set up for the final round."

"I'm sure it was nothing."

"Don't care. You're not taking any chances."

After stretching I felt looser, which was always a good thing when speed and agility were added to technique and strength. This was probably the one time in any truly dwarven pursuit that my not-so-stout physique worked in my favor.

The final round was a thing of beauty as the competitors spun and twirled, throwing the axe at randomly popping-up targets in the true tradition of the dwarven warrior.

Reede stood in front of me. "Keep your focus. It isn't too crowded or loud so you shouldn't have too difficult a time hearing the mechanics of the targets, but don't rely on what you hear. Pay attention to the gears grinding beneath the surface."

"Got it." My stomach churned as I took my place in the center of the arena one last time. I gave the signal that I was ready. The handful of spectators cheered. Within moments, the ground vibrated beneath my feet as the gears moved. I spun to my left ninety degrees and nailed the target. I twirled two-hundred degrees to my right and nailed it again. I turned once more to my left and hit the third target dead on.

The crowd roared.

I took a deep breath and retrieved my axes from the competition officials. I'd done everything I could possibly do. What happened next was out of my hands and I didn't like it. I waved to the spectators, bowed to the officials, and took my place beside Reede. She patted my knee but said nothing. I lowered my gaze. I couldn't bear to watch the final two competitors.

Third place wasn't so bad considering it had been a few years since I'd competed. Third place qualified me for the city championships. I could live with placing third. I loathed the idea of not winning.

I didn't have a choice.

I joined the top five finishers in the center of the arena for the presentation of the prize purses. One diamond for fourth and fifth. Three diamonds for third, five for second, and seven for first. No one was going to earn a grand living at these competitions, but they weren't intended for that. The real prize was moving up a level in qualifying, getting invited to compete at the city championships.

Jeff moved onto the arena floor and recorded the award ceremony, focusing on each of the winners who smiled and waved excitedly at him. I did the same, though I felt no joy.

CHAPTER 9

"MORNING, REEDE." I yawned as I entered the throwing arena in her back garden. I'd barely slept last night for thinking of Brent and the competition. He had every right not to approve of me competing in axe throwing. He didn't have to like anything I did. But if that was what he chose, then I didn't have to bow to his wishes just to please him, to stop him from scowling at me, avoiding me, hurting me.

I deserved better.

"Have a good night?" Reede was far too perky and keen to get to work. "Keep competing the way you did yesterday and there will be more wins to celebrate. Start warming up."

I was sluggish in my stretches, staying in one stretch longer than usual, taking my time before switching to the next one.

"The city championships," Reede said, "are going to be a lot harder. It's usually the warriors who come home to compete. They have the strength and little else to do but practice. You do not have their strength. There is not enough time or exercise in the world that would give you the same kind of strength."

I groaned.

"It's all right, though. We need to rely more on technique than brute strength. Are you loose? Limber? Ready to throw? Your second round technique needs improvement. We need to work on your release and follow-through. You need strength in your shoulder and upper arm, and a loose touch in your forearm and wrist. There is a different technique that might work for you. It is rarely used, but it can be very effective in the right hands. Watch me."

Reede, throwing axe in hand, reached back, pointed at the target with her free hand, and like a windmill, whirled her arms around and flung the axe forward, finishing with her arms in nearly the same position as when she'd begun. I wondered briefly as I stared in awe at her throwing prowess, if Mikey had ever planned to teach me this skill. Reede slowed down the motions, showing me each step. Then she made me try, stopping me at the key points to correct my stance or my arms. She wouldn't let me use an axe. She said there was time for that, she wanted me to get used to the feel of it first.

"Good job, Mabel," Reede said taking my axes

from me. "Tomorrow we're going to add an extra
hour to our practices. For the rest of the day, stay
loose and limber. Stretch every couple of hours."

THERE WAS no way I could stay loose as long as
I held onto my anger at Brent. Instead of returning
home, I went to his gallery. There were a few customers milling around, eyeing a few pieces. Brent
was busy going between them answering questions,
seeing to their needs. I waited until he acknowledged
my presence then made my way to his office in the
back. I sat in his office chair and put my feet up on
his desk.

"Mabel," he said coming in. "What's up?"

"Take care of your clients. I'm in no hurry," I
said as sweetly and as supportive as I could.

"Okay, I shouldn't be too long. Should I close up
once they leave?"

And be blamed for lost business? "Not at all."

Disappointment flashed across his face. Did he
really think I wanted to spend more time than necessary with him after he abandoned me last night?

He was acting like I hadn't been in an important
competition last night. Couldn't he at least have said,
"How did you do?" or "Can't wait to hear about it."
Instead, he asks me what's up. What's up? My anger,
that's what!

I shouldn't have come here. I was too upset. I

wasn't thinking clearly. I didn't want to hear what Brent had to say, what excuse he would give for not showing up to the competition. I wanted to jump on him the moment he returned to the office, to go on the offensive, accusing him of being an idiot, of hating me, of punishing me. Except I knew attacking him wasn't the right thing to do.

I stood up to leave when Brent burst through the door, grinning. "Just sold three pieces to a new client. A referral." He practically bounced over to his cash box to deposit the gems and gold pieces. "Business is finally picking up. I've been making some changes and I think they're working." He planted a kiss on my lips. "What brings you by?" He looked at me, eager to hear my news, smiling, clueless, ignorant of how he'd hurt me.

"Are you serious?" I asked.

"What?"

"I placed third and qualified for the city championships last night and you weren't there."

"Oh."

That's it? No explanation? Not good enough. I waited two whole agonizing minutes, glaring at Brent. Willing him to speak. He didn't, nor did his gaze waver from mine.

I couldn't do this anymore. I deserved better. It was time I did something about it.

I broke. "Why?"

"That's a loaded question."

"Shall I narrow it down for you? Why can't you

support my axe throwing? Why is it okay for you to hurt me like this?"

Brent became withdrawn, shoulders slumped, turned into himself. He breathed out audibly and studied his hands.

I was determined to wait him out this time.

"You know why," he said at last.

I snorted. "And you think running a successful art gallery wouldn't draw Sevrin's attention? It did, you know. Long before I ever showed up in Leitham, Sevrin was watching you. The only reason he left you alone was because you were taking Aubrey's money."

Brent shrugged and splayed his hands palm up in a gesture of surrender and frustration. "I'm sorry, Mabel. I really am. But I can't stand behind you if it means putting my business in jeopardy."

Ouch! "What can you support?"

"Mabel, I—"

"Do you want me to quit making movies, too? Should I only work at the Hammer and Chisel, tending bar? Will you allow me to at least work here in the gallery every now and then, dusting, maybe unpacking new pieces as they come in and packing up pieces as they are sold?" It was harsh, I knew.

"No. I-I don't want you to change."

Except he did. I could barely hold back the tears, or the pain from my voice. We had been so good together, once—at least I thought we had. "Fine." My voice trembled. "We're done, then."

"Mabel, no. That's not—"

I shook my head. "It was good while it lasted, but I need more. I deserve more, from the one I'm with."

I told myself to put one foot in front of the other, and again, faster, until I was running out of the office and the gallery.

I HELD back the worst of my sobs until I was alone in my room with the door closed.

Lying on my bed, face buried in my pillow, I let the tears fall, and grief wrack my body.

"Mabel?" Mam knocked on the door.

I held my breath trying to stop my weeping, hoping she would go away.

She didn't. "Mabel?" she asked again, opening the door. "Love." She closed the door and rushed to my side, gathering me up in her arms. "What happened?"

"I broke up with Brent," I choked out.

"What? Why?"

"Because of you and Sevrin. Because's he's selfish and afraid that Sevrin will ruin his gallery because of me. Because he wants me to change even though he says he wants me to be myself."

"I see. Well then, even though it hurts, you did the right thing."

"I hope so."

Mam kissed the top of my head. "I came to ask if

you want to come over for dinner, but I don't suppose you're up for it now."

I chuckled. "Not really, no."

Mam held me, letting me cry onto her shoulder. She didn't speak against Brent. She didn't defend herself or Sevrin. What she was doing was what I needed most. When I had no more tears left, I sniffed and asked, "When Da kicked you out, did you physically hurt?"

"I thought I was going to die," she said. "I felt like a piece of rock, chipped off the mine wall, left to free-fall with nothing to grab onto, nothing to keep me from tumbling into the abyss."

"How did you get over it?"

"Time. Lots of time. Sometimes I'm not sure I am over it. And then there are times, especially the last few years, when it doesn't hurt quite as much because I have you back in my life."

I curled up in my Mam's arms like I would have as a dwarfling, comforted, happy to have her there.

CHAPTER 10

MAM SAT at the table with Lil, Sam, and Hannah when Jeff and I returned to the Hammer and Chisel after a good day of practicing.

"Mabel, love." Mam stood and embraced me. "Lil tells me she and Sam are having a golden ring ceremony. Isn't that wonderful?"

"It is."

"I was hoping to speak with you, privately," Mam said.

"Of course. Excuse us," I said to my friends, and pulled Mam away from them, to the privacy of the back garden. "What's up?"

"I ran into Hannah and Aramis at Studio City. Why was Hannah with Aramis? Is he working on your movie?"

"He is," I said.

"Oh, Mabel. I really don't think it is a good idea for you to work with him."

"Why not?"

"Sevrin and Aramis have had a falling out. Aramis can't be trusted."

Aramis had said he and Sevrin weren't friends anymore, but he had left it at that. I was starting to trust him, but if Mam was concerned, maybe I should be too. "What happened?"

"He is out to ruin Sevrin. I know you don't approve of my relationship with Sevrin, but he thinks of you as a daughter. He wants to protect you. If Aramis is after Sevrin, I fear he is going to use you to get to him."

This wasn't about me at all. It was about Sevrin. "I don't understand. How would Aramis working on my movie hurt Sevrin? It isn't like they have to spend any time together, and Aramis can't really turn me against Sevrin. I have set up protection so that Aramis can't profit from my axe throwing. Or is that what Sevrin is worried about? He thinks Aramis will have access to manipulate me before Sevrin gets a chance to profit off me?"

"Mabel, that's not fair."

"How will Sevrin punish me if I continue to work with Aramis? Who will he take revenge on? Will Lil suddenly find herself without any roles? What about Jeff and Hannah? Will they be out of work in the industry?"

"Of course not."

"You know, Da had strict rules and he expected me to conform to his ideas of how and what I should be, but at least he never used me. Da's don't use daughters like that."

"Sevrin is not looking to profit off you. He promised he would leave you and your friends out of his business, just as he does my acting, and he's held to that promise. I hold him to it. He knows he would lose me if he dared use you."

"Again," I muttered.

"Excuse me?"

"Again," I said louder. "He already used me once and he didn't lose you. In fact, you were a part of it. So what makes this time different?" I held no malice toward her or Sevrin. I understood why they'd done what they'd done.

Mam hung her head. "There is nothing more I can say. Please, just please be careful."

I sighed. I'd been too harsh on her. Maybe Mam really was only looking out for me. "For what it's worth, Aramis is under a very strict contract. I don't expect to have much direct contact with him at all. He is good at making movies and I can benefit from his expertise."

Mam nodded. "If you find yourself in difficulty with him, if you suspect the slightest trouble, please come to us for help. No strings attached. I promise."

Mam walked away but I called her back. "I'm sorry, Mam. I like it when you come to visit me and my friends. Come join us for a few drinks."

"I'm not sure that's such a good idea."

"Mam, please. Just be my mam, like you were the other day."

She smiled. "All right."

I put my arm around her shoulders and walked with her inside. "You know, Jeff still has a huge crush on you."

"Does he now?" A twinkle of mischief sparked in her eyes and I smiled.

"WHY CAN'T we use this?" Hannah asked.

The image on the editing room screen was frozen on a close-up of me during the qualifying competition, my face scrunched up in a snarl as I prepared to release my axe. "Come on, Hannah. Look at me. That's hideous. If we use that for the poster, we will scare everyone away."

"I disagree," Hannah said. "It screams fierce competitor, high tension, great drama, warrior. It will be a huge draw. Don't you think, Aramis?"

He was doing a better job at keeping a straight face than Hannah was.

"I was the one who first suggested it," Aramis said with indignation. "Fierce warrior. Great drama."

I nodded. "Good points. All right. You convinced me. Let's do it. It's perfect. Fierce warrior."

That wiped the smirk off Hannah's face. "Really?" she asked.

"No." I smiled.

Hannah laughed.

"You forget I grew up with eleven brothers."

"Can't ever get one over on you." Hannah shook her head.

"You almost did, for a second." I turned on Aramis. "And you."

"What?" His eyes were wide and innocent.

"Don't let her corrupt you."

Aramis smiled, there was a twinkle in his eyes. "I will do my best. Thank you for looking out for me."

"All right, all right," Hannah said. "Back to work. Aramis, we'll need to keep what Jeff recorded on all of the top five. I want to interview them, too, get their opinions on Mabel throwing."

"I like it," Aramis said. "Let me fast-forward this to the award ceremony. I would like to see their reactions to Mabel placing third."

"Great," Hannah said.

Before Aramis had a chance to do anything, Lil burst into the room and said, "Oh! No! What is that hideousness?" She pointed at my scrunched up face on screen. "The poster for my movie," I said with pride.

"Aramis, you can't let her do that," Lil ordered.

"It was his idea." This time I couldn't keep a straight face.

Lil clutched her heart like she'd had the scare of her life. "Oh, good. Now I don't mind saying this.

Aramis, we got the house! Our offer was accepted!"

He smiled and said softly, "I am happy to have helped."

"I promise Sam and I will pay you back as soon as we can."

"That is not necessary." Aramis shook his head. "In fact, the renovations to the property will cost a fair bit and if you need help with that, ask. Anything you want, and it is yours."

My jaw dropped. So did Lil's. She recovered faster than I did.

"We couldn't possibly accept that—"

Aramis held up his hand and interrupted her. "Please, Lil. It is the least I can do for Dakkar. I do not want you to be indebted to me. My only condition is that it goes toward building a home for Dakkar. If you insist on paying me back, then I want you and Sam to consider being in my next movie, or one in the future that has parts that are suitable for the two of you. There are witnesses here. I cannot go back on my word."

I studied Aramis. He was genuinely happy for Lil and Sam. He wanted Dakkar to have a good home. I wondered if this was more than getting back at Sevrin for something. He was concerned for Dakkar's well-being.

It reminded me of when I first worked with him, in Gilliam, and he asked about my injury. He'd been so kind, trying to heal me. Of course, I couldn't tell if he had been genuine then, or if that had all been a part of his plan to win me over. I supposed I could believe the same now, that he was being so nice to Lil to win me over, but there was something different about him this time. Maybe I could read him better, but this was not a move to manipulate anyone.

"All right," Lil said. "I look forward to working with you on your next movie, and so will Sam." She shook Aramis's hand, sealing their new deal. "I have to tell Sam. And Dakkar. They are going to be so happy."

CHAPTER 11

I WALKED into Championship Sports, the official store for fans of all dwarven competitions, from battle-axe matches to boulder toss. The store was massive, with uniforms and equipment taking up three floors. I had never seen anything so magnificent. Gilliam arena, and even in Mitchum for Regionals, there had only been small stands around the concourse. Surrounded by all the gear, hanging on racks and stacked on shelves from floor to ceiling, I wished I'd come in here right after Brent had given me the ticket to see the Dragon Killers. I'd been so excited, then, but dealing with Brent's moodiness had eroded much of that excitement so I'd been postponing shopping for fan gear.

The date of the battle-axe match was fast approaching, and I wasn't quite sure what to do. Brent and I had broken up. He had never asked for my ticket back, nor had he offered me his. I didn't know if it was appropriate for me to go to the match. What if Brent showed up?

But this was only the second time the Dragon Killers had come to Leitham since I'd been here. I wanted to go. Brent hated sports. I highly doubted he was going to show up at the match. He'd probably thrown out his ticket long ago. He had told Jeff he was going out of town and I doubted he would be back in time, anyway.

I found the battle-axe section of the store in the back corner. Sadness filled me as I browsed the racks for gear in the right sizes. A part of me wished I was buying gear for Brent as well. We had been so happy. I thought we had been happy. When had it changed? Somewhere in our second year together. He'd been demanding fairly early on, for the same reason he was now: protecting us from Sevrin. I hadn't cared for it from the start, but we'd had so many good times, laughing and talking—at least I thought we had. Brent had been supportive of my movie making, as far as I knew.

I found a rack and shelf with Dragon Killers gear.

I should have offered to buy the tickets from him the moment he showed them to me. Even if we were still together, though, he'd be miserable watching a battle-axe match. I'd rather go with Sam or Jeff. They could appreciate the excitement of it.

I picked up the full uniform of breast-plate, jersey, trousers, helmet, shield, and axe. I set them down on the check-out counter.

"Dragon Killers, eh?" the clerk asked as he added up the items. "Don't sell too many of these."

"I'm surprised you sell any at all," I said.

"More of a collector's item here," he agreed. "Some fans just love the sport and want uniforms from all teams. I take it that's not you."

"I'm from Gilliam originally. Got to support my home team."

"Naturally."

I gathered up my purchases. I was finally going to get to a Dragon Killers match! I was going to have a great time. I may be going by myself, but I wouldn't be there alone. I'd be surrounded by battle-axe fans. I was going to make sure I had a good time.

I PUT my Dragon Killers gear in my room. I had a few hours before the evening crowd would show up. These were the moments I liked living here the most. It reminded me of when I first moved in and pretty much had the place to myself. It was a good time to go down and sit by the fire.

Half-way down the stairs I spotted a fellow sitting by the fire. Sophie and Otto were usually busy in the back preparing the food for the evening. They came out every now and then to check on the place. He didn't have a drink in hand so he must have arrived a few minutes ago. I sighed inwardly. So much for having some down time. "What can I get for you?"

The fellow stood up and smiled at me. My heart swelled. It couldn't be. Everything around me faded and the room spun. "Jimmy?"

"Hiya, Mabel."

I covered my mouth. I trembled, wanting to laugh and cry and hug him and ask him a million questions.

"Jimmy," I whispered and flung my arms around him. "How did you find me? What are you doing here? It's so good to see you. You're here."

He held me as tight as I held him and neither of us were willing to let go. "Max told me this was the address he had for you."

"Max remembered." I held Jimmy tighter.

"We talk about you all the time. We see every movie you make at least a dozen times."

"But he never writes. You never write."

"We write you all the time."

"No, you don't. His last letter said 'Da knows, don't write.'" I pulled it out of my pocket and showed it to him.

"Well, yeah. He got in trouble for getting letters from you, but he's been writing you letters every month, sometimes more. I've taken his letters to the trading post myself. You never received them?"

"No." My heart ached. How much had I missed from Max? Why was Da so intent on hurting me? I was out of Gilliam. I wasn't going to write back.

Why couldn't he allow me to have news from home?

"I'm so sorry. Your da hates that Max goes to your movies, he's tried to stop him many times. He's even tried to have your movies banned from the theater. He must have a connection in the trading post who stops all letters to you from getting out."

"Sounds like Da." The relief of knowing I hadn't been forgotten or abandoned tempered my ire. Da wasn't going to get his way this time, not like he had when he'd erased Mam from all memory in Gilliam. Max and Jimmy weren't going to let that happen. But if Max had been writing me... "So, um, had Max told me that you were coming here? Should I have been expecting you?"

Jimmy smiled. "He hadn't specifically said I was coming to see you, but I would have thought you might have guessed it."

"What do you mean?"

"Well." A teasing glint flashed in his eyes. He was going to keep me in suspense as long as possible. "It's an interesting story, wholly inspired by you, and now I get to tell you in person."

His beard so gorgeously thick and dark, had no braids in it. I'd inspired that. How good could this be? "Let me get you a drink and you can tell me."

We walked arm in arm to the bar. "Start talking," I said.

"I spent a lot of time thinking about what you said to me the last time I saw you."

His tone was calm, thoughtful, not angry or hurt,

yet his words were like an arrow to my heart. I'd hurt him the last time we talked, and no amount of apologizing could ever make up for it. I would try anyway. I handed him a tankard and said, "I am so sorry."

Jimmy grasped my hands. "Don't be. Please don't ever apologize for pursuing a life of happiness, doing what you love rather than being stuck in a life you hate trying to live up to expectations you don't want to meet. Watching you pursue your dreams, you were so brave to walk away from Gilliam, the mines, family and friends. It got me thinking. Max and I talked about it a lot. We wondered what we would do if we weren't miners. Neither of us could remember wanting to be anything but miners. You'd been the same way, though. I don't know when it changed for you, or what specifically made you unhappy. Thinking back, I saw it. Not necessarily that you were unhappy with mining, but you were happier elsewhere. One of the things I love about you is your willingness to try things, like axe throwing or acting."

Love. He said love, not loved. He didn't hate me like I thought he did, like he had every right to. I poured myself a tankard and brought Jimmy to a back table.

"I started trying some new things," he continued. "Not right away. It took me a couple of years. I saw all that you were doing and I started thinking about what I was doing."

"Jimmy, no. That's not—"

"It's all good," he interrupted. "There was one thing I had always wanted to do. So I trained, and I tried out, and I made it." He paused, taking a long sip of his ale, leaving me in suspense. At last he set down his tankard. Jimmy wiped his upper lip and grinned. "I'm one of the Dragon Killers."

It was a good thing my tankard was on the table because I would have dropped it otherwise. "You're what?!"

Jimmy grinned. "I'm a Dragon Killer, and I'm here for the match. I'm only an alternate, but I'm part of the team and with some hard work, I should be in the regular rotation soon."

"That's incredible!" I started laughing. "I'm going to the match and had just bought all new gear. Does this mean you aren't mining anymore?"

"I was told I can go back to the mines anytime if this doesn't work, but I get now what you were saying. I don't want to go back to mining, ever. I mean, I could if I had to, but I hope I never get to that place. I have found something I truly love doing. I want to see how far I can go with it, which, if I work hard enough, will be to the very top."

I was full to bursting with pride and joy. "I am so happy for you. So happy. How long can you stay? I want to hear about everything going on back home. I see your beard. You haven't found anyone worth your interest?"

"Ah," Jimmy blushed and ran his fingers through

his beautifully lush beard. "Actually, I think I have."

"Oh?" I leaned forward. "Who is it?"

"It's really early days. Too early for me to say."

"Come on, Jimmy, you have to tell me. It isn't Emma, is it?"

"Good gods, no, it isn't Emma," he laughed. "No. I'm not actually interested in finding a mate, but this connection has seemed to grow over the last few years, and we're both hesitant to take it to the next step. We're talking about it. Until we agree it's the right time to take that step, we're keeping it quiet."

"What's the hesitation?"

"Family."

That was something I could relate to. It couldn't be Jimmy's family, though. They'd been accepting of me even when I wasn't... "Ah. You're not a miner any more."

In Gilliam, for a miner to court a non-miner could destroy a family.

"We are both aware of what the fallout will be. We want to make sure this is the real thing before we cause irreparable damage."

"Good for you."

"Thanks. I have to say, too, that not having braids in my beard has the added benefit of keeping Emma from making Zach jealous by telling everyone that I'm interested in her. She still says it, but Zach can see otherwise."

I laughed. "She's still doing that? Wasn't she after you for a while?"

"Ugh. Relentlessly." Jimmy rolled his eyes. "Finally Zach gave her a golden ring."

"Oh good." He was crazy for it, the way Emma had messed him about. I hoped, though, that Emma was happy. She'd finally gotten what she wanted: a golden ring, and a mountain-dweller as a life-mate. The ultimate status symbols in Gilliam. "Is she happy? How many dwarflings does she have?"

"Just one so far. They're taking their time. Well, that's what they're saying. Emma is incorrigible. I don't know that she'll ever be happy with Zach. Between you and me, she pushes him away a lot."

"I'm sorry to hear that." And I was. Emma and I may have had our difficulties and I was glad to never see her again, but she had been my best friend once. I wanted her to find happiness. I suppose I thought if she found it, she would be fun and kind, the way she used to be. "How is Max? What is he doing?"

"Max is…great."

"What aren't you telling me? Is Max all right?"

"Max is…Max. He loves mining, he helps me out by watching my house for me when I'm not there, and when I am. He has practically moved in. Your da is pressuring him to find a mate, though. I think Max is jealous that you got away from your da. He resents you maybe a wee bit, for leaving the job of carrying on the family line to him."

"Oh good gods. Rescue him as often as you can."

"I try. Your da is not a big fan of mine. Competing as a Dragon Killer is barely respectable to him.

He'd prefer it if it was something I did in addition to mining. He tries to limit the time Max and I spend together."

"Poor Max." I shook my head. "But he moved in with you?"

"He has convinced your da it is easier for him to court without the whole family watching."

Max was always good at avoiding Da's demands. He wouldn't be able to do it forever, not when it comes to finding a mate.

"Max misses you. We all do. Especially Phillip and me. We aren't the only ones talking about you, which is probably the real reason your da doesn't care for me and is putting the pressure on Max."

"What do you mean?"

"He's trying to make Gilliam forget you, but we're not letting that happen. The fact that your movies show in the theater helps our cause. They routinely bring in the biggest crowds. The theater owners fought your da on banning them, and won. It also helps that we tell everyone at every opportunity that you're the one responsible for bringing down the Elven Mafia."

I couldn't believe what I was hearing. My friends were fighting to keep my memory alive in Gilliam. They were building my reputation, making me unforgettable. I didn't know what to say. I lowered my head, overwhelmed and humbled.

"We are so proud of you. You have divided the city, I have to say. While most of us think of you as a hero, some prefer to think of you as a menace to our way of life."

"A menace. I'm flattered."

"You should be." Jimmy sipped his ale and glanced around. A sadness twinged at the corner of his mouth. "I am so happy to see you, that you welcomed me. I've always wondered if you actually wanted to hear from me, after I tried to convince you to stay, to not be who you wanted to be, to guilt you into loving me."

I shook my head and reached for his hand. "I wanted to hear from you, but I thought you hated me, and you had every right to."

"I could never hate you. I was mad, yes, but mostly at myself, for not seeing you the way you needed to be seen." He rubbed the pad of his thumb over the back of my hand. My heart leapt. I was surprised at my pride and affection, and loss, sitting with him. I wish I felt half as much for Brent. It was possible that my excess of emotion was because I hadn't seen Jimmy in so long.

"How are you?" Jimmy asked. "Are you happy?"

"I'm…" I shrugged. "I've found my place, mostly. I like making movies. I've got a new project on the go. I've taken up axe throwing again and I'm making a documentary of it."

"Are you worried about injuring yourself or drawing attention from whomever is now running the Elven or Dwarven Mafias?"

"Um, a little, I can't lie, but I've got a great coach

and I think, hope, I have enough protections in place that I should be all right."

"Well then. You know I'll be cheering for you, and so will most of Gilliam." He pointed at my braid-less beard. "But are you happy?"

I shifted in my seat. I wished things had been better with Brent, but I was also relieved not to worry about his demands of me or his judgement. "Mostly. I miss my family. I miss you."

"I miss you too. So much."

"Who is this handsome fellow?" Lil asked, standing beside our table, hands on hips.

Jimmy let go of my hands, cleared his throat, and sat back.

I looked up and saw how full and busy the tavern was. When did that happen? How long had she been standing there? "Lil, this is my friend Jimmy, from Gilliam." Over Jimmy's shoulder, I saw my friends sitting at a nearby table, smiling and waving at us.

"So you're Jimmy," Lil winked. "Nice to meet you."

"Do you have time for some drinks with my friends?" I asked Jimmy, hating that we'd been interrupted, that I'd have to share my time with him, though that was preferable by far to saying good-bye. "I'd love for them to meet you."

"Sure. I'd like that."

"Great," Lil said. "Hannah's going to want to interview you."

Arm in arm with Jimmy once more, I walked him

over to my friends, and introduced him.

"Well, hello," Hannah said shifting her chair closer to his.

"YOUR FRIENDS are great," Jimmy said as we left the Hammer and Chisel.

"That they are. I'm so glad you got to meet them."

"Me too." There was a sadness to his tone.

"No you're not." I nudged him. "I've gotten a little more perceptive over the last few years. What's wrong?"

Jimmy chuckled. "I miss you, and maybe I wish you would come back home. But I love seeing you truly happy."

We strolled to the Sapphire Inn near the Leitham arena where the Dragon Killers were staying. "Jimmy—"

"I'm sorry about Brent. What happened, if you don't mind me asking?"

I puffed out my cheeks and exhaled loudly. This was Jimmy. He was my friend. We had been separated for years but he felt closer than he had ever been. "Brent isn't super crazy about me axe throwing."

"Why not?"

"He's concerned I might attract the Dwarven Mafia. He has every right to be. In my tangling with both mafias, Brent ended up in the mix and his gallery was put at risk. He's worried my throwing axes could draw that kind of attention again."

Jimmy shrugged. "So could your work in the movies. It's none of my business; maybe his concern for you is valid, but it seems to me it has more to do with protecting himself and his business than protecting you. I mean, if you were his prime concern, he would be worried about you re-injuring yourself, or he wouldn't want you making such popular movies. I know I don't know him and I've probably got it all wrong. I'm not trying to cause trouble. I think that if you're not worried, then he shouldn't be. If you're going to love someone, they should love you just as much back. To me that means supporting you in whatever you do. The way I couldn't love you when you left Gilliam. The way you loved me. You wanted only the best for me."

There was a sadness in his eyes. Did he still love me? "Jimmy—"

"I couldn't love you the way you needed. I thought I did, but you were right. I loved the idea of who you had been, who I thought you were, not who you wanted to be. I am glad you didn't stay. It would have smothered you. I never want to see you get smothered." Jimmy stroked my cheek, and tugged at my beard.

"Could you now?" I held my breath, both fearful and hopeful at the same time.

"Yes," he whispered. He took a step back. "But it must be from afar. Your life is here, and mine is in Gilliam."

I shouldn't have asked. I wished it could have been different, and I got the feeling Jimmy did too, but we were never going to be. I crossed my arms. "Do you get that kind of love from your special someone?"

"I do. And better yet, I can give it."

We walked on in silence, slowly. I didn't want the evening to end.

"Oh," Jimmy said, holding his hand up to his nose. "Do you not smell this? What is that?"

I laughed. "It's just Leitham. No, I'm not used to it, but I've learned to cope with it."

Stopping outside the Sapphire Inn, Jimmy said, "I'll be training the next few days, but if it's all right, I'd like to come by the Hammer and Chisel in my off hours, to see you."

"I'd be offended if you didn't. Bring some of your teammates with you."

Jimmy laughed. "Now the truth comes out. You just want to meet the Dragon Killers."

"What? No! Okay. You got me. But seriously, Jimmy, I'm so proud of you, for taking a risk, doing something you love." I planted a lingering kiss on his cheek. "Come to the Hammer and Chisel as often as you can. If I'm not there, I'm probably practicing, but I won't be away long. I'll let Sophie and Otto know to expect you and get you whatever you want. I would appreciate it if you let Hannah interview you for the documentary, too. It's okay to tell her everything, good and bad."

"What about the weird noises you made when you worked on your masterwork, or mining?"

"I never!"

"You very much did."

"Okay, don't tell her that part, but everything else should be fine."

I STOOD in the center of the throwing range in Reede's back garden, axes in hand. My favorite part of practice was about to begin. I closed my eyes and nodded. Eyes opened, I spun, twirled, and turned, throwing my axes at the targets as they popped up. I had joked with Aramis and Hannah about my facial expression but practicing round three throwing really did make me feel like I was a fierce warrior.

"Your reaction time is off on the third throw," Reede said, re-setting the targets.

I gathered my axes and returned to my starting mark.

"You build up good momentum from the first throw to the second and then you hesitate. You're thinking too much. Stay in the moment. Your body knows what to do. Let it. Let that momentum carry all the way through."

"Okay." I breathed deep and nodded. I let my senses take over as I hit the targets.

"Yes," Reede said.

Cheering erupted behind me. Hannah was there

with Jeff, Jimmy, and given their girth, I guessed two of Jimmy's teammates. My cheeks burned, embarrassed to be practicing my throwing in front of Dragon Killers.

"Hiya, Reede," Hannah said. "I hope you don't mind. I'd just finished interviewing Jimmy here for the movie and he and his teammates Dale and Theo wanted to see Mabel in action. I told them you were busy training for the city championships and they just insisted more."

"It's always nice to meet someone from home," Dale said, shaking my hand. "Especially after we've been on the road so long. That was impressive."

"It was," Theo said, sticking by Hannah's side. "If you change your mind about throwing axes, I'm sure we could find a spot on the Dragon Killers for you."

"She can take your place, Theo," Jimmy teased. "We won't keep you any longer, Mabel. I just wanted to see where you were practicing. We'll see you back at the Hammer and Chisel?"

"Hold on," Reede said. "Can you all stick around for a little while? We're almost done. I'd like to run round three a couple more times and it would be great to have you all here, simulating the competitive atmosphere."

"We'd love to," Jimmy said.

"Great," Reede said. "Not just cheering, though. One or two of you feel free to heckle her, too."

I gave Reede a dirty look. She grinned and

handed me my axes.

"Look at those scrawny arms," Hannah shouted.

She was going to enjoy this way too much. I glared at her.

"Stay focused," Reede told me. "Shut them out."

"Mabel! Mabel! Mabel!" Theo and Dale chanted.

"Pathetic. Wretched. Weak." Jimmy and Hannah yelled. Jeff got in on the action too.

I took a deep breath. Hannah, Jeff, and Jimmy laughed and heckled louder.

Eyes closed, I set up a mental wall around me and the throwing arena, dampening the cheers and taunts.

I nodded, opened my eyes, and threw, hesitating again on the third throw.

Reede waved her hands to keep the cheers and jeers going while she reset the targets. "Stay in the moment," she told me.

Putting up the mental wall was easier this time, shutting out my friends even more. It was just me and the targets. I nodded. I spun, and threw, nailing all three this time.

I pumped my fists and my friends cheered.

"Great job," Reede said. "I think this is a good place to stop. I'll see you tomorrow, Mabel."

I quickly packed away my axes.

"Hammer and Chisel?" Jimmy asked.

"Actually," Hannah said, "Theo wants to see some of the city so I thought I'd give him a tour. Is that all right?"

I looked at Jimmy with a raised eyebrow. He smiled. "Of course," I said. "Dale, Jimmy, we'll go back with Jeff."

The four of us piled into Jeff's cart and headed home. "What's going on there?" I asked Jimmy as Hannah and Theo headed in the opposite direction, sitting awfully close together.

"They hit it off really well," Jimmy said. "Dale's a bit jealous. He thought he had a chance with her."

"I think the golden ring I'm wearing would say otherwise." Dale tapped the ring in his thick beard.

Jeff stopped in front of the Hammer and Chisel. We hopped out but Jeff stayed in the driver's seat. "Aren't you coming in?" I asked.

"I want to take the crystal over to Aramis before I forget. I'll be back in a bit."

"Okay." I led Jimmy and Dale inside. "What can I get you fellows to drink?"

"Your stoutest ale," Dale said. "Thanks."

I fetched three pints and we sat around the fireplace. Dale tossed a log on the hearth and stirred the embers until it was blazing.

"We have a solution to our mail delivery problem," Jimmy said.

"I can't believe your da has cut you off like that," Dale said. "It's ridiculous. I have a cousin who works at the trading post. Now that we know you're not getting mail from home, I'll have a talk with him and see what's happening. No disrespect, but I think that as a Dragon Killer, I have a little more influence than your da. In the meantime, have Hannah, or any one of your friends send letters to me care of the Dragon Killers at the Gilliam arena. We get fan mail there all the time. There is no way your da can stop me receiving letters from someone he doesn't know. Any mail Jimmy, or Max, or anyone else in Gilliam, wants to send you, I'll act as the messenger," Dale said. "I'll take their letters from the arena to the trading post"

"Really? You would do that for me?"

"Of course," Dale promised. "Any friend of Jimmy's is a friend of ours."

CHAPTER 12

THE FULL Dragon Killers gear was bulkier than I'd remembered. The jersey and breast-plate gave me the stout figure I'd always wanted. Adding to it the shield and battle-axe, and I was nearly a perfect specimen. As I waddled around the concourse, I had a greater appreciation for my svelte physique.

I'd arrived plenty early, but the concourse was filling quickly. I loved being early to a battle-axe match. It gave me time to soak up the energy of the crowd, even that of enemy fans.

I took another lap around the concourse, checking out the vendors doing brisk business selling the gear of the Leitham Brigade, and the food stands selling roast mutton and deep-fried charred mushrooms. I debated getting something to eat, but my stomach was in knots. I was so excited to see Jimmy compete as a Dragon Killer.

Most of the fans were dressed in the Leitham colors of red and yellow. Every now and then I spotted one dressed in the Dragon Killer replica helmets and breast-plates of silver, emblazoned with a sapphire-blue dragon, its chest pierced by a diamond axe. I wondered who these Gilliam fans were. I didn't recognize them from home. Miners wouldn't travel to watch the team, so it was possible these fans were from other parts of Gilliam.

A smattering of cheers tumbled from within the arena. The players must have stepped in for their pre-match warmup.

I found my seat, a few rows back from the Dragon Killers bench. These were probably the best seats in the section and in the entire arena, as far as I was concerned. I was the first one to sit in the visiting team section. Because I hadn't seen a lot of others in Dragon Killers uniforms, I expected this section to remain fairly empty.

Jimmy stepped onto the arena floor to take practice swings with Dale. I was bursting with pride seeing Jimmy preparing for competition.

"You really are a fan of this, aren't you?" Brent asked, sitting beside me wearing full Dragon Killer gear.

"You came," I said, surprised to see him. I felt nothing more; no relief or joy. I hadn't seen him in a couple of weeks and his presence felt stifling rather than comfortable the way it used to. Why was he here? We weren't together and he hated sports. "How was your trip? Did you find some new art for you gallery?"

"A few nice pieces, yes. I also met with a few other gallery owners. Their galleries seem to be suffering much the same as mine. We discussed the shifting trends in art and came up with some ideas of how to change the artists we show and what we offer."

I bristled. How much more proof did he need that Sevrin wasn't after him? "That's good news, then."

"Perhaps."

Didn't he see it? "You're saying that Sevrin isn't responsible, right?"

"Unless he has set out to ruin every art gallery there is."

I rolled my eyes.

"You're right. I doubt he's that conniving."

I shook my head and watched Jimmy and the rest of the Dragon Killers. I couldn't look at Brent. I couldn't let go of my frustration with him.

"Mabel," he took my hand in his. "I'm sorry for not supporting your axe throwing. I still have my concerns, but I should be there for you. I love you. If this is what you want to do, then I will cheer you on."

I pulled my hand away. "I appreciate the sentiment, but you're too late. You should have been there for me from the start."

Brent was quiet for a moment. "I've been an

idiot. I'm sorry. I will do better. I promise. Please, give me another chance."

I wavered. I loved him. I wanted to, but…

The warmup was over and Jimmy, walking to the bench, waved at me.

"Who is that?" Brent asked, a jealous edge in his voice.

I regretted that I had almost considered taking him back. "My friend Jimmy."

Brent didn't want to be here. I wasn't making him stay. He'd bought the tickets. He'd chosen to come. I wish he hadn't. I would much rather watch the match alone.

The horn sounded, announcing the start of the match. Our section was half-full. The cheers and chants of hundreds of dwarves echoed off the smooth walls. Though our section was the smallest, it was close to being the loudest. We stood, banging our axes against our shields, and stomping our armored boots on the floor. Even Brent attempted a few half-hearted cheers. At least he was making an effort not to be a complete embarrassment.

The teams kept the score close for the first half. Soon after the start of the second, Leitham appeared to gain an extra level, becoming more aggressive, racking up hit points with greater speed. The Dragon Killers fought hard to keep the score close. But they were tiring and dangerously close to falling too far behind. We gasped when Theo took a brutal hit to the back. The coach called him off the floor and pointed to Jimmy to take his place.

I lead the section in a new chant: "Jim-my. Jim-my," beating our shields, and pounding our axe handles on the floor.

He was brilliant, swinging his axe, blocking a flurry of hits, hitting the breast plates of the opposition in a smooth, stunning attack. The momentum swung to the Killers' favor. Thanks to Jimmy, the rest of the team's energy rose and we were back on the attack, catching up in points, and taking over. By the time the final whistle blew, we had defeated Leitham by a dozen hits. Our section went wild.

Jimmy was surrounded by his teammates. He peeked out and smiled at me. I beamed with pride.

"What are we waiting for?" Brent asked as I remained in my seat.

"Jimmy invited me out for drinks after."

"Oh, that sounds like fun."

Just then an official waved at Brent and myself to join the team.

I hopped onto the arena floor and ran to Jimmy, hugging him. "You were the best! You won it! You're going to be on the regular rotation in no time."

"Thank you. It was my first actual chance to compete."

"You were brilliant." Behind me Brent cleared his throat. I backed up. "Jimmy, this is Brent. Brent, this is Jimmy."

They shook hands. "It's nice to meet someone who knew Mabel when she was younger."

Jimmy smiled though it was a cautious smile. "I've got plenty of stories if you'd like to hear them."

"He doesn't want to hear them. You don't. Trust me," I said.

Brent put his arm around my shoulder. I didn't like it. It felt heavy, possessive. "I would love to," Brent said.

I pushed his arm off me. He had no right to claim me as anything other than a friend.

"Let me just change," Jimmy said. "Theo and Dale want to join us, if that's all right."

"Sounds good," I said.

Jimmy gave my elbow a gentle squeeze and said, "I'll see you out front in a little bit."

JIMMY, THEO, and Dale joined us for drinks at the Rolling Boulder Tavern near the arena. It was late but the room was crowded with fans from the battle-axe match. Every few minutes patrons came over to our table asking for autographs and bringing us all tankards of ale. It was nice not having to worry about whose round it was. Judging by how much the fellows drank, I'd be responsible for at least four rounds and be broke by the end of the evening. Most of the fans asking for autographs wore Leitham uniforms. Jimmy and his teammates took their time talking with all the fans, but spoke longer with the few in Gilliam uniforms.

I loved seeing Jimmy get so much attention from the fans and his teammates. The interruptions made everything less awkward. Jimmy kept staring at Brent with a weird smile-but-not-a-smile. Of course I watched Jimmy with a goofy grin most of the evening. I was so happy for him.

One young fan in Killers' gear chatted with Jimmy, gushing about his skills with the axe and how she and her family were big fans. "We're sitting over there." She pointed to a nearby table. Jimmy turned and waved. They waved back. "We're from Gilliam. My da's a blacksmith, my mam is too. We're visiting my uncle and," she stopped when she looked at me. Her jaw dropped. "Ohhh," she said reverentially. "You're…Is it really her?" she asked Jimmy. "Mabel Goldenaxe?"

"That's her," Jimmy said.

"The Mabel Goldenaxe? The axe thrower? The movie-maker?"

"That's me." How did she know I'd thrown axes? Surely she'd been too young to remember me.

"I love you," she breathed.

"Oh, uh, thank you," I said.

"I want to be you." She straightened up. "Sorry, that sounds…What I mean is, I've been following your career since the Regional championships in Mitchum. My friends and I, we were the ones who first approached you for your autograph. I have a beard now." She pointed at it, as if that was the only reason I wouldn't recognize her. "I took up axe throwing for a while but I was terrible at it. Which is fine, I'm still glad I tried it. You are so incredible, coming here on your own. My friends and I see every movie you make." She turned to her family. "Mam, Da, look, it's Mabel Goldenaxe! Is it true you ran off with an elf?"

"Not exactly."

"Did you really defeat the Elven Mafia?"

"That might be—"

"Yes, she did," Brent said.

"What about the theft?" Her eyes were bright, eager for a tale.

"The what?" I asked.

"Theft," she said again.

Jimmy cleared his throat. "Your da's telling everyone that when you left with Aramis, you tried to take the family fortune but he stopped you."

I couldn't get away from his control. It didn't matter where I went, he could still hurt me.

"No. I didn't try to steal anything. I didn't even get to take what was rightfully mine."

"Oh, good." She smiled but I got the feeling she was a little bit disappointed. "What's it like living here?"

"Excuse me," her mam interrupted. "I apologize on my daughter's behalf. Leave them alone, now."

She sighed. "All right. It was amazing meeting you. You're my hero." Then, reluctantly, she returned to her family's table.

As the onslaught of fans dwindled, Theo stood.

"If you all will excuse me, I'd like to see Hannah once more time."

"Have fun," I said.

"I think I'll head back to the Sapphire," Dale said. "We've got an early start tomorrow. It was nice to see you again, Mabel, and to meet you, Brent. I look forward to getting your letters, Mabel. Jimmy, be back and ready to go by dawn."

"I will."

"Why are you writing to him?" Brent asked.

He had no right to be jealous. I was tempted to pull an Emma and say that Dale and I were now courting, but I couldn't do it. I did still love Brent and no matter how much I didn't like how he treated me, I didn't want to hurt him. "Da's been blocking any mail from my friends and family from getting to me," I said. "Dale and the Dragon Killers are my way around that."

We sat in silence for a minute or two and in that silence a sadness descended on me. This was likely to be the last time I would see Jimmy for at least a year. The Dragon Killers almost never competed in Leitham. I'd be lucky if they came back next year. I'd had a wonderful week with Jimmy. He fit in so well with my friends. We understood each other better now than we ever had: his need to stay in Gilliam, my need for independence, that I could never conform to the traditional way of life expected of me in Gilliam. We were more alike than ever before.

There were suddenly so many things I needed

to say to him and I couldn't give voice to any of it. I listened to Jimmy tell Brent about how he and I worked on our masterworks and in the mines, about the tributes given to me after my injury at Regionals. They were all stories I'd told Brent but they were completely different from Jimmy's perspective. He talked about how proud my brothers had been when I competed both at the Prospector and in official competitions. They had been so protective of me. I wish I had seen my family through his eyes.

When it was time to finally say goodbye, I gave Jimmy one last hug. Jimmy was my link to home and he was leaving me. "Tell Max I miss him. And Phillip, and Ben, and Zach, and even Emma. Tell them I miss them. No, wait, not Emma. But do tell her I hope she finds her happiness. Write me. Tell me all about your adventures with the Dragon Killers, and everything that's happening in Gilliam. Any time you're anywhere near Leitham, promise me you'll come for a visit."

"I will, I promise. And you, come home for a visit, sometime. Your da and brothers can't shut you out of the city. You can always stay at my place. Keep making those movies. You know Max and I will be watching. And your axe throwing, Mabel, you know we believe in you. You can do it. Go all the way. We'll be cheering for you. If you need anything, anything at all, just ask."

"I will." I couldn't let him go. It felt like I was saying goodbye to Gilliam, my family, my life, all

over again. I felt my tears coming and I had the need
to run and not look back. I didn't though. I backed
up, memorizing Jimmy's face. "The sun's rising.
Have a good trip home. I'm cheering for you too."

"It was nice meeting you, Brent." They shook
hands. Jimmy gave me one more quick hug. "Love
you," he whispered. "Always will." Jimmy backed
into the inn. Brent and I didn't walk away until the
door closed.

Brent tried to take my hand but I slapped him
away. "Well, that was interesting," he said, adjusting
his breast-plate and shoulder pads, clearly anxious to
take it off.

We walked on in silence until Brent said, "You
haven't answered my question."

"What question?" I asked.

He grabbed my hand and stopped me. "Please,
Mabel. I love you. Will you give me a second
chance?"

I wanted to. I wanted to believe he would support
my axe throwing, that he wouldn't continue to blame
me for Sevrin's involvement in the gallery, or be so
demanding, so controlling. I knew it wasn't possible
for him to change the way I needed him to. I shook
my head. "I want us to be friends, but we really can't
be anything more."

Brent let go of me and stepped back. The pain
that had been throbbing in my right temple, which
I hadn't noticed until that moment, flared and
disappeared.

"If that's really what you want," he said.

How dare he insinuate I didn't know what I wanted? "It is," I said. Now more than ever.

It hurt to walk away from Brent but I was also proud of myself.

CHAPTER 13

HANNAH AND Aramis were engrossed in editing, watching and making notes on my earlier competition when I walked into the darkened editing room. I closed the door softly and waited until there was a pause. I cringed at a particularly bad throw. It wasn't terrible, I reminded myself. I'd just improved since then. "How is it going?" I asked, fully prepared for them to say they had nothing to work with, that this documentary was a terrible idea.

"Quite well," Aramis said.

"Yeah, this will add some nice drama," Hannah said. "As long as you don't go bust in the city championships."

"Thanks, Hannah."

"Always happy to help," she said with a cheeky

grin. "Come and see what we've got so far."

Aramis grabbed a stool for me and I sat between them. He placed a new crystal into the projector. "Keep in mind, this is very rough. We have simply pieced together the scenes we think will serve the story. We will probably cut some and what we keep will need some refining."

"There isn't any narration yet." Hannah added. "I've been working on it, writing it, but for now I've basically sketched out what will be said for each scene. Thank you for letting me interview Jimmy, by the way. It was really, really helpful."

It had been a few days since Jimmy left and I missed him terribly. I reassured myself that I very likely would see him again, maybe not soon, but I would see him, and that made all the difference.

"It was nice to see him again," Aramis said.

"You were there for the interview?" I looked to Hannah. "The agreement was that Aramis would only be involved in the editing. When did that change?"

"Jeff was busy recording your practice so I asked Aramis to help."

"It was your choice?" I asked Hannah. "You didn't feel pressured? Because I can always make Jeff available if you would prefer."

"Aramis has been a great addition to our team. In fact, I was wondering if we could expand his involvement. We could really use him."

"No extra pay and the same protections for you," Aramis quickly added.

Hannah had asked him to help. He hadn't offered first. That meant she trusted him. Could I trust her judgment? Or was she being manipulated? "Are you sure?" I asked her.

She nodded. "I am."

I felt no tension or discomfort from her. Maybe everything was fine after all. "All right, then. I'll allow it. How did the interview with Jimmy go?"

"Great," Aramis said. "We talked about the movie in Gilliam, your friends, that he's on the battle-axe team now. He mentioned that Emma was now bonded to Zach."

"She is."

"Was Zach the one who caught her undoing the braid in her beard?"

"The one and the same."

"I though he broke up with her."

"Several times, but he always took her back. She is nothing if not persistent," I said.

"I know I shouldn't," Hannah said, "But I kind of really want to meet this Emma. She sounds like an entertaining character."

"That is one way of looking at it," I said, remembering Emma's glee as Da stormed onto the set, calling me a disgrace, disowning me. Discussing Emma was not the reason I'd come here. "Show me what you've got."

Aramis started the movie.

Hannah talked me through the scenes and the storyline they were going for: "After the interview with Jimmy, we thought with the material we recorded, we go with the narrative of this being your comeback, a second chance at a career previously cut short by injury. You came to Leitham in the search for a new career. Because of your injury you thought your life as an axe thrower was over, but it was something you couldn't let go of, so now you're trying again, seeing if you can still compete. How does that sound so far?"

I watched the screen as it switched from one practice session to another. I was pleased to see the improvement in my technique. I wondered how the comeback storyline was going to work with the material they had. "It's good, but you can't get any recordings of me throwing in Gilliam."

"We can try to do some re-creations," Hannah said. "For the full story to work, to give it substance, we really, really, really need to emphasize how unique you are as a female thrower, coming from the conservative community that you came from. It's surprising, not only that you came from there, but that you had the support of your family."

Why couldn't she leave it alone? "Hannah—"

"I know you said to leave them out of this. Jimmy said he could get your brother Max to help. If we wrote him the questions, he will answer them, and we can have someone read them. We'll leave the rest of your family out of it."

I sighed. The image switched to an interview with Reede.

"Mabel," Aramis said. "Where you come from, that is the story here."

"I know, but—"

"Let us show you the interview with Jimmy," Aramis said, changing crystals. "The entire interview. Trust...me." His voice trailed off at the last word, as I shifted in my seat.

But this was Aramis, and he did know how to tell a good story. He was so serious, so earnest. "All right."

Jimmy's face lit up the screen. At first it was simply small talk with Hannah and Aramis as they adjusted for sound and light. He talked about being a Dragon Killer, how I'd inspired him to try it.

"Let's start at the beginning—how you know Mabel, what she was like growing up."

Jimmy grinned and looked away. Oh no. How much did he tell them? How badly did he embarrass me? I know I'd said he could tell them everything. I didn't think he would have done it. How were Aramis and Hannah able to keep straight faces with me? They must be killing themselves with laughter on the inside. "I've known Mabel for as long as I can remember, but we worked in the Gilliam Toy Workshop together, which is really where we became good friends."

"I thought Mabel worked in the mines," Hannah said.

"She did. We both did. But in Gilliam—I don't know about other places, like here in Leitham—

we all start out in the toy workshop until we're old enough to work in the mines, or elsewhere if we aren't deemed strong enough or skilled enough to mine. Building toys hones our skills and our craftsmanship on the detailed work necessary for mining. Mabel and I were deemed talented enough to be selected do a masterwork, which means perfecting our skills even more than the majority of our friends."

"Our?"

"There were three of us doing masterworks at the same time; Mabel, myself, and Zach." Jimmy smiled again and I knew exactly what he was thinking. He was remembering the jokes, the stories, the weird noises we unconsciously made while we worked. I desperately hoped he wouldn't mention the noises. "They were close quarters, working together like that. We got to know each other well. I would even go so far as to say it solidified our friendship. At least it did for myself with the other two. I don't think Zach and Mabel remained particularly close, but there is still a connection, a friendship there. Zach still speaks fondly of Mabel."

He did? That was news to me. I didn't think Zach had ever really thought of me at all.

Jimmy told Hannah about the toy workshop, how all we ever talked about was becoming miners, hoping we would be good enough. He and I had a lot in common. We both came from large mining families going back generations. Everyone mined. There was a lot of pressure on us to follow their footsteps into the family trade. Gilliam viewed mining as the most respectable career possible. To do anything else is to be a disgrace to your family. He told of how I got into axe throwing during my first weeks in the mines, challenged by a colleague to see if I was like my family in other ways, given that my brother was a past Dwarf Games champion.

"Her family didn't consider Mabel a disgrace when she competed in axe throwing?" Hannah asked. "Even though it was something other than mining?"

"Right. Because she didn't quit mining. She was throwing in addition to it. There were other pressures on her, though, especially to find a life-mate. Most of the females in Gilliam settle down at a young age, having only worked a year or two in the mines. Mabel wasn't in a rush to find a mate, though. She loved mining and she loved throwing. Her da was persistent in reminding her that she needed to find a mate. Her brothers didn't seem to think she should be in a big hurry. They were proud of her accomplishments in axe throwing, and mining. I sometimes wondered if they were even aware she was female, and not just another brother. At any rate, it worked in her favor."

"How so?"

"At The Bearded Prospector, considered the miners' tavern, there are sometimes one or two of the female miners who will compete, but it's pretty clear they're only doing it to get closer to the fellow they're with. They never show any real interest in competing. With Mabel, that competitive spark was there right from the start. I think her brothers encouraged her because they didn't see her as female."

"Are you saying females aren't encouraged to compete?"

"Exactly. I thought the absence of female throwers was unique to Gilliam. Now that I'm a member of the Gilliam battle-axe team and have done some travelling, I see the same thing occurring almost everywhere. Maybe there will be one other female competing at some of the city competitions, I think there might have been one at the Black Mountain Regionals when Mabel competed, but I don't remember. If they are competing, they are not encouraged to seriously pursue it. Mabel's brothers encouraged her."

He paused, looking down. "That's not true. They knew full well she wasn't male. Mabel has an incredibly conservative family. Probably more conservative than any other family in Gilliam. It would only make sense, then, that they thought of her as a brother, but they didn't. There are certain, traditional dwarven traits that they value to the extreme. Stoutness, a thick beard, strength, competitiveness, and mining. Mabel was great at mining, and she was, is, a competitor. She was, according to them, lacking in the other areas; not as stout as they thought she should be, her beard not full by Gilliam standards. They worried that she didn't have what it took to find a mate, and they thought axe throwing would help. Her family had also experienced some hard times after her mam…left. They did not have a great reputation for many years, and they worked really hard to rebuild it. Mabel's axe throwing was supposed to help that, too."

"Sounds like she carried the weight of the family."

"She did, and she knew it. She carried it willingly. So when she injured her shoulder, she didn't tell anyone because she didn't want to disappoint them. But she pushed herself too hard, and ended up shredding her shoulder, basically ending her axe throwing and mining careers. Her family acted supportive, but they weren't. They just heaped more pressure on her to find a mate."

"Stop." I said. "Stop the crystal." I wiped tears from my eyes.

"You said you would watch all of it," Aramis said, even as he did as I asked.

"I've seen enough. Use it. Nothing too embarrassing if you can avoid it. And Max. See if he'd be willing to answer some questions. Wait. No. Hannah. I want you and Jeff to go to Gilliam. Write to Jimmy. See if Jimmy, or Theo, can find a place for you to stay. You can do your interview with Max. Ask if Jimmy can get our friends to be interviewed. Keep it quiet. At night, in the place where you're staying. Don't let anyone broadcast what you're doing or you might find yourself being run out of town by my da."

Hannah grinned. "I am so going to try and interview this Emma. I want to see what she says. I'm not going to use it for the documentary, but I'll let her think I am."

"You're crazy."

I had to do it. I had to send Hannah to Gilliam. That was the story to tell. Surely it wasn't only my story. Surely there were others who had grown up as I had. I knew there were. Emma was one of them. Maybe, just maybe, my escape could inspire some-one else.

My only hope was that sending Hannah to Gilliam wouldn't make things worse for Max.

CHAPTER 14

AXES IN hand, I swung my arms around to loosen up my shoulders. The twenty-nine other competitors and their coaches were spread out over the arena floor for their warmup. Jeff wandered among the competitors, recording the ones who had given permission, which was all of them. Soon he would find his spot next to Hannah and Aramis, the wizard's crystal mainly focused on me. Aramis stuck out in the bleachers.

To my surprise and irritation, Brent sat with Lil, and Sam near Hannah. Brent's attention was everywhere other than on what Lil was telling him. I suspected it was because he didn't care for sports so had no real interest in being here, and because to engage in conversation with Lil meant looking at her, which meant Aramis would be in his line of sight.

Now that we weren't together he could support me?

There was some movement behind Hannah. I froze mid-swing, nearly letting go of my axe. Mam and Sevrin walked to a pair of seats behind Hannah and chatted with Aramis. He didn't seem particularly happy to see them though he wasn't shying away from them, either.

"They can't be here," I muttered. "Mam maybe, but definitely not Sevrin."

"Mabel," Reede snapped her fingers in front of me. "Focus on your warmup. Visualize what you have to do to win. This is the city championships. Forget what's happening in the stands."

I lowered my arms and turned to Reede. "I can't. That's Sevrin," I whispered. "Head of the Dwarven Mafia. Here with my mam."

"I know who he is."

"He can't be here."

"Has he asked you to throw the match?"

"No."

"Has he placed any bets on you?"

"Not that I'm aware of."

"Has he threatened you? Tried to control you?"

"No."

"Then forget he's here."

"But—"

"Mabel. Forget him." Reede put her hands over mine on my axe handles. She raised them and shook them. "These axes. This competition. That is all you are thinking about."

"Got it."

During the introduction of contestants, I risked a glance at the stands. Brent wasn't there. My chest tightened. I still felt his anger at me, that he was right because Aramis and Sevrin were here. He was right to be suspicious. I was naive to believe them. I had to tell him I had nothing to do with Sevrin being here, that I didn't want Sevrin here. How could I get a message to Brent? I was about to go into a major competition that would last a few hours. I hated the idea of him being angry with me when I'd done nothing wrong.

Reede knelt in front of me and held my jittering knees, stopping them. "Look at me. We are at the city championships. You need to place in the top five to qualify for Regionals. These are the best throwers in the city. This is a tough competition. You have to set aside all distraction if you want to have a chance placing. You do not get to the Dwarf Games if you don't go to Regionals. Do you understand me?"

"I do, but—"

Reede shook her head. "Is Brent more important than competing? More important than your movie?"

I hesitated.

"Is he? Or are you going to be the first female to win the Dwarf Games? Prove your family wrong. Prove to yourself that you made the right decision pursuing this. Do you bow to someone else's will? Or will you stand up for yourself?"

I looked over to the stands where Sam and Lil

cheered. I had never let a fellow come before my career and there was no way I was going to let Brent be the first. We weren't together. I owed him nothing. "I want to be Dwarf Games Champion."

"Prove it. Focus."

I lowered my eyes, breathed deep, and shut out everything around me the way Reede had taught me. With careful, concentrated breaths, I reviewed the technique I needed for the first round. I shut out the sight of the other competitors, and the cheering fans.

My name was called. I strode to the throwing line. I could do this. I could hear Jimmy when he said to me, "We'll be cheering for you!" I tucked a lock of hair behind my ear and slapped my shoulder to keep my focus in the moment, not on my visit with Jimmy. I looked up at the target, took a deep breath, adjusted the sleeve of my tunic. One more breath, pointed at the target, and tossed.

Perfection.

I had never, ever, in my entire life, ever thrown so well. For my second throw, I repeated tucking my hair, slapping my shoulder, adjusting my sleeve. I had no idea if those moves had actually made a difference to my throwing but I'd done so well on my first throw, it couldn't hurt to repeat them. Again the blade of my axe hit dead center.

My third throw and I tucked my hair, slapped my shoulder, adjusted the sleeve, which fell over my wrist so I adjusted it again. Nope. That wasn't right. I took a step back from the line, breathed, shook out my arms, stepped up to the line and started the routine again, getting it right this time. I was glad I had; my third throw wasn't what I would have called perfection, my release was a touch off, but it still counted full points. I'd have to be more careful for round two, though.

I easily made it into round two. Reede had few words for me as the bottom ten competitors were dropped and the arena was reset. There was a tightness about her mouth, a determination. She had a lot to prove as the first female coach. She'd invested a lot of time and energy in me. I didn't want to let her down. I wouldn't, as long as I fought hard for every point. Win or lose, as long as I did my best, Reede would win, too.

Round two was always my toughest. I'd spent twice as many hours building up my strength and technique as I had before. I needed all that work to be enough to get me into round three.

My heart thudded in my chest as I stepped to the line. My throat was mine-dust dry. I hadn't practiced with the new technique as long as I would have preferred. It was too soon for me to compete with it but Reede had insisted on it. If I lost out now, that would be it for my throwing career, and my movie would be over before it really started.

"We're cheering for you," Jimmy had said.

I breathed deep and started my routine: hair tuck, slap, adjust, throw. My release was a touch late. The axe landed in the second ring. What had I done wrong? I reviewed my routine. My throat was too dry.

I stepped to the line, cleared my throat and launched into my routine. My axe landed just off center. Much better. For my third and final axe of the round, I added clearing my throat to the routine. Again I hit just outside the bullseye. I didn't know if it would be enough.

I sat next to Reede, my eyes lowered for the remainder of the round. I wanted to deconstruct round two, figure out where I'd gone wrong, but that had to wait. I had to be prepared for round three, should I make it. I couldn't be thinking about what had happened. I had to visualize what could happen in the next round. Round three was a better round for me in general, but I suspected it would go much faster than I was used to. I would need all my concentration if I was to place. If I got there.

The final round two competitor was up. Reede gripped my knees. I didn't dare look up. She squeezed every time the axe thudded into the target. She groaned after the final throw. I looked up then, expecting to have finished eleventh and out of the competition. I was close. I'd finished tenth, but tied with one other competitor.

"What happens now?" I whispered. "Do we both qualify for round three, or—"

"Tiebreak," Reede said. "You have to do round two again. Three throws each. If you're still tied, it's one throw each until one of you throws better than the other."

"No pressure then," I muttered.

"You can do this, Mabel. Keep loose, keep focused."

The officials flipped a coin. I won and chose to go first. Perhaps I should have chosen to go second so I knew what I needed to score to win, but in this case I preferred to do my absolute best and hope it was too much for the other competitor. I didn't want to take the chance that watching the other fellow do well would mess with my concentration.

I stepped to the line, rotated my shoulders, loosening my neck, cleared my throat, tucked my hair, slap, adjust, throw. Bullseye. I followed the same routine again from the rotating the shoulders to adjusting my sleeve and nailed it again. One more time, I thought. One more time. My final throw was just outside the bullseye. I'd let myself be distracted. I'd thought too much. I'd left the door open.

The other competitor was next. I stepped back to watch. I held my breath. His first throw was perfect. His second throw was just outside the bullseye. There was a chance for me. His third throw was perfect. He breathed a sigh of relief. He was still in it.

Without wasting a beat or a thought, my concentration on the target, I stepped to the line, ran through my routine and threw. The axe flew head over handle, in a straight line, into the heart of the bullseye. Though I didn't look at him, I could feel my competitor's eyes bore into me as he stepped to the line. I stood back, eyes down and waited for the thunk. The crowd groaned then cheered. I looked up. He'd missed the center. I pumped my fist and strode back to my seat with Reede. I had my work cut out for me if I was going to place. There wasn't time for celebrations.

"We're cheering for you," Jimmy had said.

My arm was tired from the extra effort. I had to control my excitement of winning the tiebreak or I would self-destruct. I could push through the tiredness. Three more throws wasn't too much to ask of myself.

I felt like the officials were showing me a little mercy as they scheduled me to throw last.

As I had before, I kept my eyes lowered, concentrating on my breathing, pulling my focus inward so I could shut out all extraneous noise and feel the vibrations in the air around me and the ground below. I had no idea what the rankings were or what score I needed to get when I stepped to the center of the arena. I went through my routine one last time, then nodded that I was ready. Less than a second later the first target popped up. I whirled and hit it. Then the second, and the third. The crowd burst into loud cheers. I checked my axes. Each throw had been perfect. I smiled and nodded to myself. Whatever the final score, I'd done my best.

Reede ran to me and scooped me up in a hug, spinning me around. "You did it! You did it! You won! We're going to Regionals!"

I finally looked at the scoreboard. My jaw dropped. I sat alone at the top by three points.

I was the champion axe thrower of Leitham!

I thought I was going to weep for joy but all that came out were screams of disbelief and elation.

"We're cheering for you," Jimmy had said.

JEFF CIRCLED the top five as we received our trophies. I beamed when the Leitham Dwarf Games Ambassador handed me a miniature throwing axe made of rubies and gold, with 'Leitham Axe Throwing Champion' engraved in the handle. I'd never won anything. Tavern competitions in Gilliam, sure, but not meaningful competitions. While I'd usually placed high enough to move on, winning, actually being named champion, was unbelievable.

I was on top of the world, full to bursting with happiness. When I thought it couldn't get any better, the ambassador announced us, the top five, as the Leitham team for Regionals, led by me, the champion, Mabel Goldenaxe! The cheers from the crowd were thunderous. The ground beneath us rumbled. I looked into the stands and waved at Lil, Sam and Hannah. My smile faltered a little, my joy diminished. Brent wasn't here for me.

He wasn't here on the biggest day of my life because of the presence of Sevrin, something completely out of my control.

I had been right not to take Brent back.

I looked over to Mam and Sevrin and Aramis. Mam was going wild waving her arms, cheering, jumping up and down. I thought she might have been wiping her eyes too. Sevrin stood, applauding, smiling. I wished I could be happy he was here. He'd been a friend to me once, until I found out how he was using me. Aramis had a broad smile as he, too, applauded. I laughed to myself. Aramis had finally seen me throw axes, and I'd won. I did like that he was here, watching me. But I hadn't won for him like I used to imagine myself doing. I'd won for myself.

And Reede.

Jeff followed me as I returned to Reede on the sidelines. A fellow with a closely-trimmed grey beard made his way to us. "Miss Goldenaxe," he said, sticking out his hand. "Drouin, of the Leitham Sporting Federation."

I shook his hand firmly. "Nice to meet you."

He glanced at Jeff and stepped between us, his back to the crystal. Jeff deftly moved around him to keep recording us. "May I speak with you, privately?"

Reede stood stone still, eyes wide, lips pressed into a tight line. My mind flashed to what she had told me about Mikey having a private meeting and then asking her to throw the tournament. I wasn't going to take any chance that this was the same kind of thing. "This is as private as it gets," I said. "This is Jeff—he's recording me for a documentary, and this is Reede, my coach."

She cautiously shook his hand. Her smile, her eyes, were almost manic.

"Fine," Drouin said. "Mabel, congratulations on your win. As Leitham Champion, we would like to speak with you about your responsibilities as city representative, team captain, and negotiate compensation in return for your service."

I looked at my Leitham teammates. No one was speaking with them about their duties or compensation. There had been no such thing as compensation when I'd competed for Gilliam. "No," I said.

"Excuse me?" Drouin asked.

"There is no need for compensation. My duties are to compete at my best, and not disgrace the city. I think you will find I am quite capable of that. Thank you."

Drouin turned to Reede. "What I was thinking—"

"We thank you," she interrupted him. Her voice was higher pitched than usual. "You heard Mabel." Reede put her hands on her hips and neither of us said another word until he left.

"Did you know him?" I asked Reede.

"Drouin was the one who met with Mikey. Jeff, did you record all of it?"

I looked to the stands. Sevrin and Mam were chatting. How dare Sevrin do this to me here, in front of Mam.

"I did." Jeff blew on the crystal ending the recording. "So proud of you," he said, giving me a hug.

"Thank you."

"Yes. Well done, Mabel." Reede said. "Celebrate tonight, but don't stay out too late. Be at my place mid-morning tomorrow. We have a lot of work to do before Regionals."

"You're not going to join us?" I asked.

"Not tonight. Have fun."

"Will do. See you tomorrow." I packed up my axes. "And thank you for the pep talk."

"You're welcome."

"Mabel!" Mam yelled, hopping over the wall onto the arena floor, running to me and hugging me. "I am so proud of you, my girl!"

At least Sevrin was smart enough to stay in his seat while Mam and I talked. "I am so glad you came, but please, don't ever bring Sevrin again."

"He's here for you, as family, nothing more."

"It doesn't matter. If anyone recognizes who he is, what he does, and they see him cheering for me, or talking to my friends, there will be suspicions."

"But Mabel—"

"Mam, I am asking you, out of respect for me, leave him at home."

Mam lowered her gaze and let go of me, clearly hurt. "You're right. I'm sorry."

"Thank you."

"I'm going to give the crystal to Aramis," Jeff said.

"Wait, Jeff. Don't give it to him yet. I want to have a look at it first."

"Sure. All right." Jeff took the crystal from the staff and handed it to me.

I tucked the crystal into my pocket. "Mam, you're welcome to join us at the Hammer and Chisel to celebrate."

"But Sevrin is not."

"That's the deal."

Mam sighed. "I'll let him know."

She was actually choosing me over Sevrin. This time.

My friends were soon on the arena floor, crowding around me, hugging me. I looked up to the stands to where Aramis sat, recording our celebrations.

"Hannah?" I asked. "Has Aramis recorded the entire event from the stands?"

"He did. I thought it would be great if we could have material from two perspectives."

I extracted myself from my friends and headed to the stands. Aramis stopped recording and met me at the wall.

"Congratulations, Mabel. Spectacular win."

"Thank you."

"Do not worry, tonight's work falls under our original deal. I will not ask for anything more."

I didn't like the wall I had put up between us. It didn't feel right. "Would you like to come celebrate at the Hammer and Chisel? I'd like to buy you a drink as thanks."

"Oh."

"Please. Mam is coming so it will be a bit awkward, for which I apologize, but I would like it if you would join us."

"Then, yes, I am honored to celebrate your win with you."

"What is he doing here?" Mam whispered as we left the arena. "He can come but Sevrin can't?"

"My party, my choice."

HANNAH AND Jeff opened the doors to the tavern for me. Sam walked in and announced my arrival. "Please make some noise-oise-oise, for Leitham Axe Throwing Champion, Mabel-el-el Golden-en-en, Axe!"

Holding my trophy aloft, I entered the tavern to roaring cheers and tankards banging on the tables. Sophie and Otto were the loudest.

"Drinks are on the house!" Otto called, bringing more cheers and stomping of feet. The floor boards rattled.

Hannah and Jeff commandeered a table in the center of the room. Otto brought over tankards of ale. Raising one himself, he said, "To Mabel."

"To Mabel!" everyone yelled and downed their drinks.

"I'm proud of you," Mam said, getting up after only one drink. "Be careful with him." She pointed at Aramis.

"Why, specifically?" I asked.

"Just be careful," she whispered, shaking her head and walking away.

I stared after her, raging inside, that she couldn't give me a straight answer, that she had to dampen my celebrations.

Hannah handed me another tankard and spun me back to the table.

"Where are the Regionals, anyway? And when?" Sam asked.

"Here in Leitham, in a month," I said.

"Oh, that's disappointing," Lil said. "I was hoping to use it as an excuse for us all to go on a trip together."

"What? You were all going to travel to Regionals to see me compete?"

"Of course," Lil said. She looked at me like I was an idiot for even considering they wouldn't be there to cheer for me.

Sam slapped her hand on the table. "I have an idea. We may not be travelling to Regionals, but why not get some rooms at an inn near the arena, like a mini trip in our own city?"

"That sounds great," Hannah enthused.

"Great. I'll book the rooms first thing tomorrow," Sam said. "If they haven't been booked up already. What should we do, two rooms? Mabel, will you and Reede be able to join us? Maybe then we should do three rooms. Except it wouldn't be right to split us all up like that."

"Hun," Lil cut in. "Mabel's probably going to

need to focus and not get caught up in too many shenanigans, at least until her part in Regionals is finished."

"That's true. Sad, but true. All right. Three rooms it is. Where did Jimmy stay? Did he like it?"

"He stayed at the Sapphire Inn and he liked it quite a bit," I said.

"Oh, the Sapphire," Hannah said. "It's really nice."

"It won't be as nice for you without Theo there," I teased, making Hannah blush.

"I'll pop over there tomorrow and see if I can book us some rooms," Sam said. "Shall I do it for the entirety of the tournament?"

"Yes!" Lil said. "Let's make an event of it. Get tickets for everyone for every sport. It's going to be so much fun."

"While you're at it, look into booking us rooms and tickets for the Dwarf Games as well," Hannah said.

"Shouldn't I qualify for the Dwarf Games first?" I asked.

"Pfft," Sam waved her hand. "We can always cancel if we have to, but that's not going to happen. Not to add extra pressure, but we want to go on this trip, so you have to qualify." Sam grinned and fluttered her eyelashes. I smiled at her cheekiness.

"I will do my best not to let you down."

"You never could," Lil said.

"Hey," Sam said. "Don't let her think she can

lose and cheat us out of a trip."

"Right. Mabel, do better than your best not to let us down." Lil wagged her finger at me.

"Understood," I said with mock solemnity.

"You lot are mad, you know that?" Jeff asked, shaking his head. "Don't you think, Aramis?"

Aramis winked and said, "Completely."

Another round of drinks arrived and Lil entertained us with a dramatic re-telling of my win, especially on the tiebreak of the second round, including my new routine. With each round of drinks, her imitation of my throat clearing and sleeve adjustment became more and more exaggerated. Aramis leaned back and smiled at me.

"What?" I asked, mid-sip of my sixth tankard. My head was buzzing.

"Reminds me of the first time I saw you at The Bearded Prospector."

Heat rose I my cheeks.

"You were a great storyteller with a fascinating story. Though I must say I like the outcome of today's story much better."

I smiled. "Me too. You know, I saw you and Sevrin walk into the Prospector that night. My friends had been begging me to tell the story of my injury. There was no way I was going to do it, then I saw you and I was so in love with you…" Oh good gods. I'd had way too much to drink.

"You were?" Aramis asked, leaning closer, his voice low, turning our casual conversation into something far more intimate.

My skin burned from embarrassment. "Haha. Ah, yes. I was desperate to impress you. So embarrassed. I'm sorry."

Aramis grinned. "You were in love with me? How long did...oh." His smile disappeared and the spark left his eyes. "Then I did what I did to you. I am—"

I waved off his apology. "Forget about it, really."

"I did not know."

"How could you? Listen, Aramis. It was silly. I'm past it."

"No thanks to me."

"What, you want me to be in love with you?" I laughed and shook my head.

Aramis remained solemn.

"Why? Do..." My heart raced. I couldn't think straight. Aramis started to talk but I held up my hand. I couldn't think about this. I had to focus on the one thing I dared give my attention to. "Make it up to me," I said. "Come with me."

I grabbed his hand and led him up to my room. "This is not what it looks like," I said closing the door.

The spark came back to his eyes, as did the breeze lifting his hair off his shoulders. "Then what is this?"

I pulled out the wizard's crystal. "At the very end of the recording, after I received my trophy, a fellow came to talk to me."

"I saw that."

"Did you record it?"

"I am afraid not. I was recording the other celebrations. Who was he? What did he want?"

"I don't know who he is. I'm hoping you do." I told Aramis about the conversation. "Reede says he's the one who talked to Mikey at the Dwarf Games. I'm hoping you can tell me if he works for Sevrin, or maybe one of Sevrin's rivals."

"Really?"

What was that in the tone of his voice? Guilt? For what?

"Let me have a look and I will be happy to tell you what I know," he continued. "And investigate who he is if needed."

I shouldn't be so paranoid.

I rolled out my screen and set it up against the far wall. I pulled out the staff I'd used for editing my first movies, practicing what Aramis had taught me. I set the crystal between the tines, tapped them and waited for the image to show on the screen. I whispered the incantation to fast-forward to the end. As soon as the second round started, Aramis stopped and made it play at regular speed.

"What are you doing?"

"We should watch this."

"What? No. Why?"

"Because you were spectacular and I would like to watch it again, with you."

"For editing?"

"No."

"Um, okay." I sat next to Aramis, flattered but thoroughly confused by what was happening. One drunken confession and he thought everything was fine?

It was fine, maybe.

I breathed deep to clear my head of this madness, but instead inhaled his beautiful, intoxicating woodsy scent. This was ridiculous.

Jeff had done a great job at capturing the competition. I was pleased to see my improved technique, though there was definitely room for improvement. I grinned like an idiot watching myself receive my trophy and be declared champion. I felt Aramis's eyes on me. I looked at him and he, too, was smiling at me, his dimples so perfect.

"May I speak with you privately?" Drouin said on screen.

"Oh," I tore my gaze from Aramis. "That's him." I pointed to the screen.

The image bounced as Jeff moved around, but he managed to maintain focus on the two fellows.

Aramis leaned forward, his attention on the action on screen. He said nothing, his expression gave away nothing, until the recording ended.

"Well?" I asked.

"He does not work for the city. His name is not Drouin. He does not work for Sevrin or any of his competitors, as far as I know. There is a familiarity about him, though I am not sure who he is. Yet you say he is the one who met with Mikey at the Dwarf

Games. I will ask around, subtly, and get back to you."

This was going far too well. "Aramis?"

"Yes?"

"You were talking with Sevrin in the stands. You didn't look happy about it, but you were talking. Mam, when she left tonight, told me to be careful around you. I need to know that you are being honest with me. That you are not working with Sevrin, or for your own gain."

"I understand your concern, especially now."

I blushed and looked away. I wished he'd forget my confession.

"Please, do not be embarrassed. It is my turn to confess."

I sank to my chair.

"Working with you in Gilliam, getting to know you on the journey back to Leitham, I...but the plan was set. I justified it by telling myself that we are of different species. It is impossible. I am ancient, you would never..."

"You told me I was like your sister."

"Your situation with your father was much like Arienne and Aubrey, and Radier. It was your situation that I used as justification for the plan. I am so very sorry for betraying you. I did my best to give you space since then. I miss you. I miss working with you, I miss talking with you. Frerin knows how I feel. She and Sevrin are unhappy with me for abandoning him and his organization. I did speak with them at the tournament, about you, and I asked Frerin about her latest role. That is all. I promise you. I am on your side. Wholly and completely."

His eyes were so blue and sincere, his voice so mesmerizing, the natural breeze that rippled his hair, intoxicating

I believed him.

"I will find out who this Drouin is, and who he is working for, and I will tell you."

I plucked the crystal out of the staff and handed it to Aramis.

At the door, he bent down and placed a lingering kiss on my cheek. The breeze that surrounded him picked up, nearly blowing me into him. I clutched the door for balance.

I remained clinging to the door long after Aramis had gone. Elation, disbelief, and the ache of his betrayal, swirled inside me. I didn't know what to think. Everything had changed and yet nothing had.

CHAPTER 15

I PULLED up in front of Lil's home and hopped out of Otto's cart. Lil came out, arms around a crate. "Hey, Lil!"

She grinned even as she labored under the weight of her burden. "It's moving day!"

I took the crate from her and loaded it onto the back of the cart. "Are you ready for this?"

"So ready."

"Even for Dakkar?" I followed Lil back to the house. The front room was crowded with crates and every piece of furniture she planned to take with her.

"Absolutely." Lil and I grabbed a crate each and carried them out to the cart. "We have a lot of work to do to get her home ready, but Sam and I are anxious to bring her home."

"Don't get me wrong. I think it's fantastic that the two of you are adopting Dakkar. But, don't you wish you had some time to live with Sam before you bring a dragon into the family?"

"I would have a couple of years ago." Lil picked up an over-sized crate. I took the other end and we walked it out together. "But Sam and I have been together for so long now, maybe not living together, but as close to it without making it official. And Dakkar is already a part of Sam's life, so not bringing Dakkar home as soon as possible, just wouldn't be right."

We heaved the crate onto the cart and returned to the house for more.

"Of course," Lil said. "That's assuming we get her."

"Fair enough. Any news on when the committee will announce their decision?"

"None. I think they were still accepting applications until a week or so ago. There was no indication as to when they would have a decision. As I understand it, they can take as long as they want, or at least until Dakkar is finished the two movies left on her contract."

"How is Sam handling the wait?" I asked.

"It is killing her. Which is kind of funny, because I'm the impatient one and I'm having to keep her calm about it."

We'd made several trips to the cart. We returned to the house and sat on one of the slowly dwindling stacks of crates. We were both huffing and puffing. I thought that with all my axe throwing training I could have at least managed a few more loads before I was out of breath. I was going to be sore tomorrow.

"Hey you lazy bones," Hannah sang, walking through the door. "Taking a break already?"

"Talk to us again when you've done as much work as we have," Lil said.

"Sure, sure. Where do you want me to start?" Hannah asked.

"Here." Lil patted the crate she was sitting on.

"With you on it? I don't think so."

Lil smiled and hopped off.

It took us a couple of hours to load up the cart. Only the furniture and a few more crates were left.

The three of us climbed into the front seat of the cart. I picked up the reins, snapped them and the pony started forward.

We traveled to the eastern edge of the city, not far from Reede's neighborhood. The homes were spread out here, on large swaths of land. It wasn't difficult to spot Lil and Sam's new place. A manufactured mountain loomed large well before we spotted the stone bungalow.

"Um, where did you say we are going?" I asked Lil, pretending not to see the mountain.

Jeff and Sam passed us.

"Follow them," Hannah said.

We reached their home. The neighbors were at least a hundred meters away on either side. A handful of scraggly lilac bushes grew in the front garden.

We each took a crate off the cart and carried them inside. "A quick tour," Lil said as we deposited the crates in the center of the cozy front room. She showed us the two bedrooms and the kitchen. The walls were made of a faded blue-gray stone, Lil's favorite color. Wood framing on the doors and windows had an intricate knot pattern that suited Sam.

"This is the best part." Sam beamed and opened the back door. Thirty feet away was a cave dug into the mountain. Dakkar's home. "It needs some work," she said. "It isn't much more than a hole right now. We're having it dug out so that she'll have a comfortable place to sleep but also plenty of room to play."

I couldn't imagine a more perfect place for Sam and Lil to start their life together, with Dakkar.

I FINALLY returned to my room. I was too exhausted to bother removing my clothes. I barely had enough energy to pull back my blankets before falling into bed. Rustling and movement on my covers caught my attention. What hadn't I seen?

I picked up a thick package. Mail. I'd received mail!

I tore open the package and out spilled a pile of parchment. There was no return address and I didn't recognize the writing. Hands trembling, hoping beyond hope. I scanned the first page.

It was from Max! Max had written me!

> Dearest Mabel,
>
> Jimmy just wrote to me, said he saw you yesterday. He said you never received any of the letters I've sent you. I have never forgotten you and I won't let anyone else.
>
> Da has been a complete tyrant. Thankfully, Jimmy is providing me some refuge in his home. How great is it that he's a Dragon Killer? Da can hardly stand that I'm still friends with Jimmy. Did Jimmy tell you the pressure Da is putting on me to find a mate? I wish you were here so that he'd be focused on you and not me. Kidding. Kind of. He is relentless.
>
> Remember how he asked us to name friends who were eligible so he could pick a mate for you? Well, he's done the same to me now, with less patience than he had with you. He made us all sit at the dinner table until everyone had named at least one eligible female, and described their family reputation and their own achievements. Kenneth and Ross, as you'd expect, have taken up the task

with great relish, coming up with new names every day. Most of them, thankfully, are entirely un-acceptable to Da, though there are enough serious contenders. It makes me think our brothers, while happy to stall for you, have decided that if they don't find me a mate soon, Da will set his sights on them and they would rather sacrifice me than themselves.

Da lets me be friends with Jimmy only because he comes from a reputable mining family, though Jimmy's support of you hasn't won him any favor with Da. Actually, it took a while for me to wear Da down on letting me be friends with Jimmy. Fortunately, no one told him we were meeting up at the mines and Prospector long before he officially allowed it.

Anyway, I've tried to cover all the news I'd written to you over the years. I'm sure I've forgotten a lot. I am devastated to report that not much has changed since the last letter you received from me. I'd hoped Da would have softened his stance by now. I know he misses you, we all do, but he's gotten worse, more narrow-

minded, since you left, if that's possible.

Jimmy said you're competing in
axe throwing again. I am so excited
for you. I'm cheering for you. Maybe
someday I'll get to watch you again,
even if it is only in your movie. Can't
wait to see it.

If you need anything from me
for your documentary, let me know.
I'll do my best. So will Phillip, Ben,
Zach, even Emma. Write me.

Forever your brother, Max.

I curled up under the covers, still hugging the
letter, a smile on my lips, happy tears in my eyes.

CHAPTER 16

STAFF IN one hand, crystal in the other, I approached Dakkar's home in Studio City. Twenty feet away from her cave entrance, I set up the equipment, whispered the spell to record, and tapped the tines. The crystal was back far enough that Dakkar and I should fit the frame as I talked with her. My hope was that it wasn't too far away to capture her expressions.

Dakkar poked her snout out of the cave before I'd reached the boundary fence. She breathed deep, sniffing out the identity of her visitor. The draft caught me and pulled me toward her. Dakkar bounded out of her make-shift cave, shaking the ground. I glanced back. Thankfully the staff remained in place.

"Hiya, Dakkar," I said. "You remember me?"

She stomped her foot and fluttered her wings,

nearly knocking me over.

"Do you remember the last time I came to see you? I was with Sam?"

Dakkar fluttered her wings again and looked from side to side, nudging me with her snout and looking again.

"Aw, sorry, love. Sam isn't with me."

Dakkar snorted her displeasure. She might not be able to breathe fire, but her breath was excruciatingly hot. Sweat coated my brow.

"Yes, I know. She wishes she could be here too. Last time I saw you, I mentioned Sevrin."

Dakkar snorted again. Sweat poured down my back.

"Right. That's why I'm here. You see, Sevrin is looking to adopt you—"

Dakkar let out a low snarling growl.

"And so is Sam."

Her wings fluttered though not as enthusiastically as when I first mentioned Sam. That didn't bode well for the plan.

"You like Sam though, right?"

Dakkar practically purred. It was a pleasant growl anyway.

"And you like Sevrin."

Dakkar snorted and hissed, as though she was trying to breathe fire.

"You don't like him?"

Dakkar looked at me and I swore it was with disdain, then turned away, like I was asking the obvious. I hoped this was coming across on the crystal.

"You do want to retire, right?"

She nodded.

"And do you want to be adopted?"

There was no reaction whatsoever.

"You don't want to be adopted? To be looked after? Have a forever home with family?"

Still no reaction.

"If it was with someone you liked?"

Dakkar grudgingly nodded.

"Well, I want to make sure you end up in the right home. So, why would Sam be good?"

Dakkar perked up, batting her wings and stomping around playfully.

"Why wouldn't she be good?"

Dakkar stopped. She didn't move at all. I hoped that meant she found no fault in Sam.

"And Sevrin?"

Dakkar snorted.

"Why would he be good?"

Dakkar didn't move.

"Why would he be bad?"

Dakkar shuffled her hind legs a moment, like she was debating whether to tell me or not. She decided in my favor and sat back on her haunches, and leaned back, exposing a massive scar on her belly where a swath of pearlescent scales were missing, the flesh below was dark, raised, rough.

"What is that, Dakkar?" I pointed to her scar.

She hissed, breathing non-existent fire.

"That's where the fire came from?"

She hissed again.

"He took your fire."

She dropped down, lying on the ground.

"He took your spirit and your fire."

Dakkar looked up at me and flapped her wings once.

"What happened? How did he take it from you?"

Dakkar hesitated, then rose up, thrashing about, tail smacking the ground, and let out an eerie, painful cry, mimicking the pain and her reaction as Sevrin pierced her and tore the fire from her. It was a devastating cry that echoed throughout Studio City and rattled my soul.

"I am so sorry. I am going to do everything I can to help you."

Dakkar sat up, flapped her wings and nudged me with her snout. I patted her and said goodbye. I removed the crystal from the staff, praying it would be enough.

THE RECORDING of Dakkar tucked in my pocket, I left Studio City and headed to the Center for the Creation and Preservation of Motion Pictures to meet with the Director of the Performing Creature Welfare Society who was in charge of Dakkar's adoption.

I checked the slip of parchment Sam had given

me. Anselm, the Director, was on the third floor. It was a long climb. The building was made to fit the tallest of beings, with plenty of head room. Thankfully, dwarves had a different set of stairs from everyone else.

At the top, I leaned against the wall to catch my breath. I didn't think it would look particularly good for me to burst into Anselm's office gasping for air.

Finally, I straightened and headed down the hall. A familiar face caught my attention. Was that Drouin leaving the Society's office? I stepped back to look again. Someone called after him: "Loughlin!" But he had vanished.

I momentarily debated looking for him. What if it was him and I found him? What would I do? I had nothing to say, nothing to confront him with. If indeed it was Drouin. I had no proof he wasn't what or who he said he was. All I had was Aramis saying his name wasn't Drouin, and that there was a familiarity about him. Besides, Sam's adoption of Dakkar was far more pressing. While Sam hadn't been given a definitive date, she expected the adoption committee would be making a decision soon. They couldn't wait forever.

I let Drouin go and walked into the PCWS office. An elevated elf-size reception desk with a solid wall in front that was as tall as I was filled the center of the room. Even if I were to hop up I wouldn't be able to see over the top. I walked around to the side and climbed up two of the three steps to the receptionist:

a beautiful elf with the classic long blonde hair, pale skin, and willowy frame. I cleared my throat. She jumped in her seat.

"May I help you?" Annoyance flashed in her eyes.

I backed off the steps. "Yes. I'm here to see Anselm regarding the adoption of Dakkar."

"The application period has closed," she droned, pivoting gracefully back to her desk.

"Oh, no, I'm not here to apply. I'm here to give a character reference for one of the applicants."

The receptionist sighed, stood up and glared at me until I backed out of her way. She glided down the corridor behind her desk, returning a minute later. "Second door on your left," she said.

"Thank you so much." I smiled, extra gracious as I bowed my way down the corridor, following her directions. I knocked on the already open door and entered.

"Come in," an elf, I assumed was Anselm, said as he sorted through pieces of parchment on a table in front of him. "Your name is?"

"Mabel Goldenaxe."

"And you are here to give a character reference for…ah, here we are," he picked up a parchment. "Sevrin."

"No, not Sevrin. I'll give one against him, but definitely not for him."

"He has you listed as one of his references."

"Well he shouldn't. I'm here on behalf of

Samantha Cuttersmith. But sure, here's what I have to say about Sevrin. He sees Dakkar as a project, something to keep him occupied. How long will that last? What happens when he gets bored and finds himself a new project?"

"Dakkar is old and needs a lot of care. Sevrin has the time and the resources to look after her."

"So does Sam. She probably has more."

"More than Sevrin, who is retired?"

"She has a regular income. She's a successful actress which means her income is increasing so she can provide for Dakkar's needs. And as for time, she has a lot of friends who will all take time with Dakkar."

"For how long? What happens when you are all working and Dakkar has an emergency?"

"Sam has arrangements in place for that. She loves Dakkar. She has been planning for this for years."

"Sevrin does not need to have a plan."

"Of course he does. He won't spend all of his time with Dakkar. Sam has bought a new home with property that she's had re-done to create an incredibly comfortable home for Dakkar. It's ten times better than where Dakkar is now. She's planned out how to provide for and look after Dakkar. She loves that dragon, and the affection is mutual."

"Loving Dakkar is not enough."

"I have seen Sam with Dakkar. She knows how to care for her. She wants to. Dakkar isn't a project for Sam. Dakkar is a part of her life. Her family."

Anselm picked up a parchment, narrowed his eyes, furrowing his brow as he studied it. "Ah, you are on her list as well. Well, thank you for coming by and giving me your opinion."

"That's it?"

"Yes." He looked up at me, eyebrows raised like he was surprised I thought there ought to be more.

"You've made your decision in favor of Sevrin, haven't you," I demanded.

"I am not at liberty to discuss the proceedings."

"Right. Sure. I understand. But perhaps you ought to know that Dakkar hates Sevrin. She's afraid of him. He hurt her and she's afraid he'll do it again."

"Miss Goldenaxe, I applaud your keenness to help your friend, but such wild declarations will not aide your cause." He stood to usher me out.

I was having none of his condescension. "Perhaps you are not aware that I make movies. I recorded Dakkar." I pulled the crystal out of my pocket.

"How wonderful for you, but it is irrelevant."

"Excuse me?"

"That may very well be you interacting with Dakkar, but there is no way for anyone to verify the accuracy. Even if we could, whatever it is you think Dakkar supposedly told you, Dakkar is a dragon, a creature. Whatever you think she feels, it does not matter. Dakkar does not need to be a part of any family, she needs to be looked after. She is work, yes, a project, not family. Thank you for stopping by and giving your opinion."

He pushed me to the door.

"Sam will provide the best home for Dakkar. Please, don't dismiss her."

"Thank you, Miss Goldenaxe." Anselm closed the door on me.

He hadn't listened to me. He hadn't cared about what I had to say. He'd made up his mind that Dakkar was going to Sevrin and there was no way to convince him otherwise. Was it possible that Sevrin held some kind of threat over him? I nearly turned back to ask Anselm, but knew he would never tell me.

There was, however, someone who might know.

ARAMIS WAS alone in the editing room. The recording of my Leitham championship win played on the screen in front of him.

Seeing him, being alone with him, was a jolt. It was as though the world around me shifted a couple of degrees, pushing my anger and frustration with Anselm to the side in favor of memories of my drunken confession and Aramis's promises that he was on my side.

His eyes narrowed. "Mabel, what is wrong?"

I held my breath a moment in an effort to keep myself together, but his kindness, the concern on his face, the softness of his voice, broke my already weakened defenses.

"Sam is going to lose Dakkar and there is nothing I can do about it." I climbed onto the stool beside Aramis. "I went to give my character reference and Anselm refused to listen to me. He wouldn't look at the recording I made of Dakkar clearly expressing her hatred of Sevrin. She showed me how he hurt her, including the scar. Anselm has practically given Dakkar to Sevrin. It is going to hurt Sam and Lil so badly, and it just might kill Dakkar." I took a breath. "Why, Aramis? Why is Sevrin doing this? What control does he have over Anselm?"

"Dakkar is Sevrin's legacy. He has been proud to show her off, show off how he saved us all from dragons, tamed them, made them malleable. He does not want anyone to know otherwise, to know how he damaged them. No one else has cared until now, and he does not like it. He does not want anyone to know how he hurt Dakkar, how he wiped out an entire species of gentle, protective beings. Dakkar is his trophy. He will do anything to keep it quiet. As for how he controls Anselm? With Aubrey and Radier gone, Sevrin has no competition. He owns everyone and everything in this city. I do not know what specifically he has on Anselm, but it does not matter. He owns it all."

"Everyone?" I asked. "He owns everyone?"

"Almost everyone. Not me. Not you or your friends. He does, however, control almost the entire movie industry. He allows it to operate with very little of his interference. As long as it is profitable, he does not care what gets produced. And as long as Frerin has work and is happy."

Of course he owned it all, and of course Mam would say otherwise. "So what do I do?"

"I suggest Sam ask for a public hearing. Sevrin wants to keep his involvement and his true history with Dakkar private. A public hearing would most likely expose it so he may settle before a hearing happens. If he fights it, he will look to have your proof dismissed, but it will at least get the public talking. The committee will have to hear your evidence. Neither the Society nor Sevrin will want to deal with bad publicity. It may not work, but it might be Sam's best chance."

His calm and reassurance eased my anxiety. It was a solid plan and Lil would be grateful. "Any news on Drouin?"

"None yet. He is keeping himself well hidden."

"I thought I saw him at the Society, but someone called him Loughlin."

"Really?" Recognition flickered across his face.

"Do you know him?"

Aramis looked away. "I am not sure. I will look into it."

"Can I ask you another question?"

"Always."

"What, specifically, did Sevrin do to make you turn on him?"

Aramis sighed and faced me, giving me his full attention. "The agreement we had was that once

Aubrey and Radier were dethroned, he would leave
my people alone. We had also agreed that he would
reduce his business dealings. He would retire. He has
done none of that. He has more power now than ever
and he likes to wield it. He has gone after my people
and I have spent the last three years fighting him. We
have reached a stalemate. I fear that I am unable to
protect my people forever. I do not have the time to
establish trust among my people and he has preyed
on that. Even with our stalemate, when we have a
tentative truce, he continues to undermine me."

My grudge for being used seemed so inconse-
quential in comparison to what Aramis had suffered
under Sevrin. "And Mam's involvement?"

Aramis looked away.

"And Mam's involvement?" I insisted.

Eyes closed, he said, "She rules alongside him."

I should have known.

"Mabel—"

I shook my head, cutting him off. "It's okay. I get
it. Everything makes sense. I should have seen it, but
I didn't. Or maybe I did and just didn't want it to be
true. Doesn't matter. We're in this together."

I stood to go. Aramis was doing so much work on
my movie, we were friends, and we were on the same
side. "Um, I don't suppose you would care to join
me and my friends for the Regionals? We've booked
some rooms at the Sapphire Inn for the two weeks.
We could get you your own room at a different inn,
one more comfortable for you."

He raised his eyebrows. "No. I mean, yes, I would love to join you, and the Sapphire is fine. Truly."

"Good."

I LEFT Aramis to tell Sam and Lil the news of my meeting with Anselm. Sam wasn't working so I headed to Dakkar's cave. She wasn't there. I'd have to try her at her new home. If she wasn't here, she was most likely there, preparing it for Dakkar.

I turned back, walking through Studio City. Sadness hit me when I neared studio twenty-two. Maybe I could convince Mam to support Lil and Sam instead of Sevrin. She had been so close to Lil. Surely Mam could wield her power for her friend, not just Sevrin.

I raised my hand to knock on her dressing room door but stopped when I heard her speaking to someone on the other side.

"She's starting to trust you again. I know you wouldn't want to risk losing her again."

"You have to tell her, Frerin."

Aramis? Why was Aramis talking to Mam?

"Leave it alone, and she will never know," Mam said.

"She is asking. She is digging. Mabel is going to find out. Tell her, or I will."

"You wouldn't dare tell her. It would destroy her."

I pushed the door open. "Tell me what?"

Mam and Aramis looked at me, eyes wide, I'd caught them conspiring. How could Aramis do this to me, again? How could I have allowed myself to trust him?

Mam crossed her arms and stood her ground, keeping silent, eyebrow raised in challenge, daring him to tell me their secret.

"Drouin—"

"Aramis," Mam cut him off.

"It will be what it must be," Aramis said. "Drouin's real name is Loughlin. He was a regular crew member of mine many years ago. He still works in movies, occasionally. Mostly, he works for Frerin. I did not recognize him at first, though he was familiar. It was not until you said his name that I knew who he was."

"Who is he?" I asked, breathless. My heart was in my throat.

"Frerin?" Aramis offered her the chance to speak.

She glared at him.

"No?" he asked. "You do not wish to give your spin on it?"

Mam looked down.

"Frerin hired Loughlin when Mikey competed in the Dwarf Games. Through him, she offered the return of the family wealth to Mikey, on the condition that he win. He was solidly in second, with no real chance. Mikey was desperate enough, he knew the only way he could win and therefore bring respect to his family, was to persuade Reede to lose."

Mam? I couldn't believe what I was hearing. My vision blurred and my jaw dropped. "But he only brought back his trophy."

Aramis and I waited for Mam to say something. She looked up and away.

Aramis continued. "After Mikey persuaded Reede to lose, he felt so guilty, he refused to take the payment."

"And me? What did you hope to gain from extorting me?"

Mam tried to change the subject. "Aramis knew about it and he never told you."

"You are my mam." I paused, collecting myself, reining in my anger. "What did you have to gain from me?"

Mam shrugged. "It wasn't personal."

She couldn't have hurt me more if she beat me with an axe.

"Okay," I whispered. "Aramis, thank you for telling me."

"Mabel," Mam said.

I held up my hand, stopping her. "You disgust me."

I walked out of her dressing room and out of the studio. I stood against the wall and bent double under the weight of what I'd heard, the lengths Mam had gone to hurt my family. I couldn't breathe. Da had banished her because she had allowed our family to be robbed, and she'd been with elves when it happened. If he only knew how much more she had done.

"Mabel?" Aramis asked, softly, crouching beside me. "I am so sorry."

I shook my head, unable to speak. I reached out, putting one hand on his shoulder, then the second, then clinging to him like my life depended on it. I needed him to hold me up. "Why does she hate my family? How can she be so cold?"

Aramis wrapped his arms around me, so warm, so comforting. "I do not know."

Being held by Aramis gave me strength. After a few moments I sighed and pushed him away. "Were you involved in Mam's attempts to extort me?"

"No. Never. Nor did I know about it."

"What about Mikey? How much did you know?"

"All of it. From the start. I saw it as a way to reverse the damage caused by my father. I helped provide some of the gems and gold Frerin planned to give to Mikey."

Aramis didn't do anything with Sevrin unless it served his interests. Getting rid of Aubrey and Radier had been his biggest interest. "What do you have to gain from going after Mam and Sevrin?"

"Justice for my people. Protection for you. Atonement for all I have done."

"Why atone? Why change? You're immortal. You can do whatever you want."

"My people—"

"Nope. You're Lord of the Elves. They will follow you regardless of what you do."

"You—"

"Nope. You may regret having used me, but you still did it."

"I never wanted to be like Aubrey. My people deserved better. I did what I thought would help them, but over time, I became complacent, and complicit. I became my father. I am Lord of the Elves now. I can no longer allow myself to do more harm than good, nor do I want to."

"Okay." I breathed deep. "And now I know who Drouin is and what he wanted with me, so, thank you."

"Will you be all right?"

"I will be."

"Will we?" Aramis asked.

I looked him in the eyes and nodded.

AS I walked up the front path to Sam and Lil's new home, I admired the blossoming lilac bushes lining the walk. This place was perfect for them.

I wished I was bringing a house-warming gift, rather than the bad news of my meeting with Anselm. I supposed Aramis's suggestion of requesting a hearing was some kind of gift, even if there wasn't much hope of it being successful.

I could still feel Aramis's hug, giving me the support I needed.

I tugged on the hem of my tunic, collecting myself, gathering my strength to deliver the news, and knocked on the door.

Lil opened the door and pulled me into an embrace. "How did it go with Dakkar and Anselm?"

"Dakkar was brilliant. Anselm was not."

"What do you mean?" Sam asked, appearing from around the corner.

"He and the committee have all but made up their minds to give Dakkar to Sevrin."

"No. No. No," Sam muttered over and over again.

"Dakkar expressed everything we could have hoped she would, her love for you, Sam, and her hatred of Sevrin," I continued, "but Anselm refused to watch the recording."

"It's over, then," Sam said.

"Not yet," I said. "I talked to Aramis, and he said you should file for a public hearing."

Sam perked up. "Do you think it will work?"

"I don't know. Aramis wasn't particularly hopeful, but you have to try."

"Absolutely," Lil said. "Come in, Mabel. We'll have some lunch, and then Sam and I will go file for that hearing. You'll have to excuse the mess. We haven't finished unpacking yet."

"I'm surprised you've done as much as you have," I said. The living room where we stood looked fully set up to me.

"Me too," Sam said.

We walked through the cozy bungalow. The space

was small yet roomy, with poufy dark blue sofa and chairs, two bedrooms, and a lovely little kitchen. The bedrooms and the kitchen were still crowded with boxes. "How is it, living together?" I asked.

"Lil's a total pain," Sam said with a smile. "I'm having second thoughts."

"All the time," Lil agreed with a laugh.

I felt a pang in my chest. I had always thought Brent and I were as happy as Sam and Lil. How much of that had been wishful thinking on my part? I didn't want to know. I preferred to believe my delusion.

"How are you doing, with the Brent situation?" Sam asked.

I blinked back my tears. I missed seeing him, talking with him the way we used to. I wished I knew where it had gone wrong. We should have split up earlier, much earlier. "I'm fine. I mean, I thought I was fine until now. It hurts, of course, and I think he's an idiot, but I decided a long time ago that I wouldn't give in to anyone's expectations of me if that wasn't what I wanted. And even though I still love him and wish he could support me, I know this is the right thing and I will be fine. I am fine. I have a great life with amazing friends. If he doesn't want to be a part of it, then that's his loss."

"It is definitely his loss," Sam said. "I expected better from him. We all did. He was never really interested in courting anyone, he was always so shy, and then he fell in love with you. I guess we all assumed he would treat you with extra care."

"Well, he might have, if there hadn't been the mess with Aubrey and Sevrin and the gallery from the start. We probably shouldn't have gotten involved after that. That was a shadow over our entire relationship."

"You're so reasoned about it all," Lil said.

Reasoned? I couldn't be further from it. "I'm in bits inside. I keep asking myself what I should have done different, how I can make it better. But I know that would mean quitting axe throwing, which I love, and even then, that shadow of Sevrin would be ever present. I'd be miserable and I don't want that. If I'm truly honest, I'd probably been miserable for a while, always trying to move us from under that shadow of Sevrin's influence. No matter what I did, it was never enough. Brent never fully trusted me."

"I'm so sorry," Lil said.

They both hugged me. They were my best friends and I was so appreciative of them, that I could talk to them without fear of judgement. I wiped my eyes. "Enough about my troubles. What is happening with your golden ring ceremony? How are your plans coming along?" I needed the distraction.

"Lil, why don't you take Mabel out back and show her what we've set up for Dakkar? I'll make us some lunch."

"Great idea. Come on." Lil grabbed my hand and pulled me out the back door.

"Is everything all right? You two are still having the golden ring ceremony, aren't you?"

Lil gave me a look that clearly said I was crazy to think otherwise. "Yes, of course we are. We want to wait until everything is settled with Dakkar, and hopefully she'll be a part of the ceremony. Come and see this."

I hovered at the entrance to the cave. They had done a lot of work on it since I was last here. It was much deeper, with plenty of room for Dakkar, with varying levels for her to move to, and stones for her to play with.

"This is incredible. Before the hearing, you should let Jeff or myself record this so you can show the committee. Or better yet, have the committee come and see this for themselves."

"Great idea. We'll put that into the hearing application. They have to see how prepared Sam is for this. No one is better equipped to look after Dakkar than she is. We want to have the ceremony back here, and we were thinking of having Dakkar come out as Sam and I put on the rings. It would have to be a much smaller ceremony than usual, but Sam and I want it to be just us and our friends, anyway. Dakkar would have to get used to the others first, of course. She likes you already. I think once we bring her home and she's settled in, we'll have a welcome home party for her and introduce her to everyone. Well, you'll all be in the house and we will make individual introductions. You know what I mean."

"I do." This had to happen. Sevrin and Mam were not going to be allowed to break my friend's heart.

They had done far too much damage to everyone I knew and cared for. "I think it would be wonderful."

"Lunch is ready," Sam called.

The kitchen table was spread with warm bread, stew, and mugs of mead.

"It isn't much," Sam said. "We're still sorting through what we have and figuring out what we don't."

"This is perfect," I said. "It reminds me of home. Da was big on making stew." Though it made me sad, it was a good memory, one I needed after what Mam told me.

"Um, before we start," Sam said, "Lil and I have something to ask you."

"O-okay." I looked to them for some kind of clue as to what they could possibly want to know. They were grinning fools which told me nothing.

"We were wondering if you would officiate our golden ring ceremony."

"Really? Me? Not Jeff or Hannah? Me?"

"Of course, you," Sam said.

"I am so honored. Yes. Of course I will!" I jumped up and hugged them both. "What do I need to do?"

"Not much," Sam said. "Basically show up on the day and acknowledge our commitment when asked."

"That I can do."

"And a speech about us," Lil said.

"That's going to be harder," I teased.

"Told you we should have asked Hannah," Lil said. "She could write the speech and do a great job.

This one," Lil pointed at me, "is going to be terrible."

"Yes, I am. But I already accepted, so you're stuck with me."

CHAPTER 17

ARAMIS RECORDED as my friends and I gathered at the Hammer and Chisel, packed bags at our feet, cart outside ready to deliver us to the Sapphire Inn.

Anxiety tightened in my chest, making it hard to focus on the cheerful chatter around me.

"Are you all right?" Jeff asked.

Conscious of the crystal recording me, I smiled and nodded. "Nervous about the competition," I mostly lied. I kept thinking about the last time I'd traveled to a Regional competition, with Da and my brothers just as cheerful, just as busy preparing, packing the carts, and me in so much pain, desperate for Emma to bring me that poison.

This time everything about going to Regionals was different. I was traveling with my friends. I wasn't injured going into the competition. I had a terrific coach. Mikey had been a good coach, but Reede had taken more time to train me and shown me new techniques. She'd worked me harder than Mikey had in a way that worked better for me. I'd been able to practice full time, not only in the evenings after a day of mining and a few drinks with friends.

"Have fun." Sophie handed out bags to my friends with snacks for the journey, even though we were only traveling a couple of miles.

"You have your tickets?" I asked her.

Otto patted the pocket of his tunic. "Right here. We'll be the loudest ones there."

Sam and Jeff began some kind of battle chant with a howl. "I think you're going to have some competition on the volume," I said.

"Let's move out," Lil shouted.

"Knock 'em dead," Sophie said.

"Thanks."

We loaded onto the waiting cart. Aramis sat up front next to Jeff who was driving. Aramis kept the crystal focused on the rest of us in the back, capturing our antics of pretending to be exhausted from the journey moments after we'd begun moving, and digging into our snack bags from Sophie. Eating our mutton sandwiches.

"Are we almost there?" Hannah whined.

"Would you lot settle down?" Jeff roared. "I will tell you when we're close. Close your eyes and sleep. It will help time pass." Jeff pulled back on the reins.

"Here we are."

"Finally!" Lil said.

I couldn't stop laughing. This was how travelling with friends to Regionals was supposed to be. Traveling with my brothers had been fun, but this was a million times better.

We jumped out of the cart and dragged our baggage inside. Sam had booked three rooms. One for herself, Lil, and Hannah, Jeff and Aramis in another, and Reede and I in the third. I wished I could have roomed with my friends, but when I had told Reede the plan, she insisted we be separate so I could have my necessary time and space to focus during the competition.

Sam checked us in and gave us each our keys. "Drop your stuff and meet back here in half an hour," she said.

We all trooped upstairs. Instead of going into their room, Hannah, Sam, and Lil followed me into mine and closed the door so that Jeff and Aramis, who was still recording, wouldn't follow.

"What's going on?" I asked as they dumped their bags on the floor.

"Seeing as Reede doesn't get here until tomorrow, we thought you could have at least one night of fun with us." Hannah said.

"You are the best," I said.

"We know," Lil smiled. "Sam, what's on the agenda?"

"First, we head out for drinks, followed by food

and more drinks. Checking out the other competitors as they arrive. Some souvenir shopping. More food and drinks. Or just food and drinks."

Lil clapped her hands. "Perfect. Do you think we can forego recording this evening, though? You don't need much more of us being idiots, do you?"

"I don't think we need any material of us being idiots," I said. "I'll ask Aramis to stop and join in on the fun."

Hannah looked thoughtful for a moment. "All right, no recording tonight. But we do need to show you with your friends, having fun, not only practicing and competing. The audience needs to know you; the real, enjoyable, loveable, you."

"With Aramis behind the crystal, I don't think that's a problem," Lil muttered.

"What's that supposed to mean?" I asked, taken aback.

"He's in love with you," Lil said. "The entire trip here, he had that crystal trained on you."

"Well, it is a documentary about me," I said.

Lil rolled her eyes. "Mabel, hun, are you telling me you haven't noticed how much he has been around lately? He didn't have to help with the movie, but he volunteered."

"He has been around us a lot," Hannah said.

"When he smiles," Sam said, "those dimples of his only come out for you. And that breeze in his hair, it's practically a wind-storm around you."

I blushed. I had noticed, after my city championship. "You don't think it's repulsive? He's an elf."

"It certainly isn't traditional," Sam said. "I don't know that it has ever been done. But if you like him…You do like him, don't you?"

I was still hurting after Brent. Was this really an appropriate conversation?

"Like him or not," Lil said, "The question is, have you forgiven him for his betrayal when you first came to Leitham? Can you trust him? Do you trust him?"

"Good question, Lil," Sam said. "Make sure you have and can before you make any decisions."

Sam and Lil made very good points. If I couldn't trust Aramis, any relationship I had with him, as friends or more, would have a rough start that we would likely never recover from. Brent and I hadn't been able to.

I shook my head. "You all are crazy."

"Of course we are," Hannah said. "That's why you like us. Now answer the question. Do you like him?"

My first instinct was to deny it. I could hear Emma mocking me, accusing me of being in love with Aramis and being so disgusted by the thought. I could say that I liked him as a friend. They knew me too well to get away with any answer but the truth. "Yes," I whispered. I couldn't bring myself to give it any more voice. "I like Aramis. A lot."

"So it wasn't just a drunken confession," Lil crowed. "What happened after you told him? You went up to your room. You didn't...you know...did you?" Lil was curious, full of mischief, not horrified.

"No! But he did tell me he cares about me. He also understood if I could never forgive him."

"He said he that?!" Lil bounced on the bed. "Mabel!"

"Can dwarves and elves even...?" Hannah asked.

"Other than the height difference, I don't see why not," Lil said.

"Do you trust him?" Sam asked. "Have you forgiven him?"

"I think I have. I mean, I always understood why he wanted his father and Radier taken out of his life. I understood Mam and Sevrin's reasons. Aubrey and Radier caused a lot of damage to a lot of us. What hurt, what made me feel so betrayed, is that they didn't tell me. I probably would have been more than happy to help them, do what they wanted, if they'd told me what was going on. But I also understand why they didn't tell me. They didn't know me. They didn't know that I would be willing.

"Aramis, he's different, though. He may have used me to get at his father, but we've helped each other a lot which counts more than anything else. And we'd both been so hurt by Aubrey and Sevrin and..." I shook my head. "This is madness. I'm competing in Regionals. I can't be distracted by this."

"Reede will be mad enough for any shenanigans we encourage tonight," Hannah said. "After Regionals, though, we are going to make this happen."

"I don't think we'll have to wait that long," Lil said. "They already told each other how they feel, so what are they waiting for? A nudge is all it will take."

"Maybe Mabel doesn't want a nudge," Sam said. "He's immortal, which means he'll be alive long after all of us are not. Before we push Mabel at him, perhaps we should make sure she isn't merely a time-filler for him."

"Good point, my love," Lil said. "Mabel, don't do anything until we've given full approval. We'll tell Jeff to help us."

"How am I supposed to face him with all of this going on? It was hard enough to be around him before."

"Don't you worry about a thing," Lil said. "He hurt you once and you've forgiven him, but if he wants to be in your life, then he needs to earn our trust. We need to be sure he won't use you, that he will support you no matter what, that his feelings for you are true. Focus on competing and we'll give you our verdict after Regionals."

"Mabel?" Aramis called, knocking on my door. My friends stifled their giggles and raised their arms in silent cheers. "We're heading downstairs."

"I told you." Lil whispered. I motioned for her to be quiet.

"I'll be right there, thanks," I said.

"Oh, and Aramis," Hannah added, poking her head out the door. "No recording tonight."

I turned on my friends. "You're assuming he's

actually interested in having a relationship with me."

"He's willing to spend the next two weeks in a cramped dwarf-sized hotel when an elven inn is next door. He is interested," Sam said as we walked out and followed the fellows down the stairs.

HANNAH LED us to The Eagle's Nest, an all-species restaurant down the street from the Sapphire Inn. The vaulted ceilings and varied heights of seating meant we would all be comfortable here. The majority of tonight's patrons were dwarves, and by their chatter echoing off the ceilings, most of them were from out of town. Their excitement of being in Leitham and at the Regionals was infectious. On the way to our table, we joined the cheers of a drunken group, not that we knew or cared what they were cheering for. I loved these moments.

Somehow Lil managed to wrangle us a table where Aramis could sit between us.

"By the way, Aramis," Sam said. "Thank you so much for recommending I apply for a hearing. The date has been set for three weeks."

"You are very welcome," Aramis said. "I would like to testify on your behalf, if you will allow me."

"That would be fantastic," Sam said.

I nearly died as Hannah and Sam beamed at us from across the table.

"How is your room, Aramis?" Hannah asked.

"Fine, thank you. And thank you for including me in your excursion."

"Happy to have you, aren't we, Mabel?" Lil asked.

No, now I was going to die. "Ah," I cleared my throat. "Yes, we are."

"You know, Aramis," Sam said. "When we first met Mabel, she told us about the movie she had made with you in Gilliam and we were in awe."

"You were?" He raised an eyebrow.

"Well, yes. We were starting out in the industry, and we wanted, those of us who haven't had the chance, to work with you. We're curious, though, what you thought of her back then?"

"Sam!" I blurted. "Why?"

Aramis gave me a wicked grin. "Should I tell them about your audition?"

How I stared at him and was so in love I couldn't tell him my name? "No."

"Yes!" everyone else said.

Aramis put an arm across the back of my chair. If I moved back a fraction of an inch, he'd be touching me. I froze in place, paranoid of appearing too intimate, terrified of what he might tell my friends.

"Mabel was so shy when she came in for her audition. It did not help that my assistant, Antinae, was a terror. Sorry about that."

"Forgotten," I said. "But she was." I faked a shiver, remembering how intimidating she'd been.

"We had auditioned several dwarves for small

parts the day before and I was prepared for another long day of it. Most who came in stood like statues. I think they had only come because they were curious about me and what it was all about. Then Mabel walked in, all fresh-faced and so eager. Antinae ordered her around, but Mabel was incredible, holding her ground. Then I threw her off by stopping her monologue and asking her instead to repeat a story I had heard her tell once in The Bearded Prospector."

"Which was beyond humiliating, by the way," I said.

"What story?" Jeff asked.

"How she injured herself." He moved his hand to my shoulder, leaving it there, warming me. "Such a storyteller. She was the only one who had any acting interest and potential. I had to have her in my movie."

"Well that was a less than embarrassing story," Hannah said. "You're holding back on us. Good job."

"Thank you?" He looked at me, confused.

I glared at Hannah. Inside I was dancing for joy. Aramis kept his hand on my shoulder.

I STEPPED over my friends passed out on the floor. Their antics last night had only escalated once the ale had arrived. I'd been upset with Mikey for not letting me drink on our way to Mitchum for the Regionals. I was glad I'd instituted that rule for myself last night. Reede would be happy too.

I closed the door as quietly as I could, though Hannah's snores made the effort pointless. I headed down to the inn's dining hall. Aramis sat alone at a tiny table. Tiny for him anyway. I stopped at the entrance, remembering all the humiliating things my friends had said.

He looked up and smiled, waving me over. I ordered a full breakfast on my way over. "Quite the night last night," he said, standing, kissing me on the cheek before we sat, me across from him.

"It was." I cleared my throat. "I apologize on behalf of my friends."

"I had a great time. They are only looking out for you."

"Wh-why would you say that?"

Aramis smiled. "I thought something was up when we first arrived at the restaurant."

"Oh." His dimples were beautifully deep. There was a bit of a wind-storm going on with his hair. I shifted in my seat, looking away, and down, and at everything but him. At the same time, I couldn't stop looking at him and his mesmerizing blue eyes.

"And then there was the comment after I told them about your audition."

Heat rose in my cheeks. "You were exceptionally kind. I was a disaster at that audition."

"You were sweet and nervous. But I figured out the protective part when Jeff warned me to never betray you or hurt you or mess with you in any way, whatsoever."

I dropped my fork. "He did? When did he say that? Why would he say that? I am so, so sorry."

"You are lucky to have friends who care so much for you."

"I am. But really, when did Jeff threaten you?"

"You had gone to the bar to get a round of drinks."

"I am so sorry."

"Mabel," Aramis reached out and held my hand. "Stop apologizing."

His arm around my shoulders last night, his hand on mine now. I gazed at it for a moment, my heart pounding, my head swimming. "D-do they need to be protective of me? With you?"

I held my breath and looked away. What was I thinking? I'd let my friends' antics get to me.

"I would like to say no, but, I think they have a good reason to be."

"Why is that?" He still wasn't letting go of my hand and I didn't want him to.

"My lifetime is infinite compared to yours. It is reasonable for them to believe that my interest in you is fleeting."

"Is it? Fleeting?"

"No. It is not."

Giggling approached us. Aramis smiled and let go of my hand. I was numb and embarrassed and boiling hot.

"What's going on here?" Lil and Sam asked, placing themselves on either side of Aramis.

"How are you two so perky after how much you

had to drink last night?" I asked.

Lil gave me a condescending look. "You speak as if you don't know me at all. Now listen, Aramis. I like you, but I haven't given official approval yet. I'm reserving my decision until after Regionals, to give us time to fully size you up. To that end, I cannot allow the two of you to be alone like this until Regionals are finished. I expect that won't be too difficult to enforce since Reede will be arriving soon and will have Mabel practicing most of the time. When Mabel is not practicing or competing, you will be chaperoned. Do I make myself clear?"

"Lil, you're being ridiculous," I said.

"If it will help me win your approval," Aramis said, "then I welcome the chaperones."

"Aramis, you do not have to go along with this," I said.

"I am happy to. It is a good thing they want me to prove I am worthy of you."

"Unless Mabel doesn't believe there is a point to proving your worth," Sam said.

I couldn't believe what was happening here. All three looked at me: Sam and Lil with an intensity that suggested they needed an answer from me right now. Aramis looked at me with a nervous hope. His smile was tense, his breath shallow. Did I really have to decide right now what I wanted? How could I decide if I didn't know how I felt, truly felt, about being with Aramis? I had to actually consider the possibility of being with Aramis? That was what they were offering: time to explore the possibility, if it was something I wanted. An evaluation of all that could go right and wrong so I could make the right decision. So much more could be at stake this time, so much more than when I was with Brent, or even when Jimmy had asked me to stay with him in Gilliam.

"Yes," I whispered. "There is, there may be, a point. I want there to be a point."

CHAPTER 18

JEFF RECORDED as Reede and I walked into the Leitham arena to register for the competition. The registrar checked off our names, handed us our passes, and the event and practice schedules, all without looking up. We took our packets and headed straight to the practice space. It was a good chance to check out the other competitors and get used to the arena.

Jeff and the wizard's crystal drew some stares, distracting the other competitors, even though they had been made aware he would be there when they had signed the releases. The coaches spent a fair bit of their time getting their charges to focus on the task at hand. The distraction worked to my advantage. Reede and I were used to Jeff recording us. The constant recording was sure to fluster some of my opponents at a key moment in the competition.

My nerves faded. I remembered being incredibly anxious walking into the practice room in Mitchum and being intimidated by the other competitors. I didn't feel that intimidation now. Being older, and having practiced more, definitely helped. So did coming in as city champion, not some runner up with not much of a hope at beating the top competitors. I suppose I had done well for myself in Mitchum, certainly better than I should have considering my injured shoulder, though I'd always believed I could have placed higher had I been injury free. I also remembered being ignored by the competitors in Mitchum. There had been that one fellow who had approached, asking Mikey to be his coach. He'd been surprised when Mikey said he was already coaching someone. That fellow never did acknowledge my presence. I smiled, remembering how frustrated I'd been with my invisibility when I'd spent so much effort hoping one of the fellows in that room would notice me and want to court me. I was far from that situation now.

We found my section of the room and Reede ordered me to warm up. "How late were you out last night?" She asked as I started on my push-ups.

"Late, but I didn't drink. My friends did, but I didn't."

"Fine. We'll do a quick practice now, then back to the room for a rest. Until your part in this competition is over, you will be practicing, competing, or resting.

Understood?"

"Absolutely."

"Good. I like your focus."

I switched to running on the spot. "You have no idea how much I want this," I said quietly.

"Redemption for last time, I know."

"If I don't win—"

"Mabel, take it one moment at a time. Warm up today, practice tomorrow. Tomorrow we'll think about the first round of competition. That is all."

"Yes, Coach."

ONE MOMENT at a time quickly became my mantra. I stood in the practice room with the other competitors, now in our uniforms, waiting to enter the arena for the first round. It was both strange and wonderful to wear the red and yellow of Leitham. I preferred the silver and blue of Gilliam simply because I looked better in them. To wear the Leitham colors, though, signified to me that I was truly a citizen in my adopted city. It was home. Where I belonged. I wanted to make my city proud of me.

The arena rumbled with the roars of the crowd, vibrations from the noise rose up from the floor. I loved it. I focused on my breathing, visualizing throwing, my technique, Aramis holding my hand. Oh, wait, no. I shook my head and shoulders and re-set my thoughts.

"Mabel?" Reede asked.

"Yes?"

"What's distracting you?"

"Excited. Can't wait to go out there," I said.

"It's Aramis," she said.

"What?"

"Lil told me what they were up to. Your focus has been great during practice. I need you to keep it that way."

"You don't have to worry. I am here. I am ready."

As I said it, the doors opened and we began the march in.

We paraded around the arena, waving to the cheering fans. Jeff had a prime spot, set up in the front row, center, recording. I waved and smiled to him, and my friends who sat beside him. Hannah had managed to get great tickets. Well behind them, in the back row, was Aramis.

I was competing at Regionals as the Leitham champion, my competing was being documented, and Aramis was watching me.

I finished the parade of the arena and felt much calmer. I had the best coach. I could do this.

I stretched as I waited. I was one of the last to go. Finally it was my turn. As always with the first round, it was close, with many of the competitors tied for first place.

I stood at the throwing line. I tucked my hair behind my ear, horribly, consciously aware that Aramis was watching me. I repeated my ritual, slapping shoulders and so on, twice, to make sure I was focused. Still, my first throw was well off the mark. My next two throws had to be perfect if I had a hope of being in the running in the second round.

Reede said nothing to me between throws. She sat back with her arms crossed, studying the other competitors. I'd hoped for some kind of gesture, a reminder to keep my elbow in.

I was letting her and everyone else down. I couldn't allow that to continue.

Lil and the others were evaluating Aramis. I didn't have to. I wouldn't think about him until after the competition.

I did what Reede had taught me to do. I set up a mental wall, blocking out the crowd, my friends, the scoreboard, and the other competitors.

I stepped to the line for my second throw, wiped my forehead, then went through my ritual. I reached back, pressing my elbow close to my ear, and threw. The release was much better this time. The axe flew and embedded in the bullseye.

I remained in my protective bubble of quiet. I did not look to Reede for help this time. I knew what I needed to do and I would not relax until I had done it.

For my third throw, I wiped my brow, tucked my hair, and finished the rest of my routine. My third throw was perfect.

I squeaked into the second round. My worst round had to be my best if I had a hope of getting to the finals.

While the arena was reset for round two, I found a spot at the back of the arena clear of competitors. I stretched. I was extra tight in my right shoulder and neck so I spent extra time on those. I rotated my arm in large circles, rehearsing the motion of the second round technique.

My name was called for my first throw of round two. My pre-throw routine was as much a part of the throw now as the actual throw itself. There were gasps and a few snickers from the crowd and some of the competitors when I threw using the windmill technique. I hit center.

My second throw and I hit center again. That silenced the snickers.

Reede continued to keep quiet between my throws. This time I was glad for it. I remained in my bubble and I didn't want anyone or anything to pop it.

I stood at the line for my third throw. I didn't have to be perfect to make the final round. I wanted it to be perfect.

I pointed at the target, rotated my arm, and threw. My release was a fraction too soon. I hit the second ring. I had over-thought my position. I had thought about my performance instead of just doing it.

Still, I made it safely into the third round.

THE THIRD round, the final round, and a clean

scoreboard. There was a pain in my right shoulder. I couldn't tell if it was real or not. I stood at the line and all I could think about was how in Mitchum I had been in so much pain in the first two rounds but had felt perfectly fine, thought myself healed, in the finals. I'd shredded my shoulder the last time I was in this position.

I couldn't do this. I was in pain and I was going to injure myself again if I threw. I didn't want to spend years trying to get my shoulder fixed, if it could get fixed at all. I couldn't throw. I was going to fail.

No. I wouldn't do that to Reede. I had to make it to the Dwarf Games. Jimmy and Max were cheering for me. Reede needed me to win.

I couldn't breathe. I flinched and the official took that as me nodding my readiness. Next thing I knew, the ground rumbled and my turn began.

I spun and hurled the first axe, and the second, and the third.

My shoulder twinged and I sat next to Reede. Having gone first, the rest of the round was going to be a long one. "I'm so sorry, Reede," I whispered, massaging my shoulder. "I've failed you."

"No, Mabel. You haven't." Reede hugged me. "I'm proud of you. You had a rough first round and you've pulled yourself together. Your throws were perfect. You are in the running."

"What?" I looked up at the scoreboard. I had a near-perfect third-round score. At worst I would have to go through a tie-break.

I grabbed Reede's hand and watched with keen interest as each of the competitor's took their place at the line, eagerly awaiting their throws, squeezing Reede's hand when an axe missed the bullseye. One by one, the names of the competitors and their scores were listed below mine.

Three qualified above me. Two others tied with me. I had to go through a tie-breaker to make it to the Dwarf Games.

I massaged my shoulder. I was back in Mitchum, facing placing fifth, being an alternate but ruining my shoulder.

"I can't do this, Reede. I can't. I'm so sorry."

"Mabel. Stretch out. You're fine. You can do this. You have the technique, the strength, the endurance, the skill, the talent. Believe in yourself. This is different. This is now, in Leitham, not Mitchum. You have it within you. I know you can do this."

The official selected me to go last.

This time I couldn't look. I kept my eyes down, the crowd's cheers were as boisterous for one throw as for the next, except for the gasp. I looked up for the gasp. One competitor had missed the target all together.

The second competitor was up. I couldn't watch.

The crowd fell silent and the rapid thunks of the axes echoed around the arena.

I looked to Reede as I took my place. She smiled. I breathed deep, ran through my rituals and nodded. I was ready. The ground rumbled, the air moved, I twirled and spun and threw. One of my axes spanned the bullseye and the next ring over. The rest were perfect. The judges had to confer on how to score the one throw. They measured the amount of the axe blade in each ring. The outside ring had the most blade. Less than perfect points.

What happened? I had been on top. I had been winning. The tiebreak. I'd been so focused during the tiebreak. "They measured it wrong," I said to Reede. "Challenge it. Make them measure again. Go. Watch them. Make sure they do it right."

"They measured it right," Reede said. "It's over."

I was out.

I had failed.

I had failed myself and Reede and everyone. I was out.

I had to at least be an alternate for the Dwarf Games. I could live with being an alternate. As an alternate, I would have done as well as I had in Mitchum. I'd expected more out of myself since I was throwing without an injury, but maybe the competition was that much better than I was. My focus wasn't where it should have been. Whatever the reason, it didn't matter.

I'd failed.

CHAPTER 19

ANGRY, BROKEN hearted, stunned, I stormed back to my room and slammed the door. The training, the recording, the planning for a documentary, was all for nothing. I broke up with Brent because of my axe throwing. For what?

How could I have allowed this to happen?

I pulled out my bag and started throwing my clothes into it.

Reede, came into the room. "What are you doing?" she asked.

"Packing," I snapped.

"Why?"

"I'm out. I'm done. There's no point in staying here."

"Regionals are still going on. Your friends are

expecting you to join them to watch the rest of the competitions."

"I can't stay and watch. I had to do it in Mitchum. I don't have to do it here."

"Fair enough. Go home, get some rest, and I'll see you back at my place in two days."

"What for?"

"To train."

"Train? I'm done axe throwing, or didn't you notice? I failed. I'm not going to the Dwarf Games."

"This year. That doesn't mean you stop training."

I stopped chucking clothes into my bag. "Yes, it does."

"Huh." Reede crossed her arms. "I thought you were an axe thrower, not only in this for a documentary, or for the glory of being Dwarf Games champion. I guess I was wrong. I'm sorry I suggested you be the subject for your movie, then, because you don't really have a story to tell at all."

"What? Why are you saying this?"

"You're a tourist. A talented one, who could have a lot of success, if you chose. But you're not interested in that, so then I'm glad you didn't win. Those who won, have worked a lot harder and a lot longer at it than you have."

"Reede…"

"The Dwarf Games are every five years, but there are a lot of competitions held every year. You could have a great career at it. Maybe you'd become Dwarf Games champion, maybe you wouldn't.

What you gain in experience, and the connections you make with other competitors, the travel, there is nothing like it. You're upset about your loss today. I get it. You were close. You were at the top. You overcame a bad first round and decent second round to have an exceptional third. It is a very tough loss to take. Believe me, I am upset about it too, but that's competition. Some you win, some you lose. You are still Leitham champion, after all.

"So I'm going to give you a chance. Be upset, let your friends buy you sympathy drinks tonight. Then decide who you want to be. Are you an axe thrower? Or are you a tourist in the sport? If you're fine with being a tourist, then great. It was nice working with you. If you want to be a professional axe thrower, then I will be happy to be your coach. Either way, let me know. I've enrolled you in a new competition being held for city champions. I'll need to withdraw you if that's what you choose."

City champion competition? That was new, and intriguing. But what was the point of competing as Leitham champion if I wasn't going to the Dwarf Games? "You might as well withdraw me," I said.

"I'd rather not."

"Why?"

Reede paused. "The competition is in Gilliam."

"What?" Why was she heaping more torment on me?

"I found out a couple of weeks ago. I didn't tell you because you've had enough to distract you. Your career is hardly over if you don't want it to be."

"I can't go back to Gilliam."

"Maybe you can."

"Reede, I'm sorry."

"Don't be. I'm proud of you." Reede patted my shoulder. "You're Leitham champion. You placed sixth in the region. That is nothing to be ashamed of. So it wasn't the outcome we wanted, this time. Take tonight, this week. Think about it."

Reede left me alone. I flopped onto my bed. I wasn't an axe thrower. I was a movie-maker, who had decided to make a movie about herself competing in axe throwing. I shouldn't have won.

If I had, though? If I had won the Dwarf Games, would I still want to compete? Or had getting to the Dwarf Games been my only goal?

What did it matter? I'd lost. I wasn't moving on. I'd wasted too much time on this. I had to get back to making movies and bring in an income again.

THERE WAS a commotion outside my room soon after Reede left. The door opened and in poured my friends. Embarrassed, I quickly sat up and wiped my eyes, though doing so was useless as the tears kept falling.

My friends ignored my crying and crowded around me, hugging me. "We're so proud of you!" Hannah said.

"You were amazing," Lil said.

"Hardly," I sniffed. "Look, I know, I should stop feeling sorry for myself. But right now, sixth doesn't feel very good. It feels like everything has been pointless."

"Why do you say that?" Jeff asked.

That's when I noticed he was recording this. I put up my hand to cover up the crystal. "Stop recording. The documentary is over."

Jeff stopped the recording. "I don't understand. Wasn't the point of it to document your story, win or lose?"

"We won't record this, but there is still plenty of story to tell," Hannah said.

"Win or lose at the Dwarf Games, not at Regionals," I said. "And there isn't that much story to tell." I told them what Reede had said.

"What are you going to do?" Lil asked.

"Why should she have to decide now?" Sam asked.

"Why wouldn't she continue throwing?"

"Because she doesn't want to?"

"Stop," Hannah shouted. "Sam, Lil, please excuse us. Jeff, Aramis, we need to talk about this." She herded the others out under cacophonous protests.

"Hannah," I said. "Do we have to do this now?"

"Yes, we do. We have to decide what you want to do with the documentary."

"There is no documentary," I said. "It's over. I'm done. I have to find something else to do."

"Don't be so quick to dismiss it," Hannah said. "We just need to regroup. Jeff and I have discussed, briefly, how we would cover things if you didn't win. Nothing was set in stone, but we have a sketch of a plan."

"It's just going to be an ongoing project," Jeff said. "Unless we want to focus more on the family aspect. Hannah, have you written Jimmy or Theo yet?"

"I have," Hannah said. "I'm waiting to hear back. I wrote both. What are you thinking?"

"I think we go with Mabel to the competition in Gilliam. It's the perfect time to interview Jimmy and Mabel's friends. We'll keep recording Mabel's competitions, but now is a great time to get the material on her family."

"Yes. I'll write them again. I'll see if they're available now that we have a specific date. I'm sure one of them will have a place for us to stay. I can't wait to see Theo again!"

Jeff and Hannah stepped off to the side, planning, re-writing the storyline they thought should be told.

I tuned them out.

Aramis sat next to me and wiped the tears from my cheeks.

"Thanks." My face burned from embarrassment.

"Am I allowed to be here, without a chaperone?" Aramis asked.

I smiled. "Technically, we aren't alone, so I think it should be all right."

"Good." He wiped another tear.

"I'm sorry. I can't stop crying."

"It was a big loss for you. You were amazing, you know. We, I, distracted you."

"No, you didn't."

"Well, Lil and the others did not help. But you recovered beautifully."

"Aramis—"

"You should take some time to think about what you want to do. There was a time when I had to take over from my father as Lord of the Elves. It was the last thing I wanted to do. At that moment I saw no other option. I thought my whole life had been a joke, a waste. You came to me and you reminded me that I did have a choice. That I should do what I love to do, what I am good at. I did not see it then. It took some time. I had gone to take over from my father and it was terrible, worse than I expected it to be."

"That's bad."

"It was. The entire battle with Sevrin, I kept thinking about what you said. That you liked my movies."

"Loved," I corrected.

"Loved. You also said that I should do what I love. I will say the same to you now. If you love axe throwing, then that is what you should do."

"What about my movies?"

"If you love making movies, then do that. Or both."

"How can I do both?"

Aramis pointed to Jeff and Hannah intensely

discussing my documentary. "You have a great team here. You can hire more to work for you, creating the story, recording, interviewing. You would still have the ideas, have as much input as you want, make sure the story goes in the direction you want it to go. Having others work for you frees up time for training. You do not have to decide now. Please, do not let today's result stop you from doing what you love."

I chuckled. "I used to read an awful lot of self-help books. I think one of them even said something like that."

"Let me guess. Dr. Thaddeus?"

"How did you know?"

"Before he started writing, he was one of my father's key advisors."

"Really? Now I'm disappointed in him, and myself, for following his advice."

"Did it help you?"

"It's the reason I auditioned for your movie in Gilliam."

"Then he is wonderful. I shall hire him back."

I sniffed. Fresh tears started falling.

"Are you making her cry?" Jeff asked.

"No." I sniffled. "He isn't. Well, he is, but in a good way."

"What does that mean?" Jeff asked.

"I'm just grateful for how supportive everyone is. I am not going to make any final decision tonight. I'm just going to enjoy the rest of the Regionals, and

I'd love to hear what ideas the two of you have come up with for the documentary, but maybe tomorrow, or the day after."

"Good," Hannah said.

"Enough feeling sorry for myself. I'm probably going to cry, a lot more, but I'll try not to. Let's go out. Because my part in Regionals is done, and you know what that means? I can have fun again."

"You sure?" Hannah asked.

I wiped at another surge of tears. "Yes. I am."

Aramis took my hand and helped me up.

"Um, I'm not sure that's allowed," Jeff said. "Is that allowed?"

"No, it isn't," Hannah said. "But I'll let it go this once."

"One minute," I said, holding Aramis back. Hannah waited in the doorway. They were really serious about this whole chaperoning thing. I made Aramis bend down. I held his hands, mine overwhelmed by his. "Thank you."

"You are welcome."

I remembered another piece of advice Dr. Thaddeus had said, about taking a chance. I leaned forward and kissed Aramis, on the lips. Not on the cheek, like a friend. Not a quick kiss. A full, lingering, I-am-in-love-with-you kiss.

Or it would have been, if Jeff hadn't cleared his throat and Hannah hadn't yelled, "Hey! Stop that. None of this until after Lil and Sam have rendered their decision. After Regionals."

"Right," Aramis said and kissed me back.

THE REST of the Regionals went by in a fog for me. My friends did an incredible job of keeping me and Aramis apart, though they could not keep the memory of the kiss from my mind, or his. We traded knowing smiles whenever we were allowed to catch a glimpse of each other. The memory of the kiss was the only clear thought I had. The rest of the time I dwelled on the axe blade that had spanned the two rings and Reede's refusal to appeal the decision.

Regionals were over and I was downstairs early, waiting for breakfast.

Aramis came into the dining hall.

"They let you come down here by yourself?" I asked as he sat across from me.

"Jeff is still asleep, and I was very quiet going past Lil's room. How are you?"

"Tired. Lost."

"No closer to making a decision?"

"No. What do you think I should do? And none of this do what you love stuff. Seriously. What should I do?"

"I am sorry, Mabel. I cannot make that decision for you."

"Good answer," Lil said, coming over to our table. "Another point in your favor."

"I'm not so sure about that," I said.

Aramis smiled. "Whatever you decide, I want you to be happy, so do what makes you happy. It is a big decision."

"But Reede will need an answer. I can't keep her waiting. I'll need to train for the city champion's competition she's enrolled me in, or be withdrawn as soon as possible to reduce the penalty. What if I start training and knowing this is it, this is my life, and it turns out I hate it? I'll have wasted more time. What if I quit and regret it? And my movies? I have a whole career. I can't make movies part time and do them justice. If I ever come up with a decent idea, that is."

"Aramis, you're giving her anxiety," Lil said. "That's working against you."

"Do not give up on me just yet, Lil," Aramis said. "You will make the right decision, Mabel, because as I see it, you cannot go wrong either way."

"Oh, I like that," Lil said.

Hannah and the others came storming over to the table. "You haven't told them yet, have you?" she asked.

"You've made your decision?" I asked.

"Wait!" Sam said. "We need to all be here. I want to see their faces."

They all grabbed their seats and ordered breakfast.

"What is the verdict?" Aramis asked.

Lil cleared her throat and whispered for a moment with Sam. Anything to be dramatic. "Aramis,

I will admit that you have been a very good sport about this. While we are not without our doubts and concerns, we like how you are with our Mabel. To that end, we give you a conditional pass."

"What does that mean?" I asked.

"No more chaperoning. We'll allow you two to be together. But Aramis, we are watching you."

"Understood. And thank you. If, at any time, I do anything that concerns you, please, talk with me."

"See? I knew this was the right decision," Sam said.

"Yes," Jeff said. "Welcome to the madhouse."

"Thank you. If Mabel wants me."

Of all the decisions I had to make, this was the easiest. "You know that I do."

I had never seen his eyes shine so bright. My stomach flipped and I couldn't stop smiling.

CHAPTER 20

I CLEANED the bar in preparation for the lunch crowd. While the monotony of the physical labor usually permitted me to dream up movie ideas, today I needed it to distract me, to stop me from thinking. It was working. A calmness settled over me as I scrubbed the tables, the floors, the bar.

I was feeling so much better I decided to organize the tankards, mugs, and other glasses under the bar. I put the tankards and pitchers within easiest reach. I then stacked the mugs and other glasses on the lower shelf.

Job complete, I stood and nearly jumped out of my skin. Aramis leaned on the bar.

"Hey," I said, my heart skipping a beat. "I didn't hear you come in."

"I just got here. I was wondering if you needed company today."

I pretended to think for a moment. Any time with Aramis was welcome. "Yes. Sure. That would be all right. Would you like something to drink?"

"Not right now, thank you."

"What would you like, then?" I wiped down the bar though it was already spotless.

"Does this mean you have made your decision?" Aramis waved at my cleaning cloth.

"If I have, are you disappointed?"

"You can never disappoint me."

"Even if I haven't decided yet?"

Aramis stopped me, holding my hand. "Not deciding is also deciding."

I looked away. "I can't—"

"You are."

Why did he have to be so persistent? And so sensible? "What if it's the wrong decision?"

"You cannot make a wrong decision."

"Then why does it feel like I can?"

"What feels wrong?"

"Not going to Reede's."

"Then why are you not going?"

"Because," I sighed. "Because it means I am changing my career yet again."

"And that is a bad thing?" He pulled me around the bar and walked me over to the fireplace.

"It isn't done. My entire family went into mining and stayed there. Even when Mikey competed in axe

throwing, he was still a miner. Always a miner first."
I perched on the edge of the chair, all calmness I'd
had now gone.

"Not everyone in your family mined." Aramis
pulled his chair in front of mine. He too sat on the
edge. He lowered his knees so he was more kneeling
than sitting. It must have been uncomfortable but it
brought him to my level.

"Well sure, Mam. But she went from mining to
acting and that's it. I've gone from mining to acting
to directing, and carving, and tending bar, and axe
throwing." I counted my careers on my fingers.

"All very admirable."

"In and of themselves, yes, but not all in one
lifetime."

"Why?"

"Aramis." I said, exasperated. Too much was
swirling around in my head. I couldn't think straight.

"Whose judgement are you worried about?
Surely not mine. Nor that of your friends."

"No. They would never—"

"Max and Jimmy?"

"No."

"Your family?"

"No." I paused. Out of all the noise in my head,
I saw Da's disgust when he found me on set in the
dining cavern of the Gilliam mines. His shoulders
bent under the weight of the shame I'd brought to
him and my entire family. His utter heartbreak at my
betrayal. "Maybe?"

"Why?"

I shrugged. "I don't know...I shouldn't worry about what they think. It isn't like they care about me."

"And yet you still hear your father's judgement."

Aramis understood me. "Yes. I do."

Aramis nodded. "If I may. As one who has changed careers several times, I can tell you there are no laws that say you can have only one or two at the most. Maybe that is how it is done in Gilliam, but you are in Leitham. We do things differently here. It is one of the things I recall you saying you love about living here. You can do what you want. I shall repeat: you can do whatever you want. The only opinion to matter, is yours. You love axe throwing. I see that joy in your eyes. You love axe throwing more than anything."

I hung my head. "I do."

"So why are you not running out that door to Reede's?"

The swirling chaos in my mind slowed. Da's disgust, Mikey's abandonment, and the absence of emotion in Reede's voice when she told me the Regional competition was over, stood out. My own heart was broken for her. "I failed. I failed myself and Reede. How can I face her?"

Aramis cupped my cheek in his hand. "You did not fail. She believes in you. She wants to continue as your coach."

I bit my bottom lip, unable to move.

"Your father has made you believe you are a failure because you are not a miner. Mikey made you believe you are a failure because you did not get to the Dwarf Games under his tutelage. Am I right?"

Tears filled my eyes, blurring my vision. I nodded.

"Emma made you believe you were a failure because you did not have fellows chasing after you. She made you feel less than everyone because your beard was not as full as hers." He tugged on my meagre beard. "I quite like your beard. Those over-grown ones are unsightly." He shivered. "Who knows what grows in them."

I laughed at that.

"Emma was simply wrong. Your brother, as I understood from Jimmy, was unable to express himself adequately. He had not expected you to necessarily make it to the Dwarf Games that first try. Your father did not understand you. You are a success, Mabel Goldenaxe. Do what you want to do and you will continue to succeed. Whatever you decide to do, I will support you. However, you do have to make a decision."

"And if I never win again? That's hardly success, no matter how much love I have for throwing."

"That is where you are wrong. As long as you love throwing, win or lose, you will have been happy. Time spent doing something that makes you happy is never a waste. That is success."

Throwing made me happier and more miserable

than I'd ever been. And I loved it. I couldn't give that up.

"What do you want?" Aramis asked.

I looked over to the bar. I loved Sophie and Otto and the thinking time I had working here, but I wanted so much more. I wasn't indecisive, I knew exactly what I wanted. Giving voice to it terrified me. I couldn't allow my fear to get in my way. "Will you take me to Reede's?"

Aramis smiled. "Your carriage awaits."

Aramis held my hand as we walked out to his cart. He helped me up before getting in himself. My heart thumped all the way to Reede's. Aramis holding my hand, kissing it every now and then, smiling at me, kept me from jumping off the cart and running.

We pulled up to Reede's house. Aramis got out and helped me down. "Are you coming with me?" I asked.

"I think not. You will be fine. Reede will be happy to see you. Come find me at Studio City after? I would like to start our courtship properly and take you out."

Now my heart was thumping because of Aramis. "I will."

I walked to Reede's back garden. She wasn't there. Was I too late? I couldn't be too late. She hadn't given me a deadline, had she?

I knocked on the door. "Reede?" I called. "Reede?" I knocked harder.

Moments later, she opened the door. "Mabel."

"I'm not too late, am I?"

"That depends." Reede put her hands on her hips.

My words spilled out. "I am not a tourist. I want to do this. I want to see how far I can go. Maybe I'll win the Dwarf Games, maybe I won't. That doesn't matter. Competing is what is important. Doing well, making a name for myself, and for you as my coach, that is what is important. That is our revenge on Mikey and my family. That is my story, whether I make it into a documentary or not, though Hannah and Jeff had some great ideas for that. Please, take me back. Let's see where this will go. If it's terrible, if you hate it, or me, then tell me, drop me, its fine. Please."

"You're sure about this?"

"I am."

"Okay then." Her demeanor didn't soften. "Get out your axes and start warming up. We have a lot of work to do before Gilliam."

I FOUND Aramis in his office. I knocked on the open door. "May I come in?"

He smiled, with his so-deep dimples and his hair whipping around his shoulders. Until Sam had mentioned it, I had never noticed how much it moved when I was around.

"Please. How did it go with Reede?" He asked.

"She worked me hard."

"And?"

I beamed. "And I loved it. Thank you."

"Always."

"What are you working on?" I climbed onto the stool beside him.

"A new story."

"Oooh. What's it about?"

"Thaddeus."

"I thought you didn't like him."

"He is not one of my favorite elves, but I also have not seen him in a long time. I started thinking about him after you told me how you read his books. I thought I would try and make one of his books into a movie."

"Which one?"

He handed me a copy of *Living Your Authentic Life*. I laughed. "This is the book! Because of this book I auditioned for your movie."

"Then I owe him my allegiance."

I blushed. "You have to change the title, though."

"I shall." Aramis set his quill down. "Before I take you to dinner, I want to make sure that you are all right with this, you and I."

My heart thumped and I looked away.

Aramis took my hand in his. "Lil can be impulsive and persistent. During Regionals, it was fun with the interrogations and chaperoning, but it felt to me that they sprung all of this on you as much as they had on me."

I nodded, unable to look at him. I didn't think I was going to like this talk.

"I want to be sure, though, that you are happy," he said. "You were with Brent a long time, and you and I have a bit of a rocky history."

"Right." It was too problematic. I knew that. I shouldn't be upset. Being with Aramis was never going to be anything more than a dream.

"Let me make my feelings plain, so there is no room for confusion or doubt." He ran the pad of his thumb over the back of my hand. "I was more than happy to prove myself to your friends. But your friends are not you. If there is more I need to do to prove myself, my worthiness, to you, my affection for you, then I will do whatever it is you ask of me."

What?

"I love you. I want to be with you."

Oh.

"I want you to want to be with me. If you want to wait, I will wait. If you do not want to be with me at all, then I understand. What I do not want, is for you to feel pressured into anything, because of me or because of your friends."

Since breaking up with Brent, I had been truly free to be myself. That didn't change when I was with Aramis. "I don't want to wait."

Aramis stood in front of me, caressed my cheek, and tucked a lock of hair behind my ear.

"I want this," I said.

He kissed me.

My head swam, all worry vanishing. "I want to be with you."

He kissed me again, his arm going around my waist.

"Aramis," Lil shouted coming in. We separated. "Sorry to interrupt. Mabel. Good thing you're here, too. You look very good together, by the way."

"What is it, Lil?" I squeaked, sadly recovering from Aramis's kiss, his hand still on the small of my back.

"I have the details for the hearing about Dakkar. It's the day after tomorrow. You have to be there to help us. You will be there, right?"

"Of course," I said.

"Great." Lil waved a parchment at us. "I'll just leave this here, it has all the details. Get back to what you were doing."

Lil closed the door behind her and I pulled Aramis back to me.

CHAPTER 21

I ARRIVED outside the conference room designated by the Performing Creature Welfare Society for the hearing. Sam paced, wringing her hands. "Hey, Sam," I said, catching my breath from the climb to the third floor.

"Mabel, you're here." She rushed to embrace me.

"Of course I am."

"I was beginning to think no one was coming."

Sam's anxiety radiated from her. "Hey, hey." I rubbed her back. "We are all here for you. There's plenty of time before the hearing. Where's Lil?"

"On her way, I hope. She wanted to fix up the house a bit, for after, good or bad result, we want everyone to come over. I was useless at helping her so she sent me here."

"Breathe. It will help."

Sam breathed deep. "This is it, Mabel. It comes down to this. If I mess up, I lose Dakkar. I can't lose Dakkar, not to—" she glanced around, "Sevrin," she whispered.

"You won't lose."

"How did you do it?"

"Do what?"

"Deal with the pressure. At the city championships, at Regionals, with all those expectations to win, everyone cheering for you. How did you stay so calm?"

"Months of Reede teaching me to stay in the moment, I guess. Dakkar wants to be with you. You have a ton of support."

"I hope you're right. Ugh." Sam waved her hands like she was erasing an image in front of her. "Change of subject. You and Aramis. Lil said she walked in on quite the kiss."

My face burned. "Sam!"

"I'm happy for you, as long as he treats you well. He is, isn't he?"

"It's only been a couple of days, but yes."

"Good. Then we made the right decision, allowing the relationship. You're welcome."

"You're crazy, but thank you."

"Mabel," Lil said, rushing in. "So glad you are here. How's she doing?" Lil nodded in Sam's direction.

"Anxious, but I'm doing my best to help her

relax," I said.

"Are you ready to testify?"

I pulled out the wizard's crystal with my recording of Dakkar. "Can't wait to get in there."

Hannah and Jeff were soon with us.

"See how much support you have?" I asked Sam.

"But I don't own Anselm," Sam muttered.

"What are you doing here?" I heard Mam ask behind us down the corridor.

I turned around, thinking she was talking to me. She wasn't. She was talking to Aramis. My breath caught and doubt flickered to life. Had he been her spy all along?

Sam held my hand to comfort me. I smiled my thanks and squeezed her hand. I was supposed to be here for her, not the other way around.

I listened, anticipating that he would tell her how he manipulated me. Aramis said nothing to Mam. He walked past her, straight to me and my friends, standing behind me and resting his hands on my shoulders, affectionately.

I squeezed Sam's hand again and let go.

Lil stared down Mam and Sevrin.

"Mabel," Mam said, coming up to me. "May I speak with you?"

She betrayed me, she extorted my brother, and she tried to extort me. The sight of her made me ill. She was my mam. I wanted to give her a chance. "Are you going to support Lil and Sam adopting Dakkar?"

"I can't do that."

She chose Sevrin, again. "Then, no."

"I just wanted to congratulate you on your sixth place in Regionals. That's all."

"Thanks." I turned back to my friends. "Should we go in?"

"Good idea," Lil said.

We filed into the conference room, my friends and I on one side, Mam, Sevrin, and what I assumed were a couple of Sevrin's henchmen, on the other.

Mam glowered at me, huffed, and marched over to me, grabbed my arm and dragged me back into the corridor.

"What are you doing?" I growled.

"I want to ask you the same thing. I warned you to be careful around Aramis."

"I don't need your approval."

"He will hurt you."

"He cannot possibly hurt me more than you have." I stormed back inside and sat with my friends.

Aramis put his arm around me.

ANSELM AND two other officials entered from a side door and sat on the other side of the conference table from us. "Everyone is here?" He sighed. We were wasting his time.

I couldn't understand why he didn't he care about Dakkar's future. Why didn't he want Dakkar to end up in the best home possible? That was the purpose of his department.

"Applications have been studied, references given and approved, and properties evaluated. Both are very strong and this has been a difficult decision for the committee."

"Decision?" Sam said. "This is a hearing, not the decision."

"Sam," Anselm spoke over top of her. "The committee is quite impressed with your commitment to Dakkar's care."

"Well, okay," Sam whispered. "I'll hear you out."

"The home you have created for Dakkar clearly has her comfort in mind, provides her with plenty of room to move, privacy as she needs it, and yet enough suitable access."

"I like where this is going," Lil muttered.

"Sevrin, you, too, have prepared for Dakkar's care. The committee is impressed with the time you are able to dedicate to looking after her."

"I don't like this," Sam said.

"Your accommodation for Dakkar is, however, lacking."

"I knew we had the best place." Sam gave a small fist pump.

"We suggest you make a good offer to Sam and purchase her place."

"What?" Lil whispered. "What?" she shouted.

"Once you have purchased the property, let us know and we will arrange—"

"No. No." Sam stood up. "You are not giving Dakkar to Sevrin. He doesn't want her. He doesn't want to care for her."

"Sam," Anselm said, sternly.

"No. Dakkar hates him. She fears him. Tell them, Mabel."

"Sam, we understand your concerns—"

"How much did he pay you for this decision? I will double it. I will triple it."

"Are you suggesting a bribe to the committee?"

"I am suggesting you took one. What did you call it? An application fee. Was there an application fee I didn't know about? How much? Just tell me and I will pay it."

"Sam," Anselm said.

"Not an application fee, then. A purchase price. He paid you, buying Dakkar, like she's a commodity, something to be owned. She isn't. She is a beautiful creature to be cherished and cared for. If you want to call it a purchase price, then I will pay it. I will quadruple whatever he paid you."

"Sam."

"Going with Sevrin will kill Dakkar. Do you want her death on your hands? Because it will be your fault. You're supposed to be the organization that cares for the well-being of creatures."

"How dare you!" Sevrin rumbled.

"Would everyone calm down," the committee member to Anselm's right said. "She's just a dragon."

"Just a dragon?" I jumped in. "She is the last

of her kind because of Sevrin. He decimated their population. He slaughtered her family, took her from her home."

"I didn't do it alone, Mabel." Sevrin was calm, as if this was a chat over tea in front of the fire. "Aramis did a fair bit of the work."

It was a decent attempt to hurt me, but the sling didn't faze me. "He isn't the one looking to own her. He isn't the one who figured out how to remove Dakkar's fire. You called it taming her, domesticating her. I've seen the damage you've done to her. It is irreparable damage. Why can't you leave her alone? Let Dakkar live out the rest of her days in comfort, in happiness, with someone who wants to look after her."

"What damage?" the committee member to Anselm's left cut in.

"There is no damage," Sevrin derided. "Mabel, your loyalty is admirable."

"You wouldn't know loyalty if it grabbed you by the beard and threw you across the room." I turned to the committee. "I have proof."

"Proof?" the committee member to Anselm's left asked, curious. Anselm fidgeted.

"Proof?" Sevrin scoffed.

I strode up to the conference table, Aramis at my side to set up the crystal, staff, and screen. I played them my interview with Dakkar. I paused it on Dakkar's scar, pointing out the physical damage. Then I let it play and Dakkar's wail echoed through the room. Sam sobbed. Lil comforted her. I think even Mam wiped tears from her eyes, though she was quick and furtive about it.

The room was silent when the recording stopped. Sevrin crossed his arms and grunted. Anselm shuffled the pages in front of him, cleared his throat and said, "While heart-wrenching, this cannot be verified."

"Excuse me?" I said.

"You are a movie director, are you not?"

"Well, yes, that's how I could record her."

"So we cannot tell how much you edited it, colored it in favor of Sam."

"I didn't have to. You heard the questions I asked. There was no slant, no favoritism in my tone. There were no questions omitted."

"We cannot—"

"You cannot deny that cry," Sam said.

"We cannot deny the cry, but we cannot verify what it was in regards to."

Aramis cleared his throat and stood. "If I may."

"It is not necessary," Anselm said.

"It is necessary," Aramis said. "I was with Sevrin during the destruction of the dragon population. As he mentioned, I did participate. I was there when Sevrin removed the gem, the source of fire, from Dakkar, domesticating her. I was with him when he perfected the process."

"Aramis," Sevrin interrupted.

"And this is the part that Sevrin does not want anyone to know. This is why he is so determined to own Dakkar."

"Aramis."

"Why he is so determined to interrupt me. He tortured dragon after dragon, as he discovered the purpose of the gem, then how to remove it. While they became docile after their gem was removed, they also lost their minds, becoming much easier for him to slay. Dakkar was the only one to come through the process relatively unscathed. Or, that is what we told everyone. She is not unscathed. That wail you heard, I have heard it before, many times. She suffered, and she continues to suffer, because of what Sevrin did. And yes, I admit, I did not stop him. I encouraged it. In my years working in movies, I have used Dakkar many times. She has done an admirable job, but she suffers. She is docile and willing to work. When I am here late at night, I hear her cry. She has worked with many an actor and director. As long as I have known Dakkar, Sam is truly the only one she likes, the only one she allows near her for more than a quick conversation. I have seen Sam and Dakkar together. That haunted look you saw in Dakkar's eyes while Mabel was talking to her, is gone when she is with Sam. There is a healing that has taken place whenever Sam is with Dakkar. Dakkar is as playful as she was when we found her, when we destroyed her. Yes, I said we. I count myself as an active participant. You cannot reasonably, ethically, morally, grant custody to Sevrin. Doing so would call the existence of this committee and the society as a whole into question.

Hearings and inquests would be demanded. Nearly every movie in production right now, would be halted indefinitely until those inquests are completed. I know that you do not want that. Sevrin, is that what you want? Think about how such a shut-down of the industry would affect your income."

"What is he talking about?" Mam asked Sevrin.

"Nothing," Sevrin hissed.

"That is a very good question, Frerin, and it is about time you asked it," Aramis continued. "I am talking about power, plain and simple. All-encompassing power. That is all Sevrin wants. He owns nearly all executives in the movie industry. A shut-down will cost him millions. And Dakkar, she is the epitome of his power, his reputation. In his eyes, she has only been on loan all these years. He believes he owns her. He must own her. She is not a hobby, a project, or something to be cared for. He must destroy her. He is the great dragon-slayer, after all. He cannot allow the last surviving dragon to live out her days in peace. If he does that, his reputation, everything he owns, his power, can be called into question. It can be taken from him."

Aramis turned back to the committee. "What say you?"

"This changes nothing," Anselm said.

"Please," Sam sobbed. "Please don't do this to her. I have done everything right. I'm the one who has created the right home for her. I love her. I will look after her. Please don't leave her to suffer."

"Anselm," the committee member on Anselm's right said. "We need to discuss this new evidence."

"You don't," Sevrin said.

Anselm sighed. "All right. Clear the room. We will call you back in a few minutes. Please, everyone wait outside."

Barely back in the corridor and Sevrin said to Sam, "How much would you like for this fancy place of yours?"

"I am not selling my place to you."

Sevrin turned to one of his henchmen. "Go to her place. Check it out. Let me know what the market value for it might be."

"Don't you dare," I jumped in.

"Don't worry, Mabel. My offer will be generous."

"I don't care. I will never accept it. You," Sam called to Sevrin's henchman. "Stay off my property."

"Lil," Frerin said. "We've been friends for a long time."

"No. I was your friend. You were only pretending to be my friend."

"You and Sam, you do not want the burden of Dakkar."

"Dakkar is not a burden to us. To you, but not to us."

"You and Sam are just starting your life together. Why complicate things so soon?"

"Again, not a complication."

"Go," Sevrin said to his henchman.

"You cannot just walk over my property," Sam said.

"Watch us."

"It's all right, Sam," Lil said. "I'll go, make sure he doesn't do anything." She hugged Sam. "Watch her?" she whispered to me.

"Of course."

"Jeff," Aramis said. "We should go with her."

"Hannah and I will go," Jeff said. "Aramis, you and Mabel stay here, in case they need clarification on what either of you said."

Sevrin snorted as Jeff and Hannah hurried off with Lil.

"Found a new plaything, have you?" Sevrin asked.

Aramis and I stuck close to Sam, our backs to him.

"He is using you to pass the time, Mabel," Sevrin continued. "When he tires of you, he will throw you away like a dragon carcass."

Sam gasped. Sevrin's choice of metaphor was not lost on me.

"You heard what he said about me in there. He blames me for all the damage done to Dakkar and her kind. He was there. Don't think he didn't have a part in it."

"Seemed to me you were perfectly happy to take all the credit for it when I first arrived in Leitham," I shot back.

We fell silent. The few moments Sevrin expected

us to be out here grew into several minutes.

"Why is it taking so long?" Sam asked.

"This has to be a good thing," I said. "They were so ready to give Dakkar to him. They have to be changing their minds."

"But what is there to discuss? Our proof is solid."

"This is Sevrin we're talking about," I said.

"That's what I'm afraid of," she said.

One of the committee members opened the door. "Come in, all of you," he said.

Sam grabbed my hand. Aramis and I practically held her up as we walked in.

"Please, please, please, please, please," she muttered.

Anselm and the others looked appropriately cowed.

"Sam," Anselm said. "We grant you full custody of Dakkar. You may take her home any time."

Sam gasped. "Thank you!"

"What?" Sevrin roared.

Anselm ignored him. "This concludes the adoption of Dakkar. This hearing is adjourned."

"What about visitation?" Mam asked.

Some nerve she had!

"Denied," Anselm said.

"I have to tell Dakkar." Sam was virtually vibrating with joy. "I'm going to get her right now. Mabel, Aramis, go to my place. Please tell Lil and the others the good news. We'll have a little party to celebrate."

"I don't think so," Sevrin said, walking out.

"Call off your henchmen, Sevrin," I shouted after him. "Leave us alone."

"What does that mean?" Sam asked, her eyes wide, panic shaking her.

"Go get Dakkar," Aramis said. "We will see you at your home."

CHAPTER 22

ANGRY SHOUTS emanated from Lil and Sam's back garden. Broken furniture and dishes, and clothes littered the front lawn. Aramis and I had rushed over both to tell Lil the good news and in hopes of heading off Sevrin and Mam, if necessary. We had not been fast enough. Mam, Sevrin, and several of his henchmen were strategically positioned around the back garden, including at the entrance to Dakkar's cave. Lil, trembling, stood her ground, shouting at Sevrin and his men to get out.

Jeff and Hannah stood beside Lil, creating a tiny wall in front of the door.

"Jeff, what's happening?" I asked.

"They'd cleaned out the house by the time we got here," he said. "They're claiming ownership. We can't get in. They have bolted the doors and changed the locks."

"Sevrin," I said, putting a calming hand on Lil's back, letting her know reinforcements, such as they were, had arrived. "The committee ruled. It was a fair process. You lost. Take your men, and leave."

"I am hurt, Mabel," he responded. "Genuinely hurt. I have been nothing but kind to you. I took you in, treated you as a daughter, gave you standing in my organization that most can only dream of, and you continually turn your back on me, betray me."

I snorted. "I care about as much for your feelings as you care for anyone else's, which is to say, not at all. What I do, or don't do, has nothing to do with the fact that the committee ruled. You are in violation of that ruling. Get off Lil and Sam's property."

Sevrin grinned. "That hearing was a farce."

"Your opinion is irrelevant. The ruling is binding."

Sevrin cocked his head to the side. "Mmm, no, it isn't."

I looked at him, dumbfounded.

Sevrin smirked. "Have you learned nothing, Mabel? I am Lord of the Dwarven Mafia. I can do whatever I want."

"Stop this, Sevrin," Aramis said. "This is beneath you."

Sevrin's eyes blazed hatred.

The ground quaked. Sam had arrived with Dakkar. The dragon's cry pierced the air. I shuddered.

Jeff and Hannah covered their ears. Lil placed a hand over her heart.

"Ah, wonderful," Sevrin smiled. "Thank you for bringing Dakkar to me."

Sam stopped beside her house, Dakkar on a lead beside her, cowering. She stroked Dakkar's snout. "It's all right," she whispered. "Get off my property," she snarled.

"I think you will find that this is my property now, and you and your friends are trespassing," Sevrin sneered.

Dakkar smacked one of her hind legs on the ground. We wobbled. Even Sevrin was caught off guard, unsteady on his feet from the rumbling earth.

"Welcome home, Dakkar," Sevrin said, regaining his balance.

Dakkar rose up on her hind legs, pulling the lead out of Sam's hands. She batted her wings and hissed. If only she could still breathe fire, she would have burned a swath and engulfed Sevrin. She hissed again and again, stomping her feet.

"Dakkar, stop," Sam said, trying to get hold of the lead, but only succeeding in jumping up and down. "Get out of here, Sevrin."

"Sam," Lil said. "They've taken over the house, too."

Dakkar stepped forward, prowling. She swung her head, knocking one of Sevrin's henchmen off his feet.

"That's right, Dakkar," Sevrin said. "Come this

way."

Dakkar charged. She snarled, smoke puffing out her nostrils. Dakkar reared back.

Aramis yelled, "No!"

Metal on metal clanged. I turned in time to see Aramis jumping in front of Dakkar, facing Sevrin. Aramis held an axe and another lay at his feet.

Sevrin had thrown an axe at Dakkar? Where had Aramis gotten an axe? I searched and spotted an unarmed henchman.

At the sound of the metal clashing, Dakkar roared. Her tail whipped back and forth, smashing a tree, cracking the trunk. Sam screamed. "See what you're doing, Sevrin? Get out!"

Another henchman pulled his axe, ready to throw. I jumped at him, tackling him to the ground. The impact of hitting him and then the ground knocked the wind from me. He rolled over, trapping me beneath him.

"Mabel!" Aramis shouted.

"Sevrin," Mam yelled. "Stop this!"

I grunted and wrapped my arms around the henchman, holding him on top of me, his arms pinned at his side. He raised his leg and stomped down, the heel of his boot connected with my knee. Pain ripped through me. I cried out and let go. He elbowed me in the ribs. I gasped, unable to breathe.

More metal clanged. Arrows flew from the trees and the rooftop, bouncing off Dakkar's scales. She roared, and though she could not breathe fire, her eyes blazed it.

I rolled out from under the henchman, kicking him as I did.

Dakkar roared and flailed. Dust storms swirled around us, blinding me, choking me.

The dust settled and the henchman was gone. Aramis had him, throwing him against the house. Three others attacked Aramis, leaping onto his back, pulling him down.

Henchmen grabbed at Dakkar, throwing ropes over her, around her neck. She roared, snapping her jaws until a rope was looped around, muzzling her. Screams echoed around me, I couldn't tell who they belonged to. I couldn't see my friends.

A discarded axe lay two feet from me. It was the one Sevrin had first wielded against Dakkar. I rose to my hands and knees, and collapsed from the pain. I pulled up to my elbows and slithered forward, inch by inch, agony overwhelming me.

I grasped the handle, rolled onto my back and threw, slicing through the rope binding one of Dakkar's hind legs. She stepped down on the henchman behind her, slapping her tail down to screams.

"Get her," Sevrin yelled.

Two sets of hands seized me, jerking me to my feet. My knee collapsed from under me. I fell, freeing me from one of my captors. My liberty was only temporary. I was back in his clutches, being dragged to Sevrin.

I kicked out with my bad leg and missed. I pulled my arms, trying to free myself again, struggling against their impressively tight hold.

A sudden impact from behind knocked one of my captors over. Mam held a thick branch in her hand. She had hit him in the head and she was pulling back, swinging at the other who let me go.

I grabbed the fallen henchman's axe and hobbled to my feet, limping forward, looking for Aramis, Lil, anyone who didn't belong to Sevrin.

Mam felled another henchman, picked up his axe and tossed it to me. I snatched it out of the air. For a fraction of a second we looked at each other and in that moment, I saw a change. Mam had finally seen Sevrin's true nature, and she didn't approve. Together we swung at two more attackers. I missed, but Mam hit them with enough impact to knock them away from us.

More ropes encumbered Dakkar.

Together, Mam and I fought to free her. Mam swung at the henchmen, moving them away from Dakkar. I hacked at the ropes. "It's all right, Dakkar," I said. "He is not going to take you. Where is Sam?"

Dakkar rumbled and prowled forward.

With Dakkar free and nothing left to hold her, several of Sevrin's henchmen fled. More axes and arrows flew at Dakkar but bounced easily off her scales. There was only one place that any weapon would penetrate, and that was the location of her scar. Even so, the projectiles angered her. She swung to the left then the right, spinning, looking for her assailants, unable to spot them for the onslaught.

"Sam," I shouted.

"Mabel," she called back.

I turned to where her voice had been. One of Sevrin's men carried her away from Dakkar. She was putting up a valiant fight, kicking and squirming. I raised my arm, axe in hand, and threw, hitting her captor in the shoulder. He dropped Sam and cried out, clutching his wound.

Sam ran to Dakkar. Sevrin was faster. He was under Dakkar, sword in hand, dodging her legs, moving with her swaying, flailing body, getting the sword into position at her scar.

I drew back and let my axe fly, knocking the sword out of his hands. At that moment, Dakkar moved, swinging her tail, catching Sevrin in the chest, throwing him several feet back.

The projectiles had stopped. A silence fell over us. The dust settled. Sam managed to grab Dakkar's lead and spoke softly to her, comforting her, soothing her, telling her it was over.

Sevrin's men were gone now. Mam hovered over Sevrin, checking his wounds. My friends lay scattered, injured but alive, moaning. Where was Aramis? I searched, hobbling from one wounded to the next. He wasn't there. Where had he gone?

A thin shadow stretched out over us from the roof of Lil's house. I looked up. He was there, bow and arrow poised, keeping watch for any stray attackers.

He didn't see the one running up behind him. I grabbed an axe from a fallen henchman and threw, hitting Aramis's attacker in the side, throwing him off balance as he raised his arm to bring his sword down. He fell.

Aramis jumped off the roof and hurried to me. "You saved my life yet again."

I COLLAPSED into Aramis's arms, pain throbbing through me. He set me on the ground and placed his hands on my shattered knee. The tingle from his healing touch replaced the pain.

"No! Don't!" I sat bolt upright. My ribs screamed out in agony.

"Mabel, this is not like before. I am the Lord of the Elves now. I have the power to heal you. I promise it will not damage you. Please."

I gazed into his blue eyes, so earnest, so full of love, for me. "All right."

"Come on, Sevrin," I heard Mam say, not too far away from me. "Let's get you home."

She'd helped me, she had seen what he was really like, and yet she was going to stay with him? "Mam. Where are you going?"

She stood, holding Sevrin up, sadness in her eyes.

"Why do you continue to choose him over me?"

"I don't—"

"You do. You walked away from your family for

him. You joined him in using me to get rid of Radier and Aubrey. You stood by him to help him adopt Dakkar. He attacked me and my friends. You know he will do it again. To me or to someone else."

Mam shrugged and shook her head. "I love him."

That hurt more than any physical pain. Tears stabbed at my eyes, then fell.

"More than me?" I refused to wipe the tears from my eyes even though they blurred my vision. "Why can't you love me?"

Mam and Sevrin started limping away. Mam stopped. My heart flipped in hope, until she tossed a bundle of keys at my feet. "For the house," she said.

I watched her leave through my tears. "Why?" I whispered.

Aramis held me and kissed my temple. "She loves you. She cannot break free of Sevrin and the lure of power."

My friends groaned. I wiped my eyes and helped them to their feet. Sevrin's men crawled away in silence. Sam emerged from the cave, cuts and bruises marking her face and hands. Her clothes, like the rest of ours, were torn and dusty.

"Sam!" Lil rushed to her.

"I'm sore, and it will look bad for a while, but I'm fine. A good wash-up will take care of most of the ugliness."

"And Dakkar?" Jeff asked, limping over.

"She's spooked, but settling in. I'm going to go back and stay with her for the rest of the night. It calms her. I want to thank you all for everything. For coming to the hearing, for fighting for me there, and especially for fighting for me here. This was the last thing I expected. Perhaps it shouldn't have been. But thank you."

"Come inside, Sam," Lil said. "All of you. I'll get us some water to wash up. And if Sevrin's men didn't eat and drink everything, we need to have our party."

"You all go on ahead," Sam said. "I should get back to Dakkar. Go. Have fun. Have an extra glass or two for me."

Before we followed the others into the house, I called after Sam. "She's home," I said.

Sam grinned. "She is."

I stood with Lil as she hovered by the back door, looking out to the cave where Sam had settled in with Dakkar. Lil's brow was furrowed and her face looked haggard. "Are you all right?" I asked softly.

Lil shook her head. "I knew Sevrin would put up a fight when I heard he'd filed for custody. I can't believe we fought him off. I am terrified he will come back."

Aramis emerged from the living room where he had been healing Jeff and Hannah. "Lil? May I have a look at your wounds?" he asked.

"Ah, no," she dismissed him. "It's just a few cuts

and bruises."

"Even so, better to have them looked at," he said. "You do not want to develop an infection or ignore a deeper injury that you might not be aware of."

"All right," she sighed.

"Let me start with your arm, please."

Lil winced and could only partially extend it.

"Not only cuts and bruises, then," Aramis said beginning the healing process. "A broken arm."

"Ooh, tingly," Lil muttered. Aramis and I smiled.

"I don't think that Sevrin will come back," I said, continuing our discussion. "But if he does, you know we will help you fight him for as long and as often as we need to."

"We definitely will," Aramis said. "But I agree with Mabel, I do not believe Sevrin will come again."

"I hope you're right. Sam and I are truly grateful for your help. I can't imagine how difficult this is for you."

"It is one of many battles I regret to have had with him. But this too shall pass," he said with a smile, though sadness filled his eyes.

I squeezed his elbow and hoped he could feel my love.

"Do you think Sam is all right out there with Dakkar?" Lil asked.

"Well," Aramis said, completing his work on Lil. "I would like to go have a look at her injuries. Come with me, and if you want, you can stay with her."

"But the house…"

"Don't worry about it," I said. "We'll stay here and defend it if needed. Go."

Lil hugged me. "You were incredible, by the way," she whispered.

I wandered to the living room where Jeff and Hannah were comparing battle wounds.

"From here to here," Jeff said, pointing to a spot on his shoulder with one hand, and to his lower abdomen with the other. "You can see where it was from the tear in my tunic. I'm lucky to be alive the way that thing went straight down the side of me. Not to mention my broken nose and the arrow sticking out of my thigh."

"That was bad," Hannah said, "but I had both my legs broken, and" she turned around, the back of her tunic was shredded, "the way I was dragged across the ground, I'm lucky to have any skin left."

"At least you could see," Jeff rebutted. "With my broken nose and shattered face, I couldn't see anything, but I still put up a fight."

"We sure did," Hannah said, grinning. "Mabel! What happened to you?"

"Shattered knee and cracked ribs, but mostly cuts and bruises." The only visible evidence there had been a battle were our torn and dirt-covered clothing.

Jeff pulled at the hole in his tunic, examining his body where the cut had been. "I think Aramis even cleaned me up a little. I was bloody and there must have been dirt on me. You saw that, right Hannah?"

She narrowed her eyes, studying Jeff. "I did. You

were disgusting. What about me?" She tugged at the back of her tunic. "Can you tell he grew new skin on me?"

Jeff took it upon himself to lift up the back of her tunic and examine her more closely, running his hand over her back. "You would never tell. And it looks like you had a nice bath, too. No dirt, no stones. Hey. Didn't you have an old scar back here?"

"I do."

"Not anymore."

"Wow, Mabel. Your Aramis is good," Hannah said. "I hated that thing."

"Are you sure you didn't mention it to him? Tell him you wanted it gone?" I teased.

"I would have, if I knew he could get rid of it for me."

"Also, I think it was lower than where your injuries were," Jeff added.

"I think he gave you better eyebrows, Jeff," Hannah said. "They're much fuller."

"Or maybe they're just finally clean," I teased. "They've fluffed out a little, now that the grime you've built up over the years is gone."

Jeff ran his fingers over his eyebrows. "Probably a bit of both."

"Where's Lil?" Hannah asked.

"Gone to look in on Sam and Dakkar," I said. "She'll probably be out there for a while. I said we'd stay here and guard the house in case Sevrin or his men come back."

"Do you think they will?" Hannah asked.

"Not likely," I said.

"But if they do, we'll be ready," Jeff said, all proud of himself, like he was a warrior now. Hannah nodded in agreement, standing firm, hands on hips, ready to jump back into action at a moment's notice.

Jeff crossed and uncrossed his arms. "Are we supposed to be sad right now? I feel like we are, but I'm not. We just had a major victory over Sevrin. We should be drinking to celebrate. Shouldn't we?"

I grinned. "We absolutely should." I led them into the kitchen. Broken dishes littered the floor. We helped ourselves to the dregs of ale Sevrin's men had left behind. I raised my mug. "To Dakkar's homecoming, and our victory."

"To Dakkar and victory!"

Jeff slammed his mug down after his sip. "Well, that was less than satisfactory. I'm going to get us a couple of kegs."

"And food," Hannah said. "Get us food."

"You two will be all right here?" Jeff asked.

"We have a dragon on our side," I said. "Of course we'll be fine."

"And the city champion axe thrower," Hannah said.

We shooed him out the door with a list of supplies to help us remain vigilant through the night without sacrificing our celebrations.

"Did Sevrin's men leave anything to eat?" Hannah asked, opening and closing cupboards.

"Probably not if they have anything close to the appetite Sevrin has." Together we rummaged through the kitchen. I found half a loaf of bread. "He could eat, I tell you."

"That's it?" Hannah looked at the pathetic state of the bread. "That's all they left? I'm beginning to think we won because the other side was too drunk and too full to put up much of a fight. Sam and Lil had all kinds of food and drink ready for us."

"Unless all the food and ale gave them more energy to fight, because they did not look sluggish to me."

"Me neither."

Hannah and I cleaned up and were exhausted by the time Jeff returned. He filled tankards with fresh ale and heaped food on plates, bringing them to us in the living room.

"I'm going to bring some out to Aramis and the others," Jeff said. "When I get back, we should have a Mage Stones tournament."

Mage Stones? I hadn't played that in years. Not since, well, my first day acting with Aramis. I missed the annual tournaments my family had. This could be fun. "Yes," I said. "But I'll need a lot more ale then."

"We'll all need more whether we play Mage Stones or not," Hannah agreed, bringing our tankards to the kitchen and refilling them.

CHAPTER 23

THE CLANGING of metal woke me.

"Wake up, sleepy-heads," Lil shouted, banging a spoon on a pot.

I opened my eyes to darkness and wondered why she was waking us in the middle of the night, until I realized I had passed out with my face buried in the pillow of her sofa. I turned my head and groaned, still drunk from the previous night's festivities. How could she be so wide awake? "Is Sevrin back?" I groaned.

The others were having as difficult a time waking up and moving.

"No, he is not. Though clearly you lot are useless at staying awake to protect my house. Sam and I have decided we don't want to wait any longer. We are going to have our golden ring ceremony now. So come on. Get up."

Golden ring ceremony? Wasn't there something I was supposed to do for it? Maybe I'd remember in an hour or two. "Okay," I moaned and closed my eyes, the fingers of sleep quickly overpowering me.

Lil banged her pot again. "No more sleep. Get up. Get up!"

"How are you so awake?" Hannah complained, rolling into a sitting position.

"We have Dakkar and I am getting my golden ring," Lil cheerfully shouted.

Jeff grunted and rose to his feet. "The Mage Stones champion is up," he said, raising his arms victoriously over his head. He'd only lorded it over us for an hour before we all passed out.

One by one we got up, straightened ourselves and stumbled outside into the bright sunshine.

"How is Dakkar settling in?" I asked as we made our way over to the cave entrance.

"It was a rough night, but she calmed down eventually, and she loves her new home."

Aramis stood at the entrance of the cave.

Dakkar bounded around, from one rock to another, one side to the other, up and down, then over to the entrance to nudge Lil and Sam with her snout, then back inside to play, repeating the pattern several times.

Aramis smiled. "I do not believe I have ever seen her this happy. And for her to become so comfortable here so quickly, Lil and Sam have done an amazing thing for her."

"Come on, come on." Lil hustled us over to where an anvil was set up with the ring molds ready to be used. Next to the anvil was a make-shift forge burning hot, melting the gold. A smith checked on the gold. "Ready?" he asked without looking at anyone in particular.

"Ready," Sam and Lil said at the same time.

The smith put on his gloves, opened the door to the forge, and pulled out the melted gold, pouring it into the mold.

Lil and Sam looked to me expectantly. Oh, right. I was their officiant and had to give a speech. I cleared my throat and stepped forward.

"Lil and Sam," I said. "It is my great honor to be the officiant at this golden ring ceremony. We have all borne witness to the commitment you two have for each other, and I can safely speak for everyone when I say, it is about time you made it official." Everyone chuckled in polite agreement. I thought of Emma and Zach. A golden ring was all she had—we had—ever talked about, and now that she had it, she wasn't happy. I knew that would not be the case with Lil and Sam. "What promises do you make to each other today and for the rest of your lives?"

"Sam," Lil started. "You are my world. You accept me in all my messed-up glory. When I'm being overdramatic, when I can't make a decision, when my emotions get the best of me for better or for worse. You encourage my creativity and my passion for my acting. You bring out the best in me, and accept me even when I am at my worst. I promise, now and forever, to always be myself with you, to love you without condition as you love me, and to prove I am worthy of your love."

Sam wiped away a tear. "Lil. I love the wild passion you have for life. You have brought that joy and exuberance into my life, and you graciously give me the space I need for solitude, reflection, and to tap my own creativity. You even let me adopt a dragon. I promise to allow you the freedom to be you, just as you allow me that freedom. I promise to cherish your creativity and your passion for life, just as you cherish mine."

I beamed. Lil had been so enamored with Sam when I first met them, but she had been so afraid to approach her. I couldn't think of anyone more suited to each other than these two.

The smith took the cooling gold out of the moulds and began shaping them into their final form.

"Sam and Lil," I said. "You have designed these rings as a sign to the world of your love and commitment to each other. These rings are a binding of your hearts, your lives, and your promises. Sam, do you accept this bond?"

"Yes."

"Lil, gather Sam's beard, please."

She did so, holding the hair in a bundle while the smith placed the ring around it, letting it seal shut as it cooled.

"Lil, do you accept this bond?"

"Yes! A thousand times, yes!"

"Sam, please gather Lil's beard."

When the smith finally pulled away, the rings shone, the noon-day sun highlighting the depressions and raised edges of the intricate knot-work pattern they had chosen as their design.

"It is with great pleasure that I declare the two of you bonded."

Lil squealed and threw her arms around Sam to loud cheers from all of us. Dakkar poked her head out of the cave, sniffed the air, then edged further out. At first I thought she was growling, but as she raised her chin and settled it over Sam and Lil and closed her eyes, I realized she was purring. Her family was complete.

I soaked it all in. The love between Lil and Sam. The love I had for them. The laughter and encouragement I had with my friends. I had a whole new appreciation for my axe throwing after last night and I couldn't wait to get back to training. I had a career I loved, my friends, and my Aramis. My life wasn't perfect, but it was so much more than I had ever expected it to be.

SOPHIE AND Otto arrived at Lil and Sam's, their cart laden with extra kegs and baskets of food just in time. Jeff had poured the last drops of ale, and we had run out of food a couple hours ago.

Sam and Lil had originally thought we would celebrate their bonding inside, but neither of them could bear to be apart from Dakkar, and the dragon didn't seem to mind the commotion. We all happily obliged and had brought everything outside.

Jeff and Aramis helped Otto with the kegs. Hannah and I helped Sophie with the food.

They hadn't come alone. Brent was with them.

"Mabel, are you all right?" Brent asked. "I heard what happened yesterday."

My celebratory spirit disappeared. It was strange to see him. I felt nothing but anxiety toward him. Did he think he had something to gloat about? "And?"

"I should have been here."

Aramis returned but stayed back.

"What is he doing here?" Brent glared at Aramis.

"He helped fight Sevrin. He was invited. He is with me."

"Oh. Um, I wanted to see you, see that you weren't hurt."

I didn't know what to say. I couldn't help but be suspicious. I kept waiting for him to rant about how dangerous Mam and Sevrin and Aramis were. He didn't. He said nothing more. "Thank you," I said.

"Are you? All right, that is."

"Yeah, I am. I had some cracked ribs and a shattered knee, but Aramis healed them perfectly. Same with the others' injuries."

Brent hung his head.

I crossed my arms, waiting, expecting the lecture to come now.

"What, um, what happened to Sevrin and your mam?"

"We ran them off."

"Good. Good."

I kept waiting for him to argue with me. It made me anxious that it didn't come.

"Lil and Sam just had their golden ring ceremony," I said. "Come around back, if you want."

"No. That's all right."

"Brent!" Lil and Sam squealed, running toward us.

"Hey. Congratulations," Brent said.

They stood on either side of him, hooked their arms in his. "You are staying to celebrate with us, aren't you?"

"I guess, sure."

I picked up the last of the baskets of food. Aramis took the basket from me and held my hand. "Are you all right?" he whispered.

It was awkward to see Brent, but I did miss him as a friend. I missed having him as a part of our group.

I made Aramis bend down to my level and kissed him. "Yes."

I SHOWED up at Reede's exhausted—stuffed from

eating too much, and still a little bit drunk, from yesterday's golden ring ceremony—but eager to get to my training.

I began with some stretches then ran laps around the throwing arena in her back garden. Each foot-fall was like a blacksmith's hammer beating against my skull. My body ached and my eyelids were too heavy to keep open. The ground looked incredibly flat and comfortable. I didn't need a pillow. I could just lie down for a little bit. I did half the number of reps I was supposed to do for my warmup. I picked up my axes and I started throwing to the nearest post, focusing on the technique of my release. I'd noticed it during the battle with Sevrin that my release was always a little too fast.

"Mabel," Reede said, coming out of her house. She stopped short. "I don't think you should be practicing today. You look as rough as a worn piece of wood."

"I feel it, too."

I told her about the battle, how I'd thrown axes to free Dakkar and save Aramis. "The exhilaration of a victory like that was something else. I hated having to throw my axes at other dwarves. I hope I never have to do it again. What I loved was the throwing itself. I loved winning. I want to compete and win. And if I don't win in a competition, then I will keep working at it until I do. Until I win them all. Even if that means returning to Gilliam. I don't care how rough I feel, I need to be able to compete at my best, especially when I feel at my worst."

"Do your warmups again. This time do the full amount, not just half," she smirked.

I sat down and got into my stretches. "When do we leave for Gilliam?"

"Two weeks."

We hadn't heard back from Jimmy or Theo yet. I figured Da had found a way to block them from getting mail, even from Hannah. Da couldn't stop me from entering the city, though. And if Jimmy wasn't home, Max would let us stay there. I made a mental note to write to Jimmy again.

"You remember my friend Jimmy? We're going to stay with him. Hannah and Jeff want to come too. Lil and Sam would, but they have to stay here for work, and Dakkar."

"And Aramis?"

We had talked about it. It was a risk for him to show up in Gilliam at my side, but I wanted him there. I needed him there for the movie. I refused to allow the stories Da was telling about me to guilt me or scare me into being anything other than myself. I was going to Gilliam to compete for Leitham. Aramis was a part of my life in Leitham. "Aramis will be coming with us."

"So the movie is back on?"

"Yes."

"And the axe throwing career?"

"I'm not going to the Dwarf Games this time, but I am going to compete for Leitham like the champion

I am."

"Good. I liked your concentration at Regionals. You pulled yourself together after that first throw. The field of competitors in Gilliam is going to be much like it will be in the Dwarf Games, so just because you haven't made it to the Games this time, this will be a great preparation for the future. It is the perfect opportunity to make everyone take notice of you as a rising talent. I want you to prove to everyone, and especially yourself, that it is a fluke that you are not at the Dwarf Games."

"Yes, Coach."

"Good. Practice your second round throws."

CHAPTER 24

I HAD forgotten how majestic the Black Mountains were. Maybe I'd never really appreciated them before. They were always only something to live and work in. It was their underbelly that we dwarves were supposed to love, not their exterior. I hadn't forgotten how oppressive the mountains were, towering over us, shutting out the sun and sky.

"Stop the cart, Jeff," Hannah said.

Jeff did as he was told at the crest of Calais Mountain. "That it down there?" he asked.

My breath caught and my heart pounded in my ears. The city of Gilliam lay visible on the other side of the valley. "Yes," I whispered.

"So this is where the famous Mabel Goldenaxe grew up," Hannah said. "Aramis, it's time to record

Mabel's homecoming.

I straightened my cap, and ran my fingers through my beard. It reminded me of the many times I left the mines and put myself in some semblance of presentability the same way, hoping for someone to show interest in me, comparing myself to Emma. My heart raced. Though my palms were sweaty, I clasped my hands tight, keeping them in my lap, sure that if I dared to separate them they would shake uncontrollably.

Aramis started recording and Jeff snapped the reins. The outskirts of the city rushed at us as we made our descent into and across the Gilliam Valley. I smiled for the recording but it was a nervous, stiff, smile.

The way Da had driven me off, the rumors he was spreading about me, were loud in my head. I couldn't wait to see Jimmy and Max. I hoped I would get to see Phillip and Ben and Zach. I dreaded the possibility of seeing the rest of my family.

"Breathe," Reede instructed me. "It will be all right."

I hadn't realized I'd been holding my breath. I let it out slowly and turned my gaze to the road ahead, and the city limits.

I half expected there to be a line of guards blocking the road into Gilliam, but it was clear. Still, I held my breath, waiting for something, an attack, Da or one of my brothers to come after me, someone to throw me out.

"I can't do this," I whispered.

"You can, and you will," Reede said, sternly.

"Give us a tour, Mabel," Jeff said. "What are we looking at as we drive into town? Any buildings of note?"

My stomach was churning and I thought it would be safest for everyone if I kept my mouth closed. I swallowed hard, willing my anxiety to subside. I had the chance to show my Leitham friends where I grew up. They would see all the places I talked about endlessly. "The wood and brick building coming up on our right, that's the trading post. All mail, all goods imported or exported, pass through there."

"Any fun stories you can tell us about the trading post?" Hannah asked.

"Um…" Stories? For the movie. Right. "I ordered an elven brooch once from here. Except I didn't know what to do so I stalked the traders who met behind the building, and gave them my order."

Aramis winked at me and I relaxed a little.

"It was also where I first discovered I had fans in Gilliam." I recounted that day, waiting to pick up something, I couldn't quite remember what, and how a young dwarfling had pointed me out to everyone.

I faltered.

"What is it?" Hannah asked.

"I had already injured my shoulder but I hadn't told anyone. Well, I hadn't told Mikey. I was secretly taking a home-grown remedy one of my friends was giving me. That wee dwarfling, she was so earnest, they all were. I didn't want to let any of them down, so I worked harder, took more of the remedy, and damaged my shoulder more and more with each throw."

"This is brilliant," Hannah muttered.

"What about this neighborhood?" Reede pointed to the small houses built close together near the trading post. "Who lives here?"

I was grateful for the change in subject. "I'm not sure. This isn't where the miners live, so it isn't an area we frequent. Trips to the trading post are the only reason we would come this way. I guess the blacksmiths and hunters, shopkeepers, pretty much anyone who isn't a miner lives out here."

I scanned the faces we passed as we drove up the main street. Everyone stared at us, strangers, and an elf, entering their city. Such a thing had been a rarity when I'd lived here.

A young female, mouth gaping, pointed me out to her friend. I recognized her from Leitham. She had been with her family, talking to Jimmy after the Dragon Killers match, at the tavern. I smiled and waved to her. She squealed and chatted animatedly to her friend.

"Looks like you still have fans here," Aramis said.

"So where do the miners live?" Jeff asked.

"See that dense forest ahead? The miners who have not inherited a home inside the mountain live in there. The thick foliage is meant to be a substitute for the darkness of the mountain. Mostly it's a painful reminder that we aren't mountain-dwellers."

"Why does it matter that you are not mountain-dwellers?" Aramis asked.

"Yeah. Who cares?" Jeff asked.

Was Gilliam that different from every other dwarven city? "In Gilliam, miners are the elite. Everyone wants to be a miner. Only the best, most skilled of us get to become miners. Mountain-dwellers are all miners, and they are the elite of the elite. They are descendants of the first dwarves to settle Gilliam. They represent the longest familial tradition of mining. The rest of us came from dwarves who settled later, after the city outgrew the mountain."

As we neared the base of the mountain, the stares of the pedestrians turned into whispers. I didn't recognize anyone, but they knew who I was. By the looks of it, Jimmy and Max had managed to keep my memory alive, but I couldn't tell if they had managed to turn public opinion as much in my favor as Jimmy said they had. Then again, Aramis was with us, which only confirmed Da's story that I had run off with an elf. If that particular tale was true, and it kind of was, what other stories of Da's might they believe?

The forest thickened and the road narrowed. Jeff slowed the cart. "Are we going to see your house?" he asked.

Panic flickered through me. "No. The road coming up on the left, that leads to my...the house

I grew up in."

I couldn't take my eyes off the intersection, wondering if I would see one of my brothers. Hoping I would and praying to the gods I wouldn't.

"This road here?" Jeff pointed to it.

"Yes." I couldn't breathe.

"Should I turn off here?" he asked.

"No," I snapped. "Keep going straight."

"Breathe, Mabel," Reede said.

I couldn't, not until we'd crossed the intersection and I hadn't seen anyone I knew.

"We're going to come up to a fork in the road," I said. "Stick to the right. If we go to the left, we'll arrive at the entrance to the mountain and the mines. We're almost at Jimmy's."

We curved to the right and snaked our way along the base of the mountain.

"On your right, see that stone building?" I asked.

"Mabel," Hannah admonished, "they're all stone."

I chuckled. "Right. I mean the one that's made to look like a mountain. That's our movie theatre. That's where I fell in love with…" I glanced at Aramis, "movies, and making movies."

"Aramis, can you focus in on the theater?"

"Got it," he said.

"Jeff, turn left," I instructed.

We headed up a narrow gravel path. I pointed out Jimmy's house.

"Mabel has a story about this house, too," Aramis

said.

"You and Jimmy?" Hannah asked as we pulled to a stop in Jimmy's drive.

"No, no." Well, kind of, but that story did not need to be a part of the documentary. "He didn't live here, then. It was his uncle's, and he rented it out to my mam when she was here to make a movie, my first movie. I ended up moving in with her."

A part of me had always thought that someday I would come back and see Da and my brothers at home, stop in at the mines, and have a few drinks at the Prospector. Returning here, to the place where I had made the decision to leave mining, my family, Gilliam, to reject Jimmy's proposal, had never been a part of that plan. It should have been. It represented my pain and my freedom.

Jimmy came out of the house, grinning. He helped me down from the cart and pulled me into a tight hug. "Welcome home. I can't believe you're here."

Home? This wasn't home anymore. Home didn't make you feel this petrified. "I can't believe it either. You got my letters?"

"A couple of weeks ago. My response must still be on its way to you. Of course you can stay here. How was your trip?" Jimmy greeted my friends. "Are you tired? Would you like to rest?" Jimmy helped grab our bags off the back of the cart and carried them in.

"I wouldn't mind washing up," Reede said.

"Of course," Jimmy opened the door. "Do you have some time before you train? I have some food ready, or we can go for drinks."

"We don't have to train until tomorrow," Reede said. "It's better to rest after so much travel. Though Mabel, at some point, I want you to stretch out."

"Yes, Coach," I said with a smile.

"Aramis, Jeff, you can put your things in the front bedroom. Mabel, I have you, Reede, and Hannah in here." Jimmy dropped our bags in the back room, the room that had been mine after Da kicked me out of the house. I had expected the space to feel gloomy and oppressive. It felt the opposite. This room had been my first refuge, my first taste of freedom to be myself.

My bed had been pushed to a corner to allow for two more. There wasn't much room to maneuver. I was grateful for the change in furnishing. It altered the feel of the room. It was a new space for a new era in my life.

"Is she here yet?" someone asked, slamming the front door open.

"Be right there," Jimmy shouted. He showed Reede where she could wash up and he and I walked to the living room where Phillip, Ben, and Zach were arguing amongst themselves about being too slow or in too much of a hurry, I couldn't quite tell which.

I gasped and covered my mouth. I couldn't believe it. Phillip was the first to embrace me. Ben and Zach came soon after, all three of them surrounding me, practically suffocating me. Their beards were soaking wet. They must have hurried here from the mines, after a quick dunk in the cleansing pool. "Welcome home, Mabel. How long are you staying? You're moving back, aren't you?"

"Let her breathe," Jimmy scolded. "She just got here."

"Besides, it's my turn," Max said from the doorway.

Max! Tears sprung to my eyes. I hurried to him, arms outstretched, nearly knocking him over. I had missed him so much. I pulled back, excited to see him, to talk to him, and the others. To hear them tell me in person, about the adventures of their lives. There was something different about Max, though. I'm sure they thought the same thing about me. A few years had passed, so we were bound to change a little. They all had more girth, their beards were thicker, too, but that wasn't it. It wasn't that he'd grown older...I stared and studied him. And then it struck me. "You have a braid in your beard!" I turned to my friends and pointed at my brother. "He has a braid in his beard. A single braid. When did this happen, Max? Who is it?"

Max blushed. "It's Jimmy," he said.

My jaw dropped. "Jim—" I looked over and sure enough Jimmy had a single braid in his beard. Jimmy and Max? Of course! Jimmy had talked non-stop about Max, how they'd become such good friends. I hadn't noticed it then, but thinking back, there might have been a twinkle in Jimmy's eyes when he'd spoken of Max. Jimmy had featured rather prominently in Max's letter, too. I guess I was still clueless when it came to romance. I grinned. "Congratulations! How is Da taking it?"

Max shrugged. "He isn't happy about it. This means our family line does not necessarily carry on, and Jimmy isn't a miner anymore which doesn't please Da at all. The only reason he accepts it is because I'm still mining. He's putting the pressure on Bobby and Bernie now to find a mate. Given how stubborn the two of them can be, he might have better luck with Kenneth and Ross. Even Frankie is more likely to be interested in mating than Bobby or Bernie."

"I almost feel sorry for Da."

"I wouldn't," Max said.

"I said almost. You all have a lot of news to fill me in on," I said, getting comfortable on the sofa. "Tell me everything. What is going on in the mines? Promotions? Gems found? Gossip?"

"Not much to tell," Phillip said. "We're all mining rubies now, and it is going fine. We go in, we mine, we go for drinks at the Prospector, we sleep, and we start over again the next day. You're the one off having adventures."

"What is it really like in Leitham?" Ben asked. "Do you see elves and trolls and others every day, or is it just once in a while?"

"Most days," I said as Aramis and my friends

emerged from their rooms.

"Percy is pretty nice," Jeff said, shaking hands.

"Who is Percy?" Phillip asked.

"He's a centaur," Hannah said. "He recently retired from the Center for the Creation and Preservation of Motion Pictures."

"I miss him," I sighed.

"Me, too," Hannah said.

"A centaur?" Zach asked, incredulous.

"A few weeks ago, we helped one of our best friends adopt a dragon." That drew grunts of disbelief and marvel. I hesitated. Should I tell them? Why would I hide it? They were supposed to be my friends. I didn't need their approval and I wasn't going to lie about who I was. I had decided that the moment Mam had let me in the door all those years ago. "And Aramis and I are together now."

"Aramis?" Jimmy asked.

"You know he's an elf, right?" Max asked.

I laughed. "Yes, I do."

Max shook his head. "If you're okay with it, then I'm happy for you."

I finished introducing my friends.

"Jeff, get out the crystal," Hannah ordered. "We should be recording this. I want to set up individual interviews as well."

It was a bit strange to have my two worlds come together like this. I wished Lil and Sam could have been here. And Emma. I actually wanted to see Emma. The three of them would have made this gathering complete.

MAX WAS the first one up. I grinned, listening him stumbling around the house, muttering to himself. I missed Max's morning noises. It was one of the reasons I remained at the Hammer and Chisel. With other guests staying at the inn, there was always someone moving around much like it had been for me growing up. I slept better, I felt safer and more comfortable with that kind of activity around me.

I pushed back my covers and snuck out of bed. Max and I had stayed up much later than everyone else. We'd only had a couple hours of sleep. I should have been out cold like Hannah and Reede, but I couldn't pass up time with my brother.

I slipped out of the room. Max stoked the fire, building it up, heating a kettle of water for tea. "Morning," I whispered.

"Hey." Max hugged me. "Did I wake you?"

"I'm not sure I ever fell asleep," I said. "Do you have to go in to the mines today?"

"Unfortunately, I do. We've been working on a very stubborn bed of rubies. I think today is the day it's going to crack. Want to come help?"

"Rubies, you say. I did always enjoy uncovering the gems." I hadn't enjoyed the tedium of swinging the axes, though, or chipping at the stone and getting coated in the mine dust.

"It wouldn't take much to persuade Phillip and Zach to let you keep the rubies you find."

It might be fun to work with my friends again. I'd be able to say I mined rubies. Getting paid with rubies was fine, but to remove them from the ore and to keep them? There was nothing like it. "You are tempting me."

"No way," Reede said, entering the kitchen. "You are not spending the day in the mines. We have to train today. You need as much practice as possible after four weeks on the road with no proper training grounds."

"Fair enough," Max said. "Think about it, though. You could always join us for a bit after the tournament."

Soon enough everyone was up and crowded into the kitchen filling our plates and our bellies with pancakes, eggs, and sausages.

"Grab your axes, Mabel. We've got to get going," Reede said as soon as we had finished breakfast.

"I'll go with you," Max said. "It's on my way."

"We all will," Jimmy said. "I was thinking I would give Hannah and Jeff a tour of the mines, the city, the toy workshop, and end up at the Prospector. Theo said he would join us there."

Hannah rubbed her hands together. "Fantastic. Aramis, will you record Mabel's practice for me?"

"I shall."

"When you're done your practice, come meet us

at the Prospector," Jimmy said.

My heart stopped for a fraction of a second. "I don't think so."

"You have to," Hannah insisted. "We can re-create your first competition."

"After the tournament," Reede said. She held up her hand, cutting off Hannah's protests. "As of this moment, Mabel's focus is on nothing but throwing axes, is that understood?"

"Yes, Coach," Hannah muttered.

"I want to hear it from everyone." Reede looked at each of us pointedly. "Do you all understand? There are to be no distractions. At all."

"Yes, Coach," we all murmured.

"Good."

Bag of throwing axes slung over my shoulder, I hesitated at the door. I didn't know what to expect, what might be waiting for me, and I wasn't ready to find out.

Jimmy held the door open. Aramis recorded. Max took my hand and said, "They can't hurt you."

Max understood this wasn't just nerves or anxiety. I was terrified Da would have my brothers and who knew how many others waiting for me, blocking me, ready to physically carry me out of the city. Max's gentle words reminded me I had the protection of my friends. I had escaped Da's control.

I nodded and stepped out onto the path leading to the mountain entrance.

CHAPTER 25

I WAS grateful Reede had insisted I concentrate only on the upcoming tournament. On the way to the mountain entrance, I set up my mental wall, allowing Reede and Aramis and Max to lead me while I allowed my thoughts to wander to the details of my throwing technique, what I needed to do, how it felt to keep my elbow in, and the perfect release.

In no time we were there. Only a handful of the keenest miners were on their way in for the day shift.

"Have a good practice," Max said, giving me a hug. "I will see you later."

"Thanks."

Aramis, Reede, and I, left Max and the others to continue on to the mines. We turned off and through the gate onto the main Gilliam road under the mountain. It was as tight and cool as I remembered it being. I could feel the weight of the mountain on top of me, pressing in on me, the weight of expectations, of having failed my family, crushing me. The number of miners heading toward us only made it worse.

"Mabel?" Someone shouted. "Mabel Goldenaxe?"

I didn't recognize them.

Everyone around us stopped.

"It's her," someone else said. "The moviemaker."

"No. She throws axes."

"What's she doing here?"

"Didn't she beat the Elven Mafia?"

"Disgrace."

"Shame."

"She brought *it* with her."

"Disgusting."

The whispers swirled around me, accompanied by scornful glares and shaking heads. It? What was the 'it'? Aramis?

"Mabel, it's me, Oliver," one brave voice stood out. He pushed his way toward me.

My mental wall fell. The blur of faces surrounding me cleared into so many I had seen in the mines or at the Prospector.

"Oliver!" I recognized him. We had started at the mines at nearly the same time. "How are you?"

"Good, good. Are you back?"

"Just for the axe throwing tournament."

"You're throwing again? Fantastic. Come by the Prospector later?"

"I'll try."

"It's so good to see you again," Oliver said.

"You too."

Reede pulled me through the onslaught of miners. Some wished me well and welcomed me home. Most bumped and shoved me, attempting to block my path.

"Use it," Reede whispered. "Prove them wrong. Prove to them how great you are. Shut them up with your axe throwing prowess."

Jimmy and Max may have kept my memory alive, but Da was succeeding at destroying my reputation. Reede's advice kept me calm and renewed my determination to win this tournament.

We reached the Gilliam arena and I could finally breathe.

Reede signed us in and we were instructed to proceed to the main arena. Aramis made his way into the stands to record from there, and we found our spot on the arena floor. All the other competitors and their coaches were there.

"What's going on?" I asked. Our competitor's package usually had all the rules, practice and competition times. We hadn't received a package of any kind.

Reede was unresponsive, her gaze fixed on the door at the other end of the arena.

"Mikey's here, isn't he," I said.

Her nod was nearly imperceptible.

"Of course he is." My confidence waned. I had stupidly thought I'd get through this without seeing him or any of my family. Gilliam wouldn't host a tournament and not have Mikey involved. He was a past Dwarf Games champion.

"When was the last time you saw him?" I asked.

"At the Dwarf Games, when he won."

"And when did you find out it would be in Gilliam?"

"Not long before I met you." Reede faced me. "Oh, no, Mabel, it's not what you think. I would have coached you anyway. I want to be your coach. You've got so much talent. This is just…"

"A bonus."

Reede hung her head. "Something like that."

"Is this why you weren't so upset I didn't place in Regionals?"

"Do not ever take my accepting the judge's ruling as being okay with what happened. You should have placed. You deserved to place. I would have told you earlier, from the start, but I thought knowing there is a city champions tournament might put too much pressure on you going into the city championships. I thought if you knew where it was going to be, you would quit throwing. I feared the anxiety of returning here would affect your throwing."

I considered her arguments for a moment. I probably would have quit or been too afraid to compete here. I'd needed to have the taste of winning, the drive to compete, before I'd agreed to come. "Fair enough."

"You're not mad?"

I shrugged. "Wish you had told me, but you were right not to have."

The door at the other end of the arena opened out walked a tournament official. He whistled to get our attention. "Welcome everyone, to the first ever Gilliam Open Axe Throwing Championships."

I knew him. I knew the official. He had won the Gilliam championship the year I'd competed. He was a warrior. I couldn't remember his name. He'd been good in the Gilliam championships, but he'd been terrible at the Regionals.

"We are pleased you all accepted the invitation to compete. I have a few things for you to be aware of and then I will let you get to your practice. The distances to targets are at Dwarf Games standard, as are the rules of competition. Because there are only twenty competitors, we have changed the format for this competition. For the first round, you will compete in alphabetical order of your city. The other major change, is that there will be no eliminations. All scores will be cumulative from first round through the third."

"No pressure there," I whispered to Reede.

"You can do it," she whispered back.

"It is expected that all of you will compete hard, but fairly," the official continued. "Failure to do so will result in disqualification. Now, I would like to introduce the judges for the tournament."

Ricky, my first ever challenger, was the first to step onto the arena floor and wave. He stopped cold when he saw me, his hand still in the air.

My heart thumped against my ribs. For the thousandth time I questioned why I had come here.

I didn't know the next two judges. They were retired warriors, both former city and regional champions, who had returned home.

"And our final judge is Gilliam's own Dwarf Games champion, Mikey Goldenaxe."

Mikey jogged onto the arena floor, looked my way and smiled for a moment when he spotted me, then quickly scowled.

He'd smiled, though. Even if for the briefest of moments. Maybe he missed me and for that moment forgot that he hated me.

Mikey wasn't going to drive me out of Gilliam. Not this time. If I could fight off Sevrin, then I could stay here and fight for myself. I leaned over to Reede. "Shall we get some revenge?"

"Oh, yeah," she said gleefully.

REEDE PUT me through my paces, extending my stretch and warm-up times, and pushing me on my technique. We'd done some basic practicing every night on the road, but this was our first chance to really work on the places I was having difficulty with, mostly my round two throws.

My unusual throwing method garnered a lot of attention from competitors, coaches, and officials. I hit the first dozen throws perfectly. I decided to miss a few of the throws on purpose. I succeeded in distracting them. They were now paying more attention to me, likely curious as to how I got to be Leitham champion with such inconsistent technique.

I caught Mikey watching. I could see the judgement in his eyes, how he wanted to correct my technique, but he didn't dare talk to me, remaining by the wall.

He wasn't just watching me, though. Reede was also in his sights. I knew Mikey and I knew exactly what he was thinking and feeling. He regretted breaking up with Reede the moment he'd done it. He'd done it because he thought it was the right thing to do.

I stopped throwing. "Reede, Mikey—"

"Forget him," Reede said. "Keep your focus on your throwing."

"But—"

She kept her voice low. "There is no revenge, there is no redemption for either of us, if you do not perform well here. Do you understand me?"

"Yes, Coach."

"Stay in the moment, Mabel."

"Yes, Coach."

Setting up my mental wall was much harder than it had ever been. Mikey, Ricky, throwing in the Gilliam arena, it was too much. My earlier confidence was gone. I threw and missed the post altogether a handful of times.

"Stop," Reede ordered. "Walk with me."

Reede put her arm around my shoulder and walked me off the arena floor. "Tell me what you need to tell me."

I sighed. "Mikey didn't want to break up with you. Mam had promised him she would return everything she'd stolen from our family if he won. That's why he asked you to lose the Dwarf Games. He felt so guilty about it after, he turned down Mam's offer and broke up with you."

"And?"

I was taken aback by her indifference. "What do you mean?"

"Mikey had said he loved me. If he really had loved me, then he should have told me what your mam had done. He didn't. I appreciate the explanation. It is nice to know, even so many years later, that he wasn't ashamed that I'd been willing to throw the Games for him. But nothing changes for me, or for you. We are here to win. To prove to everyone, not just Mikey, everyone, that you are the best. Can you do that?"

"Yes."

Reede crossed her arms and looked at me, an eyebrow raised in question.

"Yes," I said with more confidence.

"Good. Get back in there and focus."

I resumed my place at my practice post. I closed my eyes, breathed deep, tucked my hair, slapped my shoulder, adjusted my sleeve, and threw.

"That's it," Reede said. "Go again."

CHAPTER 26

EACH CONTESTANT and coach paraded into the Gilliam arena as their names were called. I wore the red and yellow of Leitham. As a sign I hadn't forgotten, that I was proud, to be originally from Gilliam, I carried my sapphire and diamond encrusted throwing axes that Mikey had given me.

"Up next we have former Gilliam resident. Leitham Champion, Mabel Goldenaxe!"

Jeff stood at the side of the arena floor and recorded as Reede and I marched in. The whispers and mutterings of the spectators were louder than the boisterous cheers coming from my friends and the entire Dragon Killers team who sat with them. A few others joined in with a smattering of applause. Da had a lot of influence, if not even the Dragon Killers could persuade the city to cheer for me. They were heroes in Gilliam. They wouldn't cheer for someone who was an enemy of the city.

I glanced up to the stands, to the where Aramis sat at the back, recording. There were plenty of seats vacant around him. No one wanted to sit with the elf that had corrupted me, who, according to Da, had stolen everything from my family. It irritated me, that he would be treated so badly. Aramis didn't seem to mind, though. He had room to stretch his legs out over the two rows of empty seats in front of him.

Following the introductions, we were each allowed a couple of practice throws. I had never felt such pressure to perform before the competition itself started. My release was early on the first throw, and late on the second. The perfect practice. I knew now what to do under the pressure of the crowds.

I stepped to the throwing line, ran through my routine of tucking my hair, slapping my shoulder and so on. I focused on the target, and threw. It spanned the bullseye and the second ring. My stomach flipped and I couldn't breathe.

Ricky was the official in charge of measuring. I hoped he would be honest and not jaded by anything Mikey might have told him. Reede and I were invited up to the post to watch. My throw counted as the second ring. My competitive spirit wanted to argue the call even though it was clear that enough of the axe-head was in the second ring for this to be a fair judgement.

Reede and I took our places at our bench and I hung my head. It was Regionals all over again.

"Put it behind you," Reede said. "Your elbow wasn't in tight enough."

I stood at the line for my second throw.

"Yeah, Mabel!" Jimmy yelled. There were a few appreciative chuckles around the arena as I smiled.

Jimmy was, indeed, cheering for me.

I ran through my routine and pulled my focus back to the task at hand. I kept my elbow in and my release was on point. The axe head split the rings again.

I held my breath as Ricky measured. This time it counted for the bullseye, but by less than half an inch.

"What am I doing wrong, Reede?" I asked.

"You're rushing your prep. Take an extra moment to aim before you throw."

At the line I pointed the axe at the target, reached back and went through the motions of the throw without the release once, twice. I ran through my routine and again aimed the axe, reached back, holding my elbow in tight, and threw.

I hit dead center, earning me cheers from a slightly greater portion of the crowd. As the number of my supporters grew, so did the volume of the murmurings about who I was and what I had or hadn't done.

I had performed well enough to sit comfortably in the top ten. In any other competition, I would breathe easier, knowing I could do well enough in round two to qualify for the finals. I could only hope now that I had done well enough to remain in a competitive position.

"Good job, Mabel," Reede said. She handed me my axes and instructed me to keep my shoulders loose with stretches and arm rotations while the arena was reset for round two.

I caught Mikey watching me. Not Reede. Me. I couldn't read his expression.

It didn't matter. I reminded myself to stay in the moment. I needed to perform at my best in round two. I couldn't allow Mikey to distract me, even if he was only observing me in his official capacity.

I breathed deep and turned away from him.

Round two started with the lowest ranking throwers. The scores were close enough that everyone had a chance of getting into the top five, if they had stellar second rounds and there were a few misses from the higher ranking throwers. Undoubtedly, round two would put a lot more separation between all of us. I was sitting with the fifth highest score. I didn't dare drop any points.

I stepped to the throwing line, aimed, ran through my routine, and windmilled. I hit the bullseye perfectly.

One down, two more throws to go.

I made the mistake of checking out the scoreboard before my second throw. So far, everyone remained in the positions they had been in to start the round.

The scores had a greater spread now than they had at the beginning of the round. The top five were close, though. I had a chance to move up.

"Focus." I told myself. "Stay in the moment. This throw. Nothing else."

I aimed, tucked my hair, slapped my shoulder, aimed again, and threw. Again I hit dead center.

I couldn't do any better with my throws. I needed their perfection to stay in fifth. I needed someone above me to miss in order to give me a chance to move up.

The only one to miss was the Mitchum champion. His axe spanned the bullseye and the first ring. It counted as less than perfect. His miss moved me into fourth position for my final throw. But it wasn't enough for me. I wanted to win this thing if I was going to feel any kind of redemption for messing up at Regionals.

My third throw was again perfect. If I finished in fourth, I could at least be satisfied with how well I'd performed in this round. It used to be my worst. So far, it had been my best.

I finished the day in fourth, behind the champions from Gilliam, and two eastern cities Dramdal and Nesfel.

"Well done," Reede said as we packed up for the day. "We'll go straight to Jimmy's and have a quiet night in."

Hundreds of fans surrounded the arena exit, pushing in on the competitors and coaches as we left.

It didn't help that Jeff walked in front of us recording. It seemed that even those who weren't a fan of mine were willing to be one if it meant getting on the recording. Reede was quick to act as my bodyguard, holding the most aggressive of fans at bay, but she was rapidly being overwhelmed.

Jimmy, Theo, and Dale stepped in and helped Reede. They walked on either side and behind me. Their presence did more to distract the fans rather than actually push them back. As soon as the crowd realized the Dragon Killers were in their midst, they became the focus of everyone's attention.

Reede and I could finally slip through and home to Jimmy's.

"Mabel." Emma waited outside the front door. "Great job today."

I tensed and my head pounded like it had when I was with Brent. "Thank you."

"I was hoping I could talk with you. For a moment. Not long."

"No," Reede hustled me into the house. "Try tomorrow, after the competition."

I HAD done my best to put Emma and yesterday's competition out of my mind. I was in a good position. It may not be a clean slate for round three, but I could still move up. I could win, if I kept my focus.

The competitors were throwing like the third

round had started with a clean slate. They all threw like they had a chance to win. The gap in points narrowed but didn't close. Unless I was a disaster, I couldn't move down from fourth.

I wanted to win.

I wanted to prove to myself that I should have qualified for the Dwarf Games. I wanted Mikey to realize what he had missed out by breaking up with Reede. I wanted him to wish he was still my coach and know that I would never go back to him because Reede was so much better.

I stood in the center, closed my eyes, and I was in Lil's back garden facing Sevrin, Dakkar rumbling behind me. I spun, slicing through the ropes, freeing Dakkar. I turned and hit the sword from Sevrin's hand, leaving him defenseless. I turned again and spotted Sevrin's henchman, sword raised, about to attack Aramis. I threw, knocking the henchman off the roof, away from Aramis.

I smiled to myself as I opened my eyes to three perfect throws. It hadn't been a fantasy this time. It had been real.

My friends cheered my victory.

Reede embraced me. "Thank you for that. You should have seen the look on Mikey's face."

"Is it different from the one he has now?" I pointed out his gargoylish pout.

"Not much."

I tied for first with the champions from Nesfel and Gilliam.

"You can do this, Mabel," Reede said.

I could barely hear her through the roar of the crowd.

I was up first. I closed my eyes, ran through my routine and nodded. I spun to my right and threw. I turned to my left and threw. I turned left one more time and threw.

I pumped my fist. Three more perfect throws.

The Gilliam champion threw less than perfect, hitting an outer ring on one of his throws.

I remained tied for first.

My shoulder was tight. I feared I would damage it throwing again like this. The strain was too much.

One more time. I could do this one more time.

I massaged my shoulder as I stepped to the line to a resounding chorus of boos.

The arena fell silent. I could hear myself breathing.

I pulled my attention away from my aching shoulder, to the three throws I had to make, listening to every noise made, absorbing every vibration in the ground.

I nodded and spun, throwing in rapid succession. I was a warrior. I was fierce. I was defeating Sevrin. I was saving Aramis. I was the greatest axe thrower ever. I was me.

The Nesfel champion threw better.

His win was deserved. I was the first to congratulate him.

"Great competition," I said, shaking his hand.

"You as well," he said. "You're the toughest thrower I've ever met. I'm going to enjoy competing against you over the next few years. You are going to be at other competitions, aren't you?"

"Definitely."

"Fantastic. I'm going to have to work hard if I want to stay ahead of you."

"Yes, you will," I said with a smile.

We were congratulated by the other competitors.

Ricky blew a horn to get everyone's attention. "The award ceremony is about to begin. Please clear the arena floor. May the tournament officials and the top five finishers come forward."

The officials faced us. I had not been this close to Mikey in years. I tried to catch his eye. He looked everywhere but at me.

"On behalf of everyone," Ricky said, "I would like to thank all of you for coming out to cheer on these great city champions. It was an incredible tournament, was it not?"

Tumultuous cheers echoed around us.

Ricky waved his hands to quiet the crowd. "I would like to thank our officials for their dedication to the sport and their hard work to make this a fair and competitive event. I would also like to thank all our city champions for coming out, embracing this new format, and competing at their very best."

The arena rumbled from the cheers.

"And now, the trophies. For the fifth place champion from Nordfoss, an iron throwing axe. For the fourth place champion from Dramdal, a platinum throwing axe with emeralds in the handle. For the third place champion, from Gilliam—"

Deafening cheers sounded. I could barely hear Ricky finish.

"For the champion from Gilliam, a bronze axe with rubies in the handle. For the second place champion, from Leitham, a silver axe with sapphires in the handle."

I accepted my trophy from Ricky, raising it in acknowledgement to the crowd. I was beaming. This was the best prize I had ever won.

The champion from Nesfel received a gold axe with diamonds in the handle.

The five of us posed for Jeff as he recorded us.

We waved once more to the crowd, then returned to our coaches to let our own celebrations begin.

Reede hugged me. "Well done, Mabel."

"Thank you."

"You're not going to threaten to quit on me because you didn't win, are you?"

"Not a chance. I did my absolute best. I couldn't ask for any more from myself. I am satisfied. For now."

"I am satisfied for now, too. We'll take a few days and get back to practicing."

CHAPTER 27

"WHAT CELEBRATION do you have planned?"
Jeff asked, still recording us.

"An evening out with my friends, I hope." I
looked to Reede who nodded her approval. "You can
stop recording now, though."

He stopped the crystal. "Oh, good. Congratulations, Mabel." He hugged me.

"Thanks."

A significant portion of the crowd had left the
stands. Only the five winners and their coaches remained in the arena. For a moment I was disappointed I hadn't had a chance to talk to Mikey, that he
hadn't come over to say anything to me. As Reede
would say, I had to put it behind me. I had friends
to celebrate with. I waved for them to join us on the

arena floor.

Max was the first over the wall. He picked me up and spun me around. "So proud of you, Mabel!"

Aramis remained in the stands recording. I waved at him again to come down. No celebration would be the same for me without him here. Hannah noticed and ran back up the steps to Aramis. He put the crystal away and came down with her.

"Spectacular win." Aramis scooped me up in his arms.

"Thank you. I am so glad you were here."

"Me too." Aramis let go of me.

"Enough of that," Hannah said. "It's time to go celebrate. Where are we going?"

"The Prospector," Jimmy said.

"The Prospector!" everyone else shouted.

Before I knew what was happening, Theo and Dale hoisted me onto their shoulders, carrying me out of the arena. If a bystander didn't know better, they would have thought I'd won.

We weren't the only ones heading to The Bearded Prospector. The road was full. It reminded me of the end of a shift at the mines when all the miners stopped at the Prospector before going home. Theo and Dale kept me on their shoulders and I was kind of relieved to be above the throngs. It was nice to be taller than Aramis for once, too. Not to mention that this perspective gave me a view I wouldn't have had if I were walking. Theo and Hannah were holding hands!

This was definitely the best trip ever.

"You can put me down now," I said when we reached the Prospector, its patrons already spilling out around it.

"Nonsense," Dale said. "Watch your head."

I ducked as they carried me through the door.

Most of the conversation ceased.

"Mabel!" Someone shouted. Oliver, it was Oliver. "Mabel Goldenaxe!"

"You're back!" Curtis called out.

No one but my friends cheered. Most everyone ignored me or whispered to their friends while glaring at me. I felt distinct hatred from the back corner where my brothers sat.

My heart thumped and my back ached. I shouldn't have come here. I knew this was going to happen. I shouldn't have allowed myself to be swept up in the moment, to think that everything would be fine.

"Put me down, please," I asked Theo and Dale.

They turned me around once so that everyone in the tavern got a good look at me. "Ready?" Theo said. He counted to three, then they lifted me off their shoulders and set me down.

"Are you all right?" Aramis asked.

I shook my head, keeping my eyes on my brothers. They sat with their backs turned to me.

"What do you want to do?" Aramis held my hand.

I felt the way I had the day my brothers had blocked me from my home, hurt and full of rage. It was pointless and stupid to let them get to me. There was nothing I could say that would ever change their minds. Max had said it. They can't hurt me anymore. I refused to let them ruin my evening. "I want to celebrate."

"I'll go get drinks," Theo said. Max went with him to help.

Dale and Jimmy managed to persuade a group to vacate their table for us.

"Max." Patrick stormed up to the bar. "What are you doing?"

He wasn't even trying to be quiet about it. Patrick was making sure everyone knew I was not to be fraternized with.

"Having drinks with Mabel," Max said without any concern.

"Hiya, Patrick," Theo said.

If Theo was trying to ease the situation, it wasn't working. Patrick ignored him. "Max, put down those drinks, now. You can sit with us, or you can go home."

My jaw dropped and I held my breath, horrified at what was about to happen to Max. "Jimmy." I grabbed his arm.

Jimmy was ahead of me, already on his feet, ready to jump in if Max needed him. I didn't want to wait. "Don't," Jimmy said. "You will only make things worse."

"I don't live with you anymore, remember?" Max said. He picked up a tray of tankards and carried them to us.

"Max, are you all right?" I asked.

"Perfectly," he said with a smile.

"But, you know what will happen—"

He held up his hand to stop me. "I am well aware, and I am fine with it. I would much rather be here with you and Jimmy and everyone else, than worried about the family's reaction."

"Are you sure?" I asked.

"Mabel Goldenaxe," Max frowned. "Do not ever ask me that again."

"Yes, sir."

Oliver and Curtis were the first of the patrons to approach us. "Hiya, Mabel," Curtis said, pulling up a chair. "Congratulations on placing second. You were terrific." The room fell silent. "Oliver and I were just talking, and I really need to know. Did you really run off with an elf?"

I cleared my throat, wondering how many times I'd have to answer these questions. "Not exactly."

Half the patrons in the tavern shuffled their chairs closer. They were all listening. I would answer these questions as often as needed.

"I left to be with my mam and make movies. Aramis," I pointed at him, "happened to be with us when we left."

"Ah," Curtis said. "And did you really defeat the Elven Mafia?"

"I did."

"What about…"

Curtis looked at Oliver who nudged him and whispered, "Ask her."

"When you left, did you really try to steal from your family?" Curtis studied his hands in his lap.

I put my hand over his, making him look up at me. "No, I did not. I had no reason to."

"Told you," Oliver said.

"She's lying," someone yelled. It wasn't one of my brothers.

"No, she isn't," Max said.

"I believe you," Curtis said. "I love your movies, by the way. It's great to see you again."

"You too. Thank you."

Someone else took Curtis's seat. I didn't recognize them. "How do we know you're telling the truth?" he asked.

"I doubt my family has been living like they have nothing unless they hid all their possessions and everything they earned. Or you can ask them." I pointed to my brothers at the table in the back corner.

All attention shifted to them. My brothers had heard the question. Danny stood and glared at me. I returned the stare, daring him to lie. After a few moments he shook his head and muttered, "She didn't."

Focus swiveled back to me. In no time we were surrounded both by those I knew from the mines, and many I didn't know at all, congratulating me on my second place finish, asking for my autograph, and telling me how much they loved my movies.

I was so busy I barely had time to drink with my friends.

Every now and then I couldn't help but glance over at my brothers. If they hated that I was here so much, why hadn't they left?

I couldn't put this behind me. I couldn't just move on. They were family and I decided to remind them of it. "Excuse me." I got up from the table, and asked a few of those around me to step aside.

"What are you doing?" Jimmy asked.

"I'll be right back," I said.

"Jeff," Hannah hissed. "Start recording."

"I don't want this recorded," I said.

"This is perfect for the movie."

"It's private," I said.

"Hannah," Aramis intervened. "This should not be in the movie."

"What are you doing, Mabel?" Max asked. "Don't go over there. They already admitted you didn't steal from us. It's enough. Let it go."

"I can't, Max. Come with me. I need to tell them something that you should hear too."

I should have done this the moment I saw them. I grabbed Max's hand and marched over to the back table. "Frankie! Patrick! Mikey! Danny!" I gave them all hugs, though they refused to turn in their seats to recognize me. "I am so happy to finally see you. I can't tell you how much I've missed you. Listen." I pulled up a chair, squeezing between Mikey and Frankie. "I have learned some things in the past few months that you might find very interesting. Mikey, you remember Reede, don't you? She's my coach?

You competed against her in the Dwarf Games? Sure you remember her. You used to court her." I patted Mikey's arm. "She told me about the meetings you had during the Dwarf Games."

Mikey shifted in his seat, his first acknowledgement that I was here, that I'd said anything.

"Mabel," Max hissed.

I ignored Max. "I did some looking into those meetings. I know what offer was made to you, and I know why you turned it down."

"Mikey?" Danny asked.

Mikey shook his head.

I wasn't going to let him keep it a secret any longer. "You need to know you have nothing to feel guilty for, or ashamed of."

"What is she talking about?" Danny asked.

"Mam," I said. That got Mikey's attention.

"Don't, Mabel." Mikey said.

I told them about Loughlin and his offer to Mikey to return everything stolen from us if he won the Dwarf Games.

"Aubrey was behind it," Frankie said.

"He was behind the theft," I said. "Mam was the one who made the offer to Mikey, through Loughlin."

"Mam?" Frankie asked. "How do you know?"

"She told me. Not willingly, but she told me."

Mikey hung his head.

"I get it. You all hate me. That's fine. I'm not here to apologize, or to have you take me back into the family. I wanted you to know the full story of what happened at the Dwarf Games. Mikey shouldn't have had to keep this secret all these years. It is too much of a burden to bear and he shouldn't have to carry it by himself because you all are blinded by your pride. I also wanted to tell all of you, that you will always be my brothers, whether you talk to me or not."

I stood.

"Mabel," Mikey said.

I froze. I couldn't believe he was talking to me. My heart had been thumping before. The blood was roaring in my ears now. "Yes?"

"You were great today, at the tournament. Congratulations."

The one thing, the only thing, I had ever wanted to hear from Mikey. "That…" My voice caught. I cleared my throat. "That means everything to me."

"And," Mikey paused. "Please tell Reede I'm sorry."

"Tell me yourself," Reede said, standing beside me.

I hugged my brothers again. Though they still didn't return my embrace, they did at least pat my arm and Danny whispered, "I'm proud of you."

MAX AND I returned to our table. Platters of deep-fried mushrooms and roast pork had arrived. Emma and Hannah were deep in conversation, with Aramis recording. I sat beside Zach. "How are you doing?"

"I'm…" he paused, "I'm all right. I'm so happy to see you. Are you going to stay around for a while before you return to Leitham?"

"I think so. I think Hannah has a lot of plans, things she wants to record, interviews, and all that. It might also be very difficult to get her away from Theo."

"I saw that," Zach said. "Maybe she'll stay here."

"I wouldn't blame her, but I would hate to lose her."

"You'll just have to come back more often, then."

Tonight had changed everything for me. Da had lost. I was no longer banned from Gilliam. He could no longer hurt me. "I think I might."

"Good. We miss you."

"I miss you all too. I'm glad the competition is over. I hope I can spend the next few days with everyone, catching up. I desperately want to meet your's and Emma's dwarfling. Max has told me nothing about him? Her?"

"Him." Zach glowed. "Marlin, named after my da."

"Aww." I rested an elbow on the table and relaxed. "How old is he?"

"Two." Zach helped himself to a mushroom. "I gave him his first toy axe just the other week. He loves it. Definitely a miner in training."

"I am so happy for you."

"Thank you. I love him. Leaving him is the hardest thing I have ever done, and I have to do it every day." He had another mushroom. "I appreciate you not asking, but I know Max told you, Emma and I are not in a great place. She moved out a year ago. I am back with my family, so they can help look after Marlin."

"I'm so sorry, Zach."

He shrugged. "It was inevitable. I stupidly thought giving her a golden ring would make her happy enough that she would finally settle down with me. I knew better. She was never satisfied, always looking elsewhere. I hoped, though. She was happy for a while, and I am very happy to have Marlin."

"So how are you with her sitting here?"

Zach watched Emma chat animatedly to Hannah, playing up to the crystal, and Aramis. "Emma's happy. It's fine. I do want her to be happy. I love her. I always will."

"But…?"

"But I'm glad we're not together any more. I have finally learned my lesson."

"You should come to Leitham," I said. "Bring your Marlin. We'll snag you a mate in no time."

"I'm all right. For now. Don't be surprised if I show up on your doorstep in a couple of years, though."

"I'd look forward to it."

Zach grunted. "You are sweet. I don't know how you put up with Emma, or me. She was horrible to you. I always thought you were a good friend to Emma, and I'm sorry if I didn't acknowledge all you did for her, especially in helping her mine. I knew it was you who had found the gems, not her, but, well, at the time I didn't want her to think I didn't believe in her."

I remembered the pain of that day as she vocally declared to everyone within earshot that I didn't know how to mine. Zach and Ben had defended her and congratulated her on her accomplishments as a miner. "It was a long time ago and long forgotten, but thank you."

"What are we talking about?" Phillip asked, sitting beside me.

"Marlin, and mining," I said.

"Are you coming back?" Phillip asked. "I'm sure we could convince the foreman to let you join our team in rubies."

"Not a chance." I laughed. "Mining is the last thing I want to do."

I had a great evening with my friends. I signed several more autographs. Before I knew it, the tavern had all but cleared out, preparing for the next shift of miners to arrive. My brothers stood up from the table, Mikey and Reede hugged, and said goodbye.

Frankie waved to me on their way past our table.

After a few moments, Reede said she was going to head back to Jimmy's as she was exhausted. "I'll take these," she said, picking up my bag of throwing axes and my prize.

"We should get going, too," Phillip said. Zach agreed. "Will we see you tomorrow?" Phillip asked me.

"Yes. I think we're staying for a few days, right, Reede?"

"Absolutely. I have no great desire to be stuck in a cart travelling for four weeks just yet."

I hugged my friends. "See you tomorrow, then."

"We should go, too," Jimmy and Max said. "We'll walk you home, Reede."

I stood up to go with them.

"Mabel, can I talk with you a moment, please?" Emma asked.

I'd had enough ale and food to tolerate anything Emma might throw at me.

I sat back down. Hannah urged Aramis to keep recording. "Please don't," I said.

"Mabel," Hannah scolded.

"I do not think so, Hannah," Aramis said, putting the crystal away.

Jeff pulled Hannah away to give Emma and me some privacy. Aramis left with them.

"So, you and Aramis?" Emma said with a smile, as if we were still best friends.

"What do you want, Emma?"

She cleared her throat. "I just wanted to say I am happy for you. You seem to have a good life."

"I do."

"Good. That's great."

I waited for her to say more, to apologize for running to Da when I was in the movie, for poisoning me when I'd injured my shoulder.

"Good," she repeated. "Any dwarflings in your future? Oh, no, I guess there wouldn't be, not with Aramis." Emma wrinkled her nose in disgust when she said his name.

She hadn't changed at all. She had sought me out in an effort to make me feel bad one more time. I wasn't going to let her succeed. I wished it could have been different. I wished she was nicer to me. Then again, her behavior justified my disinterest in being her friend. "Speaking of dwarflings, Zach was telling me about your wee Marlin."

"I can't imagine my life without him. I would kill me to never have dwarflings. Thank the gods I had Marlin. At least I'm not barren."

It saddened me that she pushed so hard to prove how much better she was than me. I had never thought it was necessary. I'd thought she was better than me, until I left Gilliam. It wasn't a competition for me because I was happy with my life.

I leaned in close as a way to let her know I intended to break through her defenses to say what I had to say, and then I'd be done. "Emma, I want you to be happy. I hope you find what you're looking for."

"Right." Emma crossed her arms and sat back.

I inched closer. "When I'd heard you had a golden ring from Zach, I thought you'd found it. You finally had a golden ring from a mountain-dweller. But clearly what you thought was supposed to make you happy hasn't. There's nothing wrong with that."

"There is everything wrong with that."

She hadn't denied her unhappiness. That was something. "Emma, look at me. I am living the most unconventional life for anyone from Gilliam, and I have never been happier. All I am saying is, be true to yourself. Remember what's his name, Mark, was it? The blacksmith?"

"Yes." Emma blushed.

"You were happy with him. You couldn't stop talking about him. I'm not saying you have to be with him unless you want to. I'm saying you should be with someone who you want to be with, not someone you think you have to be with. Zach is great, but you never really wanted to be with him."

"You want to be with him, don't you?" Emma flipped her hair over her shoulder. "Well you can't. He's mine."

I had been an idiot to think I could break through her defenses. Whatever friendship we'd once shared had disappeared years before I'd ever left Gilliam. I threw up my hands as I stood. "Forget it. I hope you have a good life. Or don't. I don't care."

"Have a nice life with your elf," she spat.

I shook my head and walked out.

Aramis met me outside. Without a word, he took my hand and gave it a gentle squeeze.

"Well," I sighed. "This has been quite the day. An amazing day. I won a tournament. I'm in Gilliam with my friends. I talked to my brothers. Mikey said he was proud of me. Emma, well, she was just classic

Emma. I could have done without that, but…"

I canted my head back, turning my face to bask in the thick foliage surrounding us, the birds twittering in the branches. "I used to hate these trees, living in the forest," I said. "Everyone in the Prospector hates them. Such a shame, too. They are so beautiful and they smell so good. I should ask Otto to plant trees around the Hammer and Chisel."

"What changed?" Aramis asked.

"To make me love the trees? Meeting you. I was so star-struck. I think too, by that point, I realized there was more to life than mining, that I didn't like everything dwarves are supposed to like, including being under the mountain. I am very happy I came here. I have missed my friends, and I'll be happy to have some time here, but this isn't home."

"It seems that Gilliam has not been your home long before you left."

I smiled. "I think you may be right."

"Is there anything about life in Gilliam you do miss? Besides your friends, of course."

"It smells so much better here than it does in Leitham," I said. We strolled down the path toward Gilliam Mountain.

"That is true."

"I am very tempted to join Max in the mines tomorrow."

"Really?" Aramis kissed the back of my hand.

"The chance to find rubies might be fun. Ugh. Of course, then I'd have to deal with all that dust and my beard is far from being thick enough to protect me from it. I would give almost anything to be able to walk one more time through the entrance cavern."

"Is there a reason we cannot go in there?"

"Into the mines?"

"Yes."

"No one ever goes into the entrance cavern unless they are going through to the mines themselves."

"Is that a law here?"

I adjusted my cap as I thought. "I don't know. It just isn't done, that's all."

"Since when has that ever stopped you?" Aramis smirked.

We were near the fork in the road. I stopped walking. Did we turn right and walk on to Jimmy's, or could we continue on the road to the mines? The night shift was well under way. There wasn't likely anyone left in the entrance cavern, and chances are, no one else would be going through it until the shift-change, and we would be long gone by then. "Never. Would you go with me?"

"Of course."

My heart raced as we walked to the door to the Gilliam Mines. I hesitated, excited and fearful. I took a deep breath and pulled the door open. I felt like a young dwarfling sneaking into someplace I shouldn't be. Aramis and I stepped into the Gilliam mine's entrance cavern. The stalactites and stalagmites were as beautiful as I remembered, glittering and colorful, scattering prisms on the walls and floor.

Such majestic beauty.

I was in the one place I never thought I'd get to see again, the one piece of the mines I had missed, where my little dwarven heart had always been happy.

I took my time, soaking in the colors, the scent of the mountain, the stone. I appreciated the wonder of it. I was glad to have the chance to return to a place I once loved. It would always hold a special place in my heart.

Something was missing, though. It wasn't the absence of my mining axes. The crystals, everything was as enchanting as I remembered, that wasn't it. It wasn't that Aramis and I were the only ones there.

It was me. Something was different about me.

I smiled, and then I grinned.

I no longer felt the weight of the mountain. It no longer crushed me.

"What is it?" Aramis asked.

"I'm free," I whispered. "I'm free!" I said, louder.

I spread my arms, spun in a circle and yelled, my voice bouncing back to me from every surface. "I. Am. Free."

Thank you for joining me on this journey with Mabel Goldenaxe!

If you loved the book and have a moment to spare, **I would really appreciate a short review on the site where you purchased it.** Your help in spreading the word is gratefully received!

If you'd like to keep up to date on what Sherry is up to, please sign up for Sherry's newsletter at www.sherrypeters.com. You will receive exclusive content, special offers, news on release dates, and more, just for signing up! And I promise not to inundate you with e-mails. Just the important stuff!

ABOUT THE AUTHOR

Sherry Peters attended the Odyssey Writing Workshop and holds an M.A. in Writing Popular Fiction from Seton Hill University. Both *Mabel the Lovelorn Dwarf* and *Mabel the Mafioso Dwarf* were short-listed for the Aurora Award for best YA novel. *Mabel the Lovelorn Dwarf* won the 2014 Writer's Digest competition for Self-Published ebooks in the Young Adult category. For more information on Sherry, visit her website at: www.sherrypeters.com.

ABOUT THE AUTHOR